Burial Mound

Phillip Strang

D1617529

BOOKS BY PHILLIP STRANG

DCI Isaac Cook Series

MURDER IS A TRICKY BUSINESS
MURDER HOUSE
MURDER IS ONLY A NUMBER
MURDER IN LITTLE VENICE
MURDER IS THE ONLY OPTION
MURDER IN NOTTING HILL
MURDER IN ROOM 346
MURDER OF A SILENT MAN
MURDER HAS NO GUILT
MURDER IN HYDE PARK
BURIAL MOUND
MURDER WITHOUT REASON

DI Keith Tremayne Series

DEATH UNHOLY
DEATH AND THE ASSASSIN'S BLADE
DEATH AND THE LUCKY MAN
DEATH AT COOMBE FARM
DEATH BY A DEAD MAN'S HAND
DEATH IN THE VILLAGE

Steve Case Series

HOSTAGE OF ISLAM
THE HABERMAN VIRUS
PRELUDE TO WAR

Standalone Books

MALIKA'S REVENGE

Copyright Page

Dedication

For Elli and Tais who both had the perseverance to make me sit down and write.

Chapter 1

Archaeology was never of much interest to Detective
Inspector Keith Tremayne, a man whose idea of a fun
weekend was not ferreting around on his hands and knees
with a small trowel and a soft brush.

Not that Clare Yarwood, his sergeant, saw it that
way. She revelled in the history of Salisbury and the area
– its acknowledged pinnacle for the hordes of tourists,
Stonehenge. However, the thought of the monument,
built high on Salisbury Plain by Neolithic ancestors five
thousand years previously, brought out negative emotions
in her, as it was the site of a murder earlier in her career.

Theirs was an unlikely partnership, most would
agree: the recalcitrant detective inspector, closing in on
retirement age, a man who loved nothing more than a
pint of beer and a cigarette, the chance to plan his next
bet on an invariably losing horse, and his thirty-four-year-
old female sergeant. Chalk and cheese in personalities, but
their relative strengths played off each other.

'What is it with these people?' Tremayne said as
he prowled around the burial mound.

1

'What people?' Yarwood said. It was a cold morning, a chill wind blowing off the hills at their backs. She was wrapped up in a coat with a scarf around her neck.

'Digging around in the dirt, disturbing the long dead.'

'History. The chance to find out where you came from, who were your ancestors.'

'And why would I want to know that? You get one chance at life, make the best of it. And if someone who lived in the distant past had eaten fish for breakfast, what does that do for you and me?'

'The fount of knowledge, the chance to learn, to improve our knowledge of the human condition.'

'Over here,' a voice called from across the field.

The two police officers walked over to where an anoraked, ponytailed man stood. Tremayne felt like commenting on how a man in his fifties, bald on top, could look so stupid, but he did not. Even though he was the inspector and Yarwood the sergeant, she'd still berate him for too many negative comments.

'You've had your ration for today,' she would say.

Clare, warm enough in appropriate clothing, had no reason to complain about the cold; Tremayne did, having chosen to arrive at the exposed site wearing his suit and black leather shoes; definitely not the clothes to be standing around in an open field looking over at an archaeological dig.

'It was Bob that found it,' Gerard Horsley, the ponytailed man, said.

'Are you certain about this?' Tremayne said. Clare could see him shivering, moving his feet up and down, attempting to maintain circulation. She'd have a chat with Jean, his wife, later on, to make sure that he received the necessary care when he finally returned home later that day.

It was the two of them, Tremayne's sergeant and his wife, who cared about him. One had become his partner at Bemerton Road Police Station seven years previously; the other, Jean, had met the inspector when they were both young. True love it had been, but a police officer's vocation didn't make for a harmonious home life and after several years of wedded bliss – Tremayne's estimation of the marriage – Jean had left, taking the dog with her, just after the animal had learnt to make itself useful and fetch his slippers when he walked in the door.

Both Tremayne and Jean were now older and wiser, although Jean would debate the latter description being ascribed to Tremayne: the man was still susceptible to too many pints of beer, one too many cigarettes of a day, and he had had one scare that had put him in the hospital due to his late hours at work, the boozy pub lunches. They had reunited after twenty-one years. Tremayne had never remarried, although Jean had married another, had two children and then been widowed. After a while, and without the stress of the demands of their earlier lives, they had moved in together again. They had recently sealed their relationship by marrying again, Jean's elder son giving her away, the other son acting as best man.

'You said a body on the phone,' Clare reminded Horsley.

'There are two. It's not often you find anything other than a few implements, the occasional piece of jewellery. You can begin to understand how excited we were. I take it you've heard of Sutton Hoo?'

'Not me,' Tremayne replied. Clare was not surprised by his response.

'We learnt about it at school,' she said.

'It was 1939, that's when they opened Mound 1 and discovered the form of a ship. The timbers had rotted away, but it had left an impression, the iron rivets still in their places. This mound's a lot older, at least three and a half thousand years, probably four.'

'A cold case if they've been murdered,' Tremayne said sarcastically. 'I doubt if there's much point us being here, is there?'

'That's what we thought, but they didn't wear watches back in the Bronze Age.'

Tremayne had seen burial mounds before; there were hundreds throughout the area. Most had either been looted soon after the deceased had been buried in there with their valuables or else they had been deemed of little value and left alone. Or, as in the case of Gerard Horsley and his team, they were opened up, offering a chance to search for history and knowledge of how the past inhabitants of the area lived; poorly Tremayne would have said, judging by the reconstructed Bronze Age village near to Stonehenge.

To Tremayne, five thousand or one thousand, even one hundred made little difference. The present was for living, not for dwelling in the past.

'The body, how did you find it?' Clare asked. She was intrigued by the work at the site, undisturbed for millennia, until Horsley and two of his associates arrived.

'Ground-penetrating radar, the same manufacturer that the police use. For amateur use, not the heavy-duty equipment that the police have. It showed us the easiest way in, the direction that would minimise the damage to the site. We're not cloth-capped diehards steeped in the past. When there's a better way, we'll take it. Unfortunately, too often it's slow and tedious work.'

'If there's a recent body in there, then how did it get there?'

'That's where you come in, sorry to say. We don't know, and we're baffled, unless the man's a time traveller,' Horsley said, a smile on his face. Clare thought that it transformed the man from eccentric to normal; Tremayne thought it was weird.

'We deal in hard facts, not make-believe,' Tremayne said.

'Sorry, a poor attempt at humour. Whoever the body is, it's been put there for a reason.'

'You mentioned two bodies,' Clare reminded Horsley.

'The other one's someone of importance, over four thousand years old, can you believe it? The burial site is not in good condition, and at first we thought it was just the one body.'

'Any weapons?' Clare asked.

'We've not got that far yet. We could see the original skeleton, or what was left of it. Unfortunately, the badgers have been in there. Some might see them as furry country wildlife, but to us they're a damn nuisance.'

'The second body?' Tremayne asked, more anxious to bring in the team than to debate the historical value of what had been discovered.

'As we were coming out, backwards as it's tight in there, a part of the shaft that we had constructed collapsed and an arm came out, almost hit me in the face.'

'And you believe it not the same period as this warrior?'

'Wearing a watch?' Horsley replied indignantly.

'Yarwood, you know what to do,' Tremayne said, looking over at his sergeant.

***

Tremayne would have preferred somewhere cleaner, less muddy, and definitely somewhere more agreeable than a field that was soggy underfoot. Clare had donned coveralls to get a closer look of the more recent of the two bodies; Tremayne had not. As far as he was concerned, there was a perfectly good team of crime scene investigators who could do that, reporting back to him what they found.

It was an unusual case; he'd have to admit. Gerard Horsley, well-respected in Salisbury, had a reputation as an eccentric, a man who spent his time at archaeological digs or making presentations to schools around the area on the heritage that the children were part of. Not that many were interested, Tremayne was sure of that. As part of his community responsibility, he had been asked to make the occasional speech about modern policing, and how the general public could assist, and if it was for the pre-teens, it included the inevitable warning about people, men usually, who attempted to cajole them into their cars, and where to phone in an emergency. Not that any of them would have any trouble with phoning, as all the children carried mobile phones, not like in his day.

He still remembered the first day a phone had appeared in his parents' house, and the old-style phone boxes, money in the slot, press button A to connect, button B to reclaim left-over coins. He had gained a few extra pence by pressing the reclaim button every time he passed a phone box. But now they were gone, as were the days of his childhood when he would pedal his bike wherever he wanted to go, not worrying about cars and trucks, and definitely not wearing a helmet. Jean, now his wife again, had tried to get him back on a bike, more for his health than anything else, but he had resisted.

'I'd look a complete fool in those Lycra outfits they wear, and I'm not going to wear one of those helmets. It's only bike riding, I'm not entering the Tour de France.'

Jean had given up persuading him to ride, but she had instigated a walk around the block every other day, rain or shine, murder or no murder. She didn't always succeed, and as Clare, his sergeant, as well as being Jean's friend, knew, Tremayne would be using the latest murder as a way out of the every-other-day walk.

Murder had not been confirmed yet, but the watch that Clare had seen was analogue and looked to be old.

The question according to her when she rejoined Tremayne was how a body had ended up in there.

Horsley was excited. Not only was there a Bronze Age skeleton inside the mound, but there was also the possibility that the person had been someone of note, and potentially there would be weapons, jewellery, even clothing fragments, although that was a long shot.

'It could be a find of great significance once you've retrieved your body,' Horsley said.

Tremayne looked at the man, wondered how the archaeologist could be intelligent yet so naïve.

'That's not how it works,' Tremayne said. 'It's a crime scene, modern day. That takes precedence over your – how many thousands of years old did you say the body was?'

'We'll need to conduct tests, but at least four thousand, possibly more. Do you realise that the person inside could have seen Stonehenge in its prime when it was of importance, not a tourist attraction?'

'We'll be careful,' Clare said, 'but you can't expect us to hurry up just because of what you've found. There'll be no more work by your team until we've concluded our investigation.'

'I'm willing to help, but this is an important historical site. Pressure will be applied to maintain the integrity of it.'

'You can do what you like,' Tremayne said, annoyed by Horsley's attitude, 'but it's a murder enquiry. We have total authority over this site.'

'But, but…'

'No buts,' Tremayne said. 'Our people will be sensitive to what is here, but they will conduct their investigation thoroughly and without hindrance. Do I make myself clear?'

Horsley moved away, a resigned look on his face. He took his mobile phone out of his pocket and made a phone call.

'Phoning the heavies,' Clare said.

'He's right, of course,' Tremayne said. 'Let the uniforms know that they are not to go stomping around on the area with their hob-nailed boots.'

'I think they know that already.'

'I know it, just remind them. Horsley and his people have obtained authority to be here, and we're bound to get a few phone calls to take care of the area.'

'We will.'

'Don't ask Jim Hughes and his crime scene investigators to start ferreting around with a small trowel, down on their hands and knees, sifting through the soil.'

'But that's what they do.'

'Okay, I'll grant you that,' Tremayne said. 'Just make sure they don't take too long before they give us an update on who it is and how long he's been in there.'

'A long time, at least ten to fifteen years, possibly more.'

'Any updates on missing persons from the period?'

'I've got people looking into it, but so far we can only give them a male adult. It's not a lot to go on.'

Tremayne walked away, trying to avoid the mud, not succeeding entirely. Back at his car, he switched on the engine and then the heater. He took out his phone and called Pathology. 'I need an answer as soon as possible on this one,' he said.

'What's the condition of the body?' Stuart Collins, the pathologist, asked. He was a decent man, Tremayne knew that, always offering a comment on Tremayne's inevitable pressure to prioritise his case over any others.

'Not good, in the ground for a long time. It'll take some time to get the body out; it's a damn archaeological site, and we'll have to be careful, or we'll have the heritage society or whoever it is on to us.'

'Get the body to me by seven this evening, and I'll start on it at 8 a.m. tomorrow.'

'Good man,' Tremayne said. He stretched out his legs, conscious of the aches and pains, fearful of his mortality. One major health scare so far, and his father had died in his fifties. And with Jean back in his life, he intended to enjoy many years more with her.

Not that he'd ever tell Clare, his sergeant, how he felt about his wife. She'd be on the phone to Jean in an instance. The two of them were as thick as thieves, and they were always comparing notes about his health and what they should do to keep him on the straight and narrow.

Clare Yarwood had suffered in her short life. She had seen death the same as he had, – a woman drowned in a horse trough, another hanging from a beam, a man shot dead in a church. She had seen plenty, even the love of her life when he had forfeited his life for her. The man had turned out to be bad but had redeemed himself in that one selfless sacrifice. She had tried to move on since, but her attempts had failed. There was a doctor who had been keen on her, and she on him, but it wasn't to be. He had subsequently married someone else. Since then she had been on her own.

Clare came and sat in the passenger seat of the car, a late-model Toyota. She was feeling cold as well.

'There's not a lot to go on,' she said as she rubbed her hands in front of the heater vent.

'What's Horsley got to say?'

'He's complaining, worried that the site will be destroyed.'

'He's right, but the recent have precedence over the long dead. How long did he say?'

'The mounds' ages vary from 2100 to 1500 BC. It's interesting, don't you think?' Clare said, knowing full well that Tremayne didn't.

Tremayne took out a cigarette from the packet that was inside his jacket pocket.

'Not in here,' Clare said. 'You know the regulations.'

'Give me a break. You're as bad as Jean; do this, do that, wipe your feet when you enter the house.'

'She's the best thing in your life, and don't you forget it.'

'I know that. Just don't let her know what I just said. Life's good with her, not so much with this murder.'

'Are we certain that it is?'

'What else can it be? Do you think the man dug a hole, put himself in it, then backfilled the soil, and patted down the earth so no one would see that he was there?'

'He could have died under unusual circumstances, and his disappearance, rather than his death, was beneficial to all parties.'

'Inheritance laws, death duties, questions someone didn't want answering.'

'I'm just raising the possibility.'

'I've got my money on murder. The pathologist will open him up tomorrow. We should start to get some answers then. In the meantime, I'm going back to the office.'

'I'll stay here,' Clare said, 'although I could do with something to eat. Pub lunch?'

'The most sense you've made all day,' Tremayne said.

There were others who didn't understand the relationship that existed between the two: a great deal of respect, a lot of sarcasm. Clare gave as good as she got. And Tremayne liked people who could be feisty. Jean was feisty, that was why he loved her, and Clare, not that he would ever admit to it, was the daughter that he never had.

Chapter 2

Jim Hughes, the senior crime scene investigator, didn't like the crime scene, although for once there was no blood to deal with, only mud. He wasn't sure which was worse, and to be alongside a burial mound with his team, slowly excavating the soil, careful not to disturb the archaeological dig, was proving difficult.

Clare, who had remained at the site, thought that the retrieval of the body was slow. Horsley and his team, in frustration, had moved to another burial mound close by. The tourists continued to arrive in the area in droves, lured by Stonehenge, the most prominent ancient site in England. But as she knew, there were other interesting places nearby: Avebury with its stone circles, the present-day village built in and around it, and then there was Salisbury Cathedral, the spire over four hundred feet high. Wherever you travelled, there was history to be found. Clare had to admit to being interested in taking part in an archaeological dig, but she knew it was just a thought, for when would she have the time.

Seventy miles from London, it appeared that for all its quiet charm, Salisbury and its environs had more murders than Homicide could handle, and invariably it was the villages that supplied the majority of them. She wondered if this was to be another village investigation. Tremayne would have said it was a certainty, but he was an unemotional sort of man, always expressing a negative outlook on life, or trying to convince others that that was his natural demeanour. Clare knew it was not, so did Jean, both having seen him when his guard was down. He had even shed a tear when he had made a speech at his second marriage to Jean, regretting the time that they had spent apart, the happiness that he felt.

Clare had chuckled to herself when he had said it, knowing that happy and Tremayne were two words that were not mutually compatible. Yet he had said them, and Jean had been delighted, so had Clare. Her relationship with her father was fine; her mother not so. They lived in Norfolk, hopeful that she would join them and take over the running of the hotel that they owned. She had tried it for a few months after the love of her life, Harry Holchester, had died for her – not before he had killed others, though. It was a bitter-sweet memory for her, and still the man remained in her mind, complicating her ability to move on, to find another man, to settle down and have children. To her, it seemed as though the police force was to be her partner in life.

It left her melancholy at times, especially when at home in her cottage in Stratford sub Castle, a small village not far from Salisbury, close to where a woman that she had regarded as a friend had died. Her death, the reason for it mysterious, and with a shade of the macabre about it, had left her saddened. Up the hill from her cottage, a pleasant walk of an afternoon, was the Anglo-Saxon fort of Old Sarum. There wasn't much left up there now, but it was an attractive place, although it had been the scene of another murder.

Wherever she looked, Clare could see misery and despair, yet she had not become inured to it, and she agreed with Tremayne on one thing – life was what you made of it.

However, she knew that he had wanted to make chief inspector, but hadn't. Not so much for himself, as he wasn't the most ambitious of men, but for Jean. She deserved better than the house he owned in Wilton, three miles from Salisbury. A two-storey red-brick house, it had no redeeming features, not even a pleasant outlook. It was circa 1950, a housing estate, where every house had the same look; the only apparent differences were the paint colour on the windows and the doors, the attic conversions, the garages added on later.

All in all, Tremayne regarded the house as suitable for him, but not for his wife. Clare would have to agree. It was a charmless house, but Jean had been over the place, cleaning here, painting there, buying new furniture, throwing out Tremayne's old clothes, buying him new ones.

'Over here,' Hughes shouted. 'You might want to have a look at this.'

Clare, already kitted out in coveralls, walked over to where the crime scene team were at work.

'You can't see anything from down there, can you?'

Hughes, not much older than she was, was an enthusiastic, eager man; a man she admired, as did Tremayne. The relationship that Hughes had engendered with the detective inspector was based initially on standing up to Tremayne, giving as good as he got in a verbal debate. However, Tremayne, always critical of someone wet behind the ears flashing their university degree, their professional qualifications, had to agree that Jim Hughes was a smart man, knew what he was talking about, could conduct a top-rate investigation, and there were no long-winded words when he spoke to you, although there were when he wrote up his report. And what Tremayne and Clare wanted was up at the top of the mound, slippery to negotiate, muddy underfoot, and altogether unpleasant.

'Any easy way up?' Clare said.

'We left the red carpet back at Bemerton Road Police Station, unfortunately.'

Tremayne's type of sarcasm from the mouth of the senior crime scene investigator. Not that Clare minded. A murder scene always affected those involved in investigating it, and humour helped to bring the tensions into context.

'We've rigged up a rope on the far side,' one of the other CSIs said. 'You can pull yourself up.'

Clare walked around and followed instructions. It was good that Tremayne was back at Bemerton Road – no doubt warming himself on the radiator in his office, attempting to put in place the paperwork for the investigation, shouting at others to get on with it. She knew what his reaction would have been if he had been asked to pull himself up a slippery bank with a rope – negative in the extreme – and she doubted if he could have managed it. Jean had done a great job in looking after him, but he was looking older by the month, and sometimes by the day. Clare was sure there was more to it than age: a hitherto unrevealed illness, mortality that would defy his staying until the official retirement bell was sounded, the reality that he was dying before his time.

***

Clare stood at the top of the mound. Around her, a panoramic view, Stonehenge over to the east, no more than a mile, its purpose obscured by time. And the mystery of why bluestone had been used in its construction, the larger stones over four tonnes in weight, brought from Wales, a distance of nearly two hundred miles. Some saw it as a sacred burial site, some as a site for celestial or astronomical alignments, a way to mark the seasons, and others as a place for healing. The truth was that no one was sure, not totally. It was the same with the mounds. Who were the people buried inside them? Were they the leaders of their society, warriors of note? The druids claimed Stonehenge as their own, but they weren't there when it was built – they had missed out on that by two thousand years.

Jim Hughes did not concern himself with such matters. He had a job to do, and it was down a shaft that had now got wood supports lining its sides. Clare knew that Horsley would be distressed at the desecration of England's heritage, but it was a crime scene, as Tremayne had said.

'We've uncovered more of the body,' Hughes said. 'It's male, as you had surmised.'

'The wristwatch and the shirt sleeve were good indicators,' Clare said.

'No cross-dressing back then?'

'It depends on how long we're talking about.'

'That's the point, isn't it? Forensics will do their work, and Pathology will probably be able to tell you what the man's diet was, ailments he may have had. Dentistry is always a good indicator, so are any operations that the man may have had, broken legs, that sort of thing. The procedures have changed over the years.'

'A guess?'

'I'm not keen to,' Hughes said. 'So far, we've cleared around the man's arm, up as far as his shoulder. We've also found a leg, dark-coloured trousers.'

'Shoes?'

'Leather, look expensive.'

'Any more?'

'The problem is that we'll collapse the mound if we pull him out. We'll be accused of vandalism, lambasted in the local press, and Horsley's got influence.'

'Murder?'

'The circumstances lead us to that conclusion. What do you suggest we do?'

'I'll check with DI Tremayne, but the body's been here a long time. Any chance of a tentative identification?'

'We can try and find a clothing label, and if the shoes are expensive, then that may help.'

Clare phoned Tremayne, put her plan forward, finding him to be in agreement. After that, she and Hughes left the mound and walked over to where Horsley was hard at work. 'A deal,' she said.

'You can't imagine what you could be destroying,' Horsley said.

'Fortunately, we can,' Hughes said. 'Sergeant Yarwood has a compromise. I suggest that you listen to what she has to say.'

'Very well, Sergeant, what is it?' Horsley responded. He was a man with few social graces, an obsession with the past, little care for the modern world. His vehicle, parked twenty-five yards away, was a pre-sixties Land Rover, and with his anorak removed, it was clear that fashion didn't interest him either. He was wearing a pair of jeans, the knees no longer present, not as a fashion statement, purely worn away through use. The shirt that he wore had a frayed collar, and even discounting the surroundings and the work being conducted, it had not been washed for some time. He also, once the three of them had distanced themselves from the dig, smoked a pipe. The type of man they would have assumed not to be married, the type of man who

17

would prefer his books and his antiques and his history to the joy of a woman by his side, but he did have a wife, Clare knew that. In fact, she had met her on more than one occasion, and she was a delightful woman in her fifties, prim and proper, and very clean.

'It's been there for that long, we can wait a few more days. We want to give you a chance to examine the Bronze Age skeleton, alongside the crime scene investigators. It's unusual that we'd agree to this, but it seems the only option,' Clare said.

'We'd get precedence?' Horsley asked.

'Whoever you nominate, no more than two people. They would need to be kitted up: coveralls, nitrile gloves, overshoes.'

'You'll make the entrance secure?'

'We'll do our best. We'll bring up some additional equipment, whatever will help.'

'I agree. When can we start?'

'It's unstable, so you'll need to take the lead from us. We could get our body out easily enough; yours is more of a challenge.'

'Understood. I'll be one, and I've got a good person who'll work with me.'

'The mound you moved to?' Clare asked.

'A lot of them were ransacked in the seventeenth and eighteenth centuries. It's one of those, I'm afraid. We can't explain why this one hasn't, but it looks intact.'

***

An archaeological dig was not big news in the Salisbury area. There were always at least two or three, sometimes more in the summer, peopled by eager university students, local school children bored by long holidays or raked in as part of a school project. Then there were the elderly, enjoying every moment of being down in the dirt and uncovering past histories, complaining about their sore backs and their calloused hands later. And at the centre, a core group of professionals taking advantage of the extra manpower, but worried that the enthusiastic amateurs would miss something, or go in too aggressively with the trowel, and break something fragile. Horsley remembered such an occurrence, two summers past. A twenty-five-year-old university student, bleary after a night at the pub, had prodded something difficult to remove, a stone he thought, breaking it in two. Not realising until later that the brooch, a perfect example of first-century Roman jewellery, had gone from unique to damaged. Not that the value of the piece had concerned Horsley, but it was vandalism, and he had allowed the person onto the site. Since then, he had instigated stricter controls on who was allowed on and who wasn't, who was to be given a trowel, and who was to be offered the job of sifting through the debris removed. Numbers of assistants were down as a result, and now he had a pristine site with two bodies, one of interest, the other of no concern to him.

It wasn't that a murdered man didn't deserve more respect; Horsley knew that he did, but he was a pragmatist. A man who was thousands of years old, his name long forgotten, his occupation unclear unless there was armour with his body, was significant in that he represented a link with the past; a modern man did not.

And now he had a lifeline from the police, a chance to successfully search the mound, with the additional skills of a police crime scene investigation team, professionals every one of them.

19

Clare did not tell Horsley that Tremayne had been reluctant to comply with her compromise, and he had run it past Superintendent Moulton, his superior. Moulton – a man who hankered after Tremayne's retirement, a degree-educated and younger police force his primary objective. The two were combatants over the retirement issue, respectful of each other otherwise.

Common sense had prevailed, a better outcome than Clare had expected, and now Horsley intended to take advantage of the situation. They would still have to attempt to avoid the detritus of years gone by, making sure not to get an insect inside their clothing, a cobweb in the face, and hopefully not to disturb a badger, cute and cuddly when wandering around at night, not so when there were young in the sett. A new word for Clare; she had always assumed that a badger had a den, but it appeared that there was a more correct term.

Hughes brought up more people from Salisbury, including a mining engineer on contract to advise on the best approach to protect both teams' best interests. The senior crime scene investigator was delighted. He, like Clare, was interested in local history, and the chance to be on site when important discoveries could occur excited him.

Clare was also keen, and even though there was other work she could be doing, in the comfort of her car if necessary, she was glued to the spot. The weather was inclement, not unusual for the time of the year. The mud was not so bad after a brief interlude of sun, and the CSIs had brought up metal stepping stone-style plates, ensuring a common approach path, with the crime scene manager charged with ensuring that anyone entering or leaving the crime scene was logged.

The crime scene manager, if asked, would have stated that it was one thing to have trained professionals to deal with, it was another matter with keen amateurs. Clare knew him to be a man with an attitude, and she had not asked whether he approved or not, only telling Jim Hughes and the manager that the decision had been made by Superintendent Moulton and Detective Inspector Tremayne, and what they said was what was going to happen.

The manager, a miserable man from near the Scottish border, not popular at Bemerton Road due to his surly nature and his inability to smile, would do his job, Clare knew that. He was a consummate professional, and affability or lack of it meant very little. There would be no contamination of the site, that was for sure.

Horsley was pleased to see two crime scene tents being erected, one of them over the shaft entrance into the mound. For once, he was sure that the area would not be devalued after thousands of years by an unfortunate and ill-timed thunderstorm.

Floodlights were brought up close, a generator set twenty yards back, the cables carefully laid in position.

It was six in the evening, and the light had faded, the temperature was dropping, and there was a light drizzle. Jim Hughes called his team around him. Horsley and Clare, along with Sue Boswell, a local historian and Horsley's nominated assistant, attended as well.

'Tomorrow, seven in the morning sharp,' he said. 'We've got time to conduct this correctly, and as long as we have our body out by tomorrow night, then there's no need to work through the night.'

Horsley wanted to protest, but Hughes was right, there was no need. If the man had died recently, then there would have been no discussion, no bringing the team's day to an end. It would have been to carry on until the body was out and with Pathology.

Clare phoned Tremayne who phoned the pathologist to tell him one more day before the body was with him. Stuart Collins was not disappointed with the delay. He'd had twelve hours straight on his feet, and he didn't want another day like the current one.

Chapter 3

Clare was glad of the early night, the chance to catch up on some sleep and to spend time by herself, her cat by her side – not that it did much, old as it was – and the chance to finish the book she had been reading. A whodunnit, but she had figured it out after the first chapter, or she thought she had. It didn't matter either way, whether it was the butler or the doctor or the ex-wife; it was after all a substitute for her life, devoid of a man. When she was out of her cottage, it didn't worry her; inside, it did. Not a lot, she would have to admit, and there were benefits, no one to argue with, an easy maintenance life, sufficient money to pay the bills, the mortgage, to indulge in the occasional luxury. She still missed Harry, the man who had moved her more than any other. She had met him at the pub that Tremayne frequented – he had been the licensee – and it hadn't been long before they were lovers, planning their future together. Then came the night in Avon Hill when she found out that his family were steeped in ancient history and ritual, and that violence in the pursuit of a belief – not something that she could ever understand – had caused Harry and others to commit terrible acts, murder even.

He had given his life for her, an act of redemption, of love, and she realised that if he had lived, then he would now be in prison, not in her arms, nor her bed, nor would the two of them be married and with children.

Clare stroked the cat at her side. It gave her little consolation, as with the doctor she had gone out with, loved even. She met him occasionally, unavoidable in a market town of just over thirty thousand; inevitable as he was a doctor at the city's hospital. Their meetings were always professional, always to do with her work.

As she sat with the cat, she wondered if she should have compromised and accepted the doctor's proposal.

With Harry the love had been pure, even though he had turned out to be evil. It was Catch-22, she knew that. She wanted to move on, but she couldn't. The attempts not to visit his grave had failed miserably, and although she only went there every few months, it was inevitable that she would go again. She knew that Tremayne wanted her to stop, so did Jean, but she couldn't, not yet. Her book stayed open, but it was not being read. Clare, a detective sergeant, a person with a future in the police force, the chance to become an inspector, left the room and went upstairs to her bed. She knew that the cat would follow soon after. She felt sad.

***

Tremayne left Bemerton Road Police Station at eight in the evening. In the past, it would have been a good time to go to the pub and have a few pints of beer. Instead, he drove home to the house that he shared with Jean; on the table, a hot meal for him, a bottle of beer.

'Home early,' Jean said. Tremayne remembered when they had first met, a pub in the country. He had been with some fellow junior officers, indulging in drinking too much, checking out the local females, not worrying too much about drink-driving, feeling immortal as young people do. He remembered little of the night the day after, apart from the pretty young woman who had preferred him to the others in the pub that night. He was not a vain man, he knew that he was not attractive, certainly not the sort of man to draw women to him. None of the others had had much success, either, as they were more interested in devoting time to the pursuit of alcohol.

After six months, him getting drunk on occasion, she chastising him when he did, they were married in a small village church.

Three years as he rose in the police force from constable to sergeant. The promotion to inspector came later, after Jean had left that eventful day.

It was several months after she left before he managed to control his drinking, going into Bemerton Road not just hungover, but still drunk. It was only because of Inspector Grimley that he had survived. Grimley had seen the value in the young Tremayne, sat him down and had a few words with him, making sure that the drinking reduced. Grimley was dead now, the result of a stroke at the age of sixty-eight. A chain smoker, and a reformed alcoholic, the man had preached the lesson to Tremayne, conscious of his own failings.

'Yarwood will have the body tomorrow,' Tremayne said as he poured his beer. He appreciated what Jean had done with the house, glad that she was back with him.

'We don't want to talk about murders, do we? I thought we'd have a quiet night in, just the two of us. Maybe watch the television.'

Tremayne had to admit that a quiet night would have been anathema to him not so long ago, but with Jean, it sounded just fine. The health scare had changed him unalterably. He had tried drinking again with the same gusto, but it didn't excite him as it once had, the thought in the back of his mind that the next drink could be his last. The cigarettes were not proving as easy to cut back on, but he had tried, Jean and Yarwood in his ear all the time about them, and he still managed to sneak in the extra one when neither of them was looking.

He could feel the futility in holding out against Moulton and his retirement offer, and it was seriously on his mind, the chance of extra time with Jean, the possibility of regaining some of his lost vigour. He had been checked out by his doctor three months previously, the same lecture about exercising and drinking less, smoking less. But Tremayne knew that he was getting older and his joints were stiffening, his hair thinning, a permanent state of exhaustion.

He looked over at Jean. 'A quiet night in, that would be fine,' he said.

***

At seven in the morning, sharp, Jim Hughes's instruction from the previous day did not hold the appeal that it had previously.

Gerard Horsley was there, as was his assistant Sue Boswell. Some of the crime scene investigators were still to arrive, but that wasn't a concern, not yet. Firstly, the mining engineer, Lance Atterton, needed to give his opinion of the site. He was a red-faced man, not on account of the cold, although that helped, but due to his obviously unfit condition.

Clare knew that he would not be entering the mound, as he was rotund, almost as round as he was tall.

'No one's entering into that mound until I give the all-clear,' Atterton said. His accent sounded South African, although it would later be found to be Zimbabwean.

The wind was biting, and a light mist covered the area. Stonehenge, down below, was barely visible. Although the day was cold, there was no forecast of rain.

Clare was dressed for the occasion with a ski jacket, the legacy of a skiing holiday to Switzerland. Not that her skiing had amounted to much as she had twisted her ankle on the second day, and had spent the rest of the time either at the bar or in the heated indoor pool in the hotel. It had been an enjoyable holiday, she remembered that, and she had always had an aversion to the cold anyway.

'Lance has full authority here,' Jim Hughes said. 'We don't want any accidents, no one stuck in a collapsed shaft, no destruction of the body at the bottom.' Horsley, a man who did not smile that often, did at that.

Atterton led the way to the mound. He had put on police-issue coveralls, as had the others. He had had trouble closing his it due to his girth, but in the end one of the CSIs had helped him complete the task. The crime scene manager hovered, ensuring that no one disturbed the site, everyone followed the rules.

On top of the mound, Atterton looked down the shaft. Only two others were allowed up, Clare and Hughes. Clare had to concur with Atterton on that one. Horsley had wanted to come up as well, so had his assistant, and some of the CSIs, but the mound had been weakened after the shaft had been excavated.

'It's not safe, but then I assume you know that,' Atterton said. He seemed impervious to the biting wind, to the frost. Clare was not, and her feet were unpleasantly cold.

'We need to act quickly on this,' Hughes said. 'We've got to get one body out today, and Horsley needs to get down to his warrior or whoever he is.'

'That's understood. You've already used timber planks for shoring.'

'It helped.'

'Without complicating what we have here, I suggest we get some more and then use screw jacks to hold them apart. Not sure that ponytail's going to like it; not much I can do about him, though.'

'Damage to the mound?' Clare asked.

'Some. Can't be helped. We'll shore up to where the first body is, and then you can retrieve it. The only problem, as far as I can see, is that any loosened soil will drop down. It'd be easier to go in from the side of the mound, a horizontal tunnel, but that'll take time. Not much of that, I suppose.'

'There never is,' Clare said.

'Does anyone have the planks? We can rent screw jacks in Salisbury.'

'How many planks?' Hughes said.

Clare could see that Atterton was a no-nonsense man, used to making quick decisions, comfortable with delegating authority.

'If you've got some spare, we can use them. Mind you, it's not going to be pleasant down there. Glad it's not me, but I'll not fit,' Atterton said.

Clare shouted down to Horsley. 'How long do you need?'

Five to six days, possibly more, the reply.

'That seals it,' Clare said. 'We take out our body first.'

The three left the mound. Clare headed off to her car to warm up, Hughes went to get one of the CSIs to bring the spare planks closer to the mound. Atterton phoned the hire company in Salisbury and asked them to send up a vehicle with the jacks.

As they waited for the all-clear, Clare spoke to Horsley, asked him why the dig was being conducted in the winter, and not the summer when the weather was more favourable.

'It's like this,' Horsley said. Sue Boswell was standing close to him, disarmingly close. 'Getting permission can be difficult, and then after research into the mound showed that it could be significant, well, I had to act, winter or no winter. Sue was keen to get started as well.'

Clare thought there may have been something between the two, other than a love of ancient history. 'Someone put the other body there. Any ideas?' she asked.

'Hardly. Our interest is in ancient history,' Sue Boswell said.

'If, as you say, there's significance in the mound, something the Bronze Age inhabitants of the area recognised, isn't it possible that someone more recent would have recognised that as well?'

'It's always a possibility,' Horsley said. 'It's not something we've considered. I can't see it, not really.'

'Nor can I,' Sue Boswell said.

At ten minutes past eleven, Atterton returned to the tent set up as the temporary headquarters. 'We'll break for one hour, allow the soil to stabilise, and then I'll make a final check. After that one person can go down.'

'Can I check our site first?' Horsley said.

'I'd suggest that your assistant goes down, she's slimmer than you, less weight as well. She'll have to wear a harness in case we have to pull her up,' Atterton said. 'If you want to place a covering over your area, that's fine.'

'Ten minutes only,' Hughes said. 'I'd prefer it if they didn't, but under the circumstances, I'll agree.'

A mobile canteen waited where the cars were. Even though the area was exposed, the food was hot. Some benches had been set out for people to sit down, although most didn't. The temperature was just above freezing. The sun as forecasted was shining, not a cloud in the sky. In the distance, the tourists were out in force at Stonehenge, a privileged few allowed to approach and to touch the stones.

'You're a mining engineer,' Clare said. A dumb way to instigate a conversation with Lance Allerton, she thought, seeing that she knew that already.

'In South Africa mainly. The last fifteen years in England, but mining's not what it used to be, not in England, anyway.'

'But you're from Zimbabwe.'

'I left there when I was in my teens. It was a good life there, and then the rebels became the government. It was okay for a while, and then Mugabe lost the plot, started kicking out the whites, giving their land and property to his people.'

'South Africa?'

'I went to university there, got my qualifications and ended up in a few gold mines. Good years, although a few cave-ins, a few too many people dying unnecessarily.'

'Is that where you learnt about shoring up tunnels?'

'It's where I learnt everything. I saved a few lives in my time, but my wife was born in England, so we

30

headed over here. The climate's not the greatest, but it's calm, and we're happy enough here.'

'Zimbabwe, any chance of returning?'

'Not now. The land is still there, probably the house, but that's for a younger man. Now I consult out, advise the police if they need me, not that often though. It's nice out here, the fresh air, the history. Did you know that Zimbabwe is named after some ruins there? Built in the eleventh to the fifteenth centuries. I went there once, massive stone walls, the centre of a civilisation, a population of up to fifteen thousand. There was progress back then, long gone in Zimbabwe now.'

'You must have formed views of the people and what's happened there.'

'When you're kicked off your land, out of your country, then of course. So would you, if it happened to you, but now I hold no grudge, no prejudices. Live and let live, that's my motto. As long as the wife and myself have our little house, and I can go fishing, visit the local pub, then I'll not be making waves, not anymore.'

Chapter 4

Sue Boswell was suitably harnessed and wearing, in addition to the police-issued crime scene paraphernalia, a hard hat and a warm jacket under her coveralls. Lance Atterton, concerned about her going further down than where the shoring was, further than where the arm and leg of the more recent body were exposed, also ensured that she had lightweight breathing apparatus.

'This is against my better judgement,' Atterton said. 'I hope this has been noted.'

'It's against the crime scene manager's as well. Your concerns have been documented,' Clare said.

'I'll be fine,' Sue Boswell said. The woman looked ludicrous, Clare thought, trussed up like a Christmas turkey.

A frame had been rigged over the opening, a rope strung over it. Atterton and one of the younger and fitter CSIs slowly eased the rope, Sue Boswell dangling momentarily in space.

'Keep your hands clear if you can on the way down,' Atterton said.

Clare could see that was not so easy as the jerking motion of the rope was swaying the woman to one side and then to the other. Horsley stood by, anxiously looking at his assistant as she dropped below the lip of the opening. A light shone down from above, another was attached to Sue Boswell's hard hat. She also had two pocket torches tied by cords around her neck.

'I can see the body,' Sue shouted back. No one doubted which body she was referring to.

'Secure the area, make sure you use the plastic you have to cover it well,' Horsley excitedly shouted down to his assistant. Atterton had to pull him back; his exuberance was causing loosened dirt to fall down the shaft.

'I'm here,' Sue Boswell shouted. In her enthusiasm to move the soil close to the ancient body, something she hadn't been instructed to do, she disturbed the earth above it, causing the earth to cascade down on her from above. As she was momentarily obscured, Atterton went into rapid extraction mode, reminiscent of his time back in South Africa in the gold mines.

'Pull her up, now!' he shouted. He took a firm hold of the rope, as did the CSI who was holding it too. The men tensioned it.

'It's okay,' came a voice from down below. 'It's incredible.'

'Are you safe?' Atterton asked, his voice slightly calmer.

'I can see you up above. I can see the upper body of the skeleton.'

'What else can you see?' Horsley yet again moved too close, disturbing the soil. 'Take some photos.'

'I can see a dagger, as well as a breastplate. It's a treasure trove. This is someone of great importance. There could be more here than at Bush Barrow.'

'What does it mean?' Clare asked.

'In 1808,' Horsley said, 'William Cunnington excavated Bush Barrow. It's not far from here, three hundred yards. There was so much retrieved that the find became known as the crown jewels of the "King of Stonehenge".'

'King?' Atterton queried.

33

'Not literally, but a chieftain of great importance. If what Sue is saying is correct, then that places this site in a whole new light.'

'I'll cover what I can and come back up,' Sue said.

'Bring something with you, marks it position,' Horsley shouted back. The man was beside himself, like a child with a new toy.

Sue emerged after ten minutes, the returning heroine. In a plastic bag securely held around her neck was a diamond-shaped plate from over four thousand years ago. Once free of the harness, and after she had caught her breath, she handed it over to Horsley. The man held it with reverence.

'There's more down there,' Sue said. 'I'm certain that it's more important than Bush Barrow.'

Clare could foresee delays, knowing full well that a historical find of great significance would bring out the heavyweights from the historical societies, the local councillors, the member of parliament, those in favour of preserving the area, others who saw progress being inhibited by undue reverence for a past long gone. Clare knew who would win, and the plan to take out the more recent body would need further consultation, further agreement. She climbed down from the top of the mound, past the crime scene manager, ensuring that she was signed off from the site, and walked over to her car.

'It's a major find,' Clare said to Tremayne on her phone once she had warmed up. 'Gerard Horsley's prior agreement with us will not hold. He's right, of course, we can't deny him that. The only issue is how to get our body out.'

'Damn nuisance,' Tremayne said. 'Any idea what's been found?'

'A dagger handle, as well as a diamond-shaped plate which Horsley's assistant brought up. He's trying to clean it up, but it could be gold.'

'What's Jim Hughes's opinion?'

'I've not sounded him out. I'm running the possibility through you first. If we act now, even with Horsley's reluctant agreement, we could be lambasted for the desecration of a historically important site. The police could be shown to be heavy-handed and uncaring, the usual criticisms.'

'You're right. Superintendent Moulton needs to be informed. Leave it to me. In the meantime, sound out Horsley and Hughes, get the mining engineer onside, and prepare to act ASAP.'

***

Tremayne, not as insensitive as he portrayed himself, realised the dilemma. On one hand, ancient history, and on the other, a recent body. There was no doubt that it was there as a result of foul play. One thing was clear, the body had to be sent to Pathology. Murder was murder, no matter how long ago it was, and the perpetrator could still be alive, still capable of murdering others, possibly already had.

'How important is this body?' Superintendent Moulton said as Tremayne entered his office.

'It's dead, and it didn't get there on its own. I'd say it was important,' Tremayne replied.

'It's a hornets' nest you've stirred up.'

'It wasn't us who opened up the mound. It was Gerard Horsley, odd character.'

The two men sat looking at each other across Moulton's expansive desk. They respected each other: the older police officer, plenty of experience under his belt; younger the superintendent, a stickler for following procedures, reporting, and key performance indicators. The man had irked Tremayne when he had first entered Bemerton Road Police Station eight years earlier, the new broom aiming to sweep clean, to dispense with the old, bring in the new. But in time, an uneasy peace had developed between the two men: Moulton mellowing, gaining an understanding that gut instinct, policing by investigation out on the street, still had its place; Tremayne understanding that a modern computer-driven world needed a different approach to policing than his.

'Odd he may be, but the man knows the right people. I've already had the Wiltshire Heritage Museum on the phone, that's where the Bush Barrow treasure is displayed, and the museum in Salisbury's been on the phone asking what I'm going to do. What am I going to do, Detective Inspector? Override them, incur their wrath, or do you have a better solution?'

'You agree that we need to get our body out?'

'Of course. As you say, the death has to be suspicious. We can't just forget about it because it's too difficult.'

'Stonehenge is World Heritage Listed.'

'Is the site close enough to be part of that?'

'Close enough to have significant historical interest from Stonehenge. If it's as important as Sergeant Yarwood believes it is, we'll have to get permission to continue.'

'Phone up Yarwood, tell her to secure the site while we consider what to do.'

'Stand down Hughes and his people?'

'Not yet. Ensure the site is secure, and make sure no one, not even Horsley, goes near; not until we've resolved this impasse.'

Clare took the news well, fully understanding the reasoning; Lance Atterton walked away from the site with a smile on his face – he was on contract, pay by the day, and the meter would keep running until the police officially signed him off from the site.

Gerard Horsley was not sure what he felt. He was on the verge of a great discovery, his name up there with William Cunnington, a nineteenth-century man who had seen beyond the greed of taking what he could for himself and had approached archaeology as a noble pursuit. And if what Sue Boswell had discovered in the burial mound was an indication of future finds, then the man lying there was more important than the one in Bush Barrow.

The Bush Barrow chieftain, the treasures proudly displayed in Devizes, in the Wiltshire Heritage Museum, stood unique amongst the discoveries in the region.

In Salisbury, the forces rallied. Tremayne, keen for a quick resolution, knew that it was for him to be the antagonist in any discussions. Clare wanted all care to be taken, and Jim Hughes, the senior crime scene investigator, had left the site, not concerned either way, only saying for her to call him when it had been resolved. The entrance into the mound had been sealed, and the frame that had lowered Sue Boswell remained in place. Atterton had spent time checking that the shoring was secure, and if there were to be more rain, then there would be no water ingression. Inside the shaft, the lower air temperature was freezing the previously loose soil.

***

Three hours after Clare had left the site, a group met at Bemerton Road Police Station. There had been an attempt, a result of phone calls by Gerard Horsley, to meet at a neutral location. Tremayne did not consider the museum in Salisbury as neutral. And it was his insistence that it was still a police matter, and the present held sway over the ancient.

The local newspaper had now been tipped off, and there was to be a news item on the television that night. Stonehenge and ancient history were big news, and buried treasure stirred up the public imagination. Even in the time since Horsley had announced – unwisely, Clare thought – that there was gold in the burial mound, there had been two fossickers close to the mound with metal detectors, and the police had warned them off. Extra police had been seconded to assist the two officers already there – not the effect that Horsley had wanted. And now the police were feeling the wrath of the Stonehenge World Heritage Site Coordinator, Cecil Hardcastle, a precise man in a tweed jacket and a cravat, who sat at one end of the table in the police station's conference room.

'Ladies and gentlemen, could we bring this to order,' Superintendent Moulton said over the hubbub as everyone wanted to say their piece.

'The regulations are clear in this matter,' Hardcastle said. 'A find of this magnitude takes precedence over any other activities.'

'There's no mention of what to do in the case of a police investigation,' Clare interjected. She had had a chance to read up on the subject, but even so, it was still vague as to what should be done.

'We shouldn't have stopped, it's too important.' Horsley said, on his feet. Sue Boswell was sitting close to him.

Lance Atterton sat quietly surveying the scene. He had changed out of his work wear and was dressed in an open-necked shirt and a pair of loose-fitting trousers held up by braces, the man not having any discernible waist.

'We need to put this to our executive,' Hardcastle said. The director of the Wiltshire Museum in Devizes nodded his head in agreement, as did his counterpart at the Salisbury Museum. The Bush Barrow treasure was displayed in Devizes, a city more distant than Salisbury from Stonehenge. Clare assumed that the two men would be disputing which museum would be displaying the latest find.

'We can't leave a body there while you conduct your work,' Tremayne said. He was surprised how diplomatic he had been. Typically, he would have forced his point, but even he had to concede that matter being discussed in the conference room was not a murder enquiry, not yet.

'Detective Inspector Tremayne's right,' Moulton said. 'We'll work with you on this one, but we need our body first.'

'If I may make a suggestion,' Atterton said.

'The floor's yours,' Tremayne said.

'The temperature's still cold in the mound, and another cold night should assist. What I suggest is that we form a cage around where the Bronze Age man is, nothing too elaborate, but sufficient to prevent any more soil falling down onto it. Also, we need to ensure that whatever soil is dislodged from around the more recent of the two bodies is extracted.'

'How?' Moulton asked.

'The second body was not placed there from the top, but from the side. How it was done, and how no one noticed, is another issue. We know the approximate position on the side of the mound where we should work. I'll set up a method to dispose of the soil, and also a way of enhancing the plastic down below with something more suitable. It'll take a couple of days to complete, and then we'll remove the first body with due care and attention, maintaining the integrity of the other.'

'Two days?' Tremayne asked.

'Two days for the body you want.'

'I don't like this,' Horsley said. The others on his side of the discussion nodded their heads in agreement.

'When can you start?' Moulton asked. He knew that further discussion would not resolve the impasse and that it was for him to assert his position. He hoped that he was making the right decision. He had had the benefit of checking out Atterton, including his successful recovery of over one hundred men from one of the deepest mines in South Africa. If Atterton couldn't solve the dilemma, nobody could.

'This cannot be allowed,' Horsley said.

'Unfortunately, Mr Horsley, it is the only compromise possible. None of us wants to do this, but we have no option. We have a duty to the present; your duty lies in a time long past. We're all sympathetic to what you have discovered, but we will have our body.'

Atterton leant over to Horsley, placed his hand on the man's shoulder. 'Don't worry, it'll be fine. I know what I'm doing.' It did not appease the archaeologist's frustration at what to him was vandalism.

Chapter 5

With the battle lost, Gerard Horsley resigned himself to the decision, although Lance Atterton still found that he was becoming a nuisance. A few sharp words from Atterton, a plain-speaking man, not with the delicacy of the English language that Horsley would have used, soon resolved the situation.

The weather continued to be cold, and no one was smiling up at the burial mound, apart from Atterton. He had confided to Clare that his proposal was fraught with difficulties, one of which was that he was dealing with soil and not rock. The plan he had laid out at Bemerton Road Police Station on the day when Moulton had made his decision, and then again as the site in the tent to one side of the mound, was simple in theory, complicated in actuality.

'I need to isolate the body at the bottom. The logical way would be to insert pipes above the lower area at a height sufficient not to disturb either body,' Atterton said to those assembled. Horsley nodded his head, not indicating whether he approved or not.

Clare's instruction from Tremayne had been succinct. 'Two days, no more. And if Horsley causes trouble, evict him from the site until we have what we want.'

Not ideal, Clare would admit, and she was determined to avoid taking such action at all cost. And besides, the word had got out. The importance of the find had been known by the media for over a day, enhanced dramatically by Horsley, a man who should have known better but who was determined to have his five minutes of fame. He had featured on the television the night before after the meeting at the police station. At least he'd had the common sense not to criticise the police, although he had told the interviewer that what was in the mound was of the greatest significance and the police presence was unfortunate.

Tremayne, sitting at home with Jean, another quiet night in, had let out an expletive when Horsley had appeared on the television, sounding off as if he and William Cunnington, the hero of Bush Barrow and the discoverer of the 'King of Stonehenge', were kindred spirits.

Clare had laughed when Jean had told her Tremayne's reaction. She had also seen the interview, and thought that Horsley had good reason to be pleased with himself. She was as excited as the others at the site at the prospect of finding out what else lay hidden at the bottom of the mound, knowing full well that when the other body had been extracted, she would be off the site.

The early morning frost, a regular winter feature on Salisbury Plain, showed no sign of clearing. It was ten in the morning, and it was still heavy on the ground.

'I've changed my plan,' Atterton said. 'This cold, if it continues, should hold the soil stable enough for all of us. What I suggest as an alternative is for a plate or plates, if we have the space, to be placed over the lower body and supported by screw jacks. Now by my reckoning, and if we're very clever, with a certain amount of luck as well, we should be able to create a platform for one of the CSIs to stand on, and for him or her to work on the other body, and if possible send up a very fine rod to the outside of the mound. That way we'll know where we need to extract the soil. Otherwise, we progressively dismantle the mound, but that would require heavy equipment and time. Neither option will be too popular, I suppose.'

'How soon before we can start on the first option?' Jim Hughes said.

'Ten minutes. I'll grant that you'll not be able to conduct your investigation to the degree that you normally would.'

'Any soil we remove will be sifted and checked, but there won't be any blood, not after so long, and any loose items we should be able to pick up.'

'I'm in agreement,' Horsley said.

In the end, Atterton phoned another mining engineer. The man, a wiry Welshman, as thin as Atterton was fat, arrived at the site within the hour.

'Sorry, Sue, not this time,' Atterton said, looking over at the young archaeologist.

'Don't worry,' the Welsh engineer said. 'I've worked with Lance before. He knows my ability.'

Clare wasn't sure of the plan, as it seemed fraught with danger to her, but no one had anything else to say.

On the top of the mound stood Jim Hughes, Sue Boswell, Dafydd Evans and Lance Atterton. Clare and Horsley were relegated to watching from below.

Evans, Atterton's colleague, peered down the shaft, letting out a gasp at what he could see. 'No chance for you, Lance,' he said.

'Can it be done?' Atterton asked.

Evans turned to Sue Boswell. 'How far does the body extend at the bottom?' he asked.

'I've only seen the top half. We need an area of at least a foot around the whole body.'

'Not possible, as you've probably realised. I suggest we take some of the metal plates or spares that we've just walked on and place them over what's exposed and use screw jacks to hold them up. Unfortunately, there's no room for two, so it'll have to be me,' Evans said, his accent noticeable.

'I could do it,' Sue insisted.

'I suggest you let her,' Atterton said. 'We need to be cooperating here, and I don't want to be accused afterwards of rejecting a perfectly reasonable suggestion.'

'Are you sure?' Hughes asked.

'No one's hundred per cent on this one, but yes, it should be okay.'

'A compromise,' Evans said. 'The plates and the jacks are cumbersome. Sue can go down, prepare the area, no more ferreting around. We'll pull her up, and then I'll go down and secure the area.'

Sue took her place at the entrance to the shaft. As on the previous day, she was fully kitted up, her breathing apparatus checked and working. The second time her descent was more controlled than the first, not only because she was less frightened, but because Evans was steadying the rope.

'I'm here,' Sue shouted, her voice muffled by the mask over her face.

'You know the size of the plates and the jacks,' Evans said. 'Don't try to find something else. If you dig into the sides of the mound, it could collapse.'

'I won't.'

Sue kept to the agreement, and soon she was back at the top of the mound. Evans followed her route down, the plates – there was only space for three – fed down on another rope, the screw jacks following.

After forty-five minutes, the area was declared safe. A sheet of plastic had now been placed over the plates, and there was a place for the CSI's feet to rest, although he would still be secured from above.

***

Ground-penetrating radar brought to the site that day was moved over the area where the first body retrieval was to be made. With patience and a good deal of skill, the outline of the body could be seen, also its position. Jim Hughes, the senior CSI, was delighted.

'We'll need our nominated CSI in the shaft to assist, and we'll dig from outside,' Hughes said.

'Agreed,' Atterton said. 'We'll set up a soil retrieval system inside the mound, nothing complex, just plastic buckets.'

'Some will fall down,' Horsley said. He was ignored. The first body extraction was going ahead.

Two CSIs stood on the outside of the mound, about half-way up. One of them made the first thrust with his fork, piercing the grass that grew there. Carefully, he and the other CSI removed the turf from an area of one square yard. Another CSI took a metal rod and prodded gently into the soil, checking for resistance. At the third attempt, he declared success.

Inside the mound, the CSI gently removed the soil around the body's exposed leg, ensuring that whatever he removed was placed in a bucket and lifted to the top for further examination by other CSIs. It wasn't pleasant, and the man knew that he could only work there for thirty minutes before a break. The next CSI to be lowered down the shaft, a twenty-two-year-old woman, relished the prospect.

By the time she was lowered down, the first leg had been fully exposed, and the ankle of a second one was visible. On the side of the mound outside, slow progress was being made as the soil was dug out, not at an oblique angle, but by cutting into the mound as if cutting a slice of cake. Horsley stood mutely to one side, not expressing an opinion.

The man's head was revealed at four twenty in the afternoon. With a clear indicator, the CSIs on the outside intensified their activity. Inside, in rotation, the two CSIs, chosen because of their physiques, continued to work. When the metal rod broke through from outside into the tunnel, their work was complete.

Dafydd Evans dropped down into the tunnel and secured the body that Horsley and Sue Boswell worried over with an additional cover, and a layer of clean soil, padding it down as best he could. On instructions from Jim Hughes that were being relayed from above him at the entrance to the shaft, he removed the last of the soil holding the body. From the side of the mound, the CSIs pulled it out, not taking any notice of the condition, only seeing that the man was fully clothed and that the skeletal remains were intact.

Afterwards, at the debriefing, Gerard Horsley was ecstatic, and he shook Atterton's and Evan's hands firmly. 'Great job. When can we start?' he asked.

'We'll need tomorrow morning,' Hughes said. 'After that, we'll hand it over to you.'

'Fine, better than I expected,' Horsley replied.

'I'll stay and help,' Atterton said. 'The equipment's rented for a month.'

'We're volunteers,' Horsley said.

'Don't worry. A pint of beer will be the payment. I imagine you can manage that.'

'Of course. Who knows what we'll discover now.'

***

Tremayne was pleased: the body was with Pathology. Stuart Collins, the senior pathologist, arrived back in his office at seven in the evening. Both Tremayne and Clare were waiting for him.

'You don't waste any time,' Collins said.

'We're anxious for any information,' Clare said. 'There wasn't much that could be done at the crime scene, just the man's removal and transportation to here.'

'I've not looked at him yet. The little I've heard so far is that he is of medium height and that he was well dressed. Apart from that, you'll have to wait. I'll not be commencing the post mortem until tomorrow morning.'

'Not tonight?' Tremayne said.

'Unlike you, I have a home to go to, and not only that, the man needs to be prepared. Those working on it know what to do, and Forensics has put a couple of people on duty to start their work. I suggest that you two come back tomorrow at seven sharp and watch me as I work. You'll gain more doing that than pestering me now.'

'Murder?'

'Probable,' Collins said.

'Positive?'

'Nothing's positive until I've given my report. It's causing quite a stir from what I've heard, buried treasure and all that.'

'It's the body that you have,' Tremayne said. 'Not the one that's still there. If the ancient body had been murdered, we'd not be opening a case; the statute of limitations is definitely in place on that one.'

'Interesting, though,' Collins said. 'I must admit to being interested in what they've found.'

'So am I,' Clare said. Tremayne said nothing. His image of an uncaring, disinterested man was to be maintained at all costs.

Tremayne and Clare left Collins in his office, aware that the man – regardless of what he had said – would be spending another hour or two there before he went home.

Clare slept fitfully that night, the cat snuggled up at the end of the bed; Tremayne went home to a meal and a couple of beers before retiring upstairs– sleep was no trouble for him, and he slept until the alarm sounded at 6 a.m.

Stuart Collins was in with the body on Tremayne's arrival, Clare was already there and kitted up. A junior pathologist stood on the other side of the long-dead man. Even though the body, or more correctly, the skeleton, was without clothes, it bore little resemblance to what had once been human.

'It's been cleaned as much as possible,' Collins said. 'Forensics have a watch, a ring on the man's left hand, not a wedding ring. They also retrieved a wallet, empty they tell me, and not much else. The clothing is with them as well. Louise Regan can help you with forensic analysis, I can't.'

'What can you tell us?' Tremayne asked.

Collins examined the body for several minutes before replying. 'A broken leg in his youth, a full set of teeth so there should be dental records. Also, he had dislocated his shoulder at one stage. He had a height of approximately five feet eight inches. Age is based on my examination and assessment of the clavicle, the pubic symphysis, and the sternal rib end, standard and verifiable tests. I would give the man's age at between 30 and 39. That's all I can tell you for now. Toxicology and DNA testing will be conducted, but the skeleton shows no visible indication of trauma. My full report will give you more, but you have, I believe, enough for you to be going on with. Decay of a body to skeleton takes between eight to twelve years depending on a number of factors. Examination of the area where the body was found may help, but you'll have a better chance with the man's effects.'

'Dental records?'

'You will have them within one hour.'

'Short, sweet and to the point,' Tremayne said. 'It shouldn't be impossible to find out who this man was.' Clare nodded, having been down that road before, knowing that the dead don't always give up their secrets that easily.

Chapter 6

Forensics did not take long to come back with some indicators. The clothing, tattered remnants that had been severely affected by their time in the ground, proved, as previously thought, to have belonged to someone affluent. The jacket that the man had been wearing was made-to-measure; a clothing label stitched to an inside pocket – readable only after Forensics had spent time with it – gave the name where the jacket had come from. It was a men's outfitters that still traded in Salisbury, a shop that Tremayne bought his suits from, ready-to-wear for him, not the luxury or the extravagance to pay for that little extra.

Louise Regan, the head of Forensics, her thick-framed glasses perched perilously on the end of her nose, had to give Tremayne his due – he was persistent.

'What else can you tell us,' Tremayne said standing with a cup of coffee in his hand. They were in a small canteen down the hall from Forensics. Clare had a juice, and Louise Regan, a mug of hot chocolate.

'The dental records are being checked,' Louise Regan said. 'Either the dental records or the man's clothing will give you a positive ID.'

'Approximate year of death?'

'It'll take time, and you, DI Tremayne, never have the time to let us complete our work.'

'I'll take an approximation.'

'The clothing would not look out of place today. Men's fashions haven't changed that much in the last couple of decades.'

'There was a wallet.'

'Relatively intact considering, but empty, nonetheless. Whoever buried him was careful to ensure that an easy ID wouldn't be possible.'

'Whoever it was,' Tremayne said, 'never intended him to be found.'

Tremayne continued, talking out loud, expressing the possibilities, the unknowns, the knowns.

Pathology had given Homicide little to assist them. There had been evidence of animals gnawing at the bones, a rat possibly. Remarkable in itself how untouched the body was, although a violent attack, a blow to the stomach, fatal damage to a bodily organ, the possible rupturing of an artery, even if the man's wrists had been slashed and he had bled to death, would all be hard to prove. The possibilities were myriad, and nothing was to be gained from further questions to Louise Regan. Tremayne and Clare left and returned to Homicide.

Clare sat at her computer. 'The men's outfitters are still in the same building close to the Guildhall.'

'Have you contacted them yet?'

'I'm going there in the next ten minutes. These days they sell only ready-to-wear, but they used to be almost exclusively made-to-measure.'

'You've spoken to someone?'

'The manager. He's in the shop now.'

'So why are you here?' Tremayne said acerbically.

***

At the men's outfitters, not far from the police station, Clare waited in the manager's office. It wasn't her first time in the shop as she had gone in on several occasions with Harry. He liked to dress well, and the shop was the best in the city. Re-entering the shop brought back good and bad memories, but mostly bad.

'Cedric's retired now,' said the manager, a tall man, probably not much younger than the man they were waiting for, Clare assumed. The shop had an old-world feel about it. Whenever she had come in with Harry, there had been time for a cup of tea and a chat, the salesman never hurrying, always willing to dispense his wisdom on the wares for sale.

'He worked here for over forty years, did Cedric,' the manager said.

'He'll know what I've got to show him?' Clare asked, making conversation while the two of them waited.

'More so than me. I've only been here for fourteen years, transferred from our store in Bristol when it closed. I'm still a junior, according to Cedric, that is. Not that I'll make much longer, though.'

'Why not?'

'I'm close to retirement, and the profit margins are hard to make, too much competition, imports from China, cost-cutting, pre-Christmas sales, and then at the new year too. We can't do that, not with our clothing only made from English or European cloth. No cheap imports here with "Made in Italy" on the label, even when it was made in a sweatshop in China or Pakistan. Comes at a cost, though, and most people don't want to pay. Look at that piece of fabric you showed me. How many years has it been in the ground?'

'Over ten. Possibly more.'

'There's not much left, but you can still make out the weave. Quality always pays, that's what Cedric would always say, not that he wasn't capable of flattering the customer to get him to spend his money.'

The door to the office opened, a small man entered. Clare judged him to be in his late seventies and not in good physical shape. For one thing, he was grossly overweight. He was dressed in a pinstripe suit with a waistcoat and around his neck hung a tape measure.

'Cedric's not good at retiring,' the manager said. 'I'm right, aren't I?' he said, looking over at the man.

'I'd still be here if I could.'

'This is Detective Sergeant Yarwood. She needs your expertise.'

A pudgy hand took hold of Clare's and shook it vigorously. 'I hope I can be of assistance,' Cedric said. The voice was still firm, although his breathing was laboured.

'You'd better take a seat,' Clare said as she moved a chair towards the man.

'You said you had a piece of fabric for me to look at,' Cedric, the former head of men's outfitting, said. He had taken advantage of the chair offered and was sitting down, his breathing improved.

'We pulled a body out of a burial mound up near Stonehenge. Not the original inhabitant of course.'

Clare showed the plastic bag containing the fabric sample to Cedric. He took out a pair of glasses from the top pocket of his jacket; it was clear that his eyesight was poor, judging by the thick lenses. According to the manager, Cedric had shrunk into oblivion after his compulsory retirement eight years earlier, and had rarely left his house other than to visit the local supermarket, and yet as he concentrated on the fabric the years started to fall away from him.

To Clare, he was the same as Tremayne, her detective inspector, her mentor. His retirement was looming, and the pressure was on again for him to accept the more-than-generous package to leave early. Jean, his wife, had been encouraging him to take it, and Tremayne was considering it, more for her benefit than his. After so many years reluctantly apart, the two of them in their later years were more like teenage newly-weds, instead of people who should be acting their age.

Clare knew from looking at Cedric that retirement for Tremayne would be anathema. She would have a word with Jean to ask her not to encourage him to act rashly. Cedric was, according to the manager of the shop, dynamic until his retirement.

Apparently, Cedric had a heart condition as well, and the excess weight and the lack of exercise were taking his life. Clare felt sad at seeing a once dynamic man fading away through loneliness and no purpose in life.

'I'll need to feel it,' Cedric said.

Clare withdrew the cloth from the bag and handed it over. Cedric rubbed the fabric between the thumb and index finger of his right hand, holding it close to one eye and smelling it, although the only smell would have been of dirt from the burial mound.

'Fifteen years,' the pronouncement.

'Can you be sure?' Clare asked.

'It's wool, although I suppose you know that already,' Cedric said. 'It came from Huddersfield, the company that manufactured it is still there. It's 280 grams, or 8.26 ounces if you want pre-metric.'

'Anything else?'

Cedric produced a small and very tattered notebook from his pocket. He opened it and leafed through the pages. After five minutes of running one of his fingers up and down the pages, he stopped. 'April 3rd, 2004, early morning,' he said. 'It's all here, my records for nearly forty years.'

54

'Do you have a name?'

'It wasn't the most popular fabric that year, although it sold well enough. What else was he wearing, this body?'

'Grey trousers, black leather shoes.'

'Shirt?'

'White.'

'Button-down or straight point?'

'Not button-down. I'm not sure whether it was straight point though.'

Cedric stood up and walked around the office. 'Any chance of a cup of tea,' he said to the manager.

It was clear that the man who had sunk into retirement obscurity was reliving his past life and he did not want it to end. Clare let him have his moment with the information that would drive the murder enquiry forward.

At last, after a suitable delay while Cedric drank two cups, ate one of the biscuits supplied, and paid a visit to the gents, he stood up proud, his posture firm. 'We sold the fabric to seven customers. Two of them had only a jacket made from the fabric, the other five had suits. One of the two purchased a pair of grey trousers.'

'Do you have their names?' Clare asked.

'You want a name, not names.'

'Yes.'

'Then indulge me. The jacket was double-breasted or single-breasted?'

'Single-breasted.'

'One or two-buttons?'

'Two.'

'One more question. Were there flaps on the pockets?'

'Yes,' Clare answered, and although she had photos of the jacket, she left the man the satisfaction that his fastidious nature, his detailed records, had allowed him to form a conclusion.

'There are more variations, but I don't need them. Although I'm sorry that the man is dead.'

'A name?' Clare asked tersely. She had indulged Cedric his moment, but now she needed to be back at Bemerton Road, updating Tremayne, and then checking on the name, who he was, where he was from, his history.

'Only one man bought a jacket with those details. His name is or was Richard Grantley.'

'The only Grantley I know is the mayor of Salisbury.'

'His brother.'

Clare left the two men in the office at the back of the shop and drove to the police station, passing the Guildhall where Clive Grantley presided. She wondered what secrets there were to be unveiled. Whatever they were, she knew that Tremayne would be excited at the prospect.

Chapter 7

The possible identity of the deceased and the reference to Clive Grantley being his brother came as a surprise to Tremayne, not that he could profess to knowing the man well. It was just that Grantley had always been a loner, not revealing too much about his personal life, not even when he had become a councillor on the Salisbury City Council, not even when he was unanimously elected as mayor. There had been a rumour of a wife, but that was some years before.

Grantley lived in a heritage listed house located in the Cathedral Close, a walled-off section in the centre of the city, and those who had visited would tell that the building was decaying, the furnishings old and the paintings hanging on the walls no doubt originals and very valuable.

Tremayne had met him on several occasions at official functions. Clare had seen the man several times, spoken to him once or twice.

Grantley had been the mayor for five years, longer than the previous incumbents, and he had a reputation for getting things done – projects which had been on the council's agenda for years, forestalled due to planning permissions, environmental concerns, and the occasional obstructionist person or group of people.

The new bypass to the west of the city had been one such project, and twelve houses had been compulsorily purchased, the owners paid the agreed valuation and moving out.

"Tremayne, isn't it?' Grantley said as he opened the door of his house.

'Mr Grantley, it's a matter of some delicacy,' Tremayne said. 'This is Sergeant Yarwood, although I'm sure you've met.'

'The face is familiar,' Grantley replied. His manner was distinctly offhand, but Tremayne took it in his stride, aware than most people resent the police turning up on their door uninvited and unexpected.

'It's about your brother,' Clare said.

'Richard's the only brother I have, and I've not heard from him for over ten years.'

'Could you be more specific?'

'Why should my brother be of concern to you? He left Salisbury a long time ago, and apart from an occasional postcard years ago, no one in this family has ever heard from him again.'

'It would be better if we came in,' Tremayne said.

'Here's as good a place as any,' Grantley's reply.

Clare could see that behind the imposing front door of the house, the hallway had a dull, tired look.

'Very well,' Tremayne said. 'A body was discovered close to Stonehenge, in an ancient burial mound. Two bodies to be more precise, but one's been there for over three thousand years, the other is more recent.'

'How does this relate to me?'

It was Clare who responded. 'We had no idea who the more recent body was, no identification, nothing to go on except the man's clothing.'

'Get to the point,' Grantley said.

'Very well. There was a label on the clothing, a shop not far from the Guildhall. I went there, met the manager and the person who had sold the made-to-measure jacket in the material discovered at the burial mound. He was definite that it was your brother, Richard.'

'Ridiculous,' Grantley said, but a shadow of doubt crossed his face as he grasped the door frame for support.

'It may be best if we come in now,' Clare said.

Grantley stood to one side, shaking his head in denial. 'Not Richard, not in Salisbury.'

As Clare had imagined, the house inside had an air of decay, and a smell of mustiness, not unusual for its age. There was also a strong smell of tobacco, indicating that Grantley was a smoker. Clare could see Tremayne sniffing the air, attempting to gain some advantage from the stale smell of nicotine. Clare imagined it was pleasant to him, but it made her feel nauseous.

'A drink?' Grantley asked as he sat down in a leather chair close to the fireplace, although there was no roaring log fire. The room was warm due to the central heating in the house.

'The same as you,' Tremayne said, noticing that Grantley was holding a large brandy.

'Not for me, thanks,' Clare's reply.

'Richard was the black sheep of the family,' Grantley said after he had given Tremayne his drink. 'If it is him, and I can't see how, it comes as a shock.'

'We'll need a DNA swab,' Clare said. 'If you don't mind.'

'No reason not to,' Grantley replied, then he rubbed the cotton bud that Clare had handed him inside his cheek to remove some skin cells.

'We may conduct a more detailed check, possibly ask Forensics if necessary.'

'As I said, I've no reason to believe it's Richard.'

Tremayne sat down opposite Grantley, took a sip of the brandy. 'Sergeant Yarwood will get the DNA checked soon enough, but in the meantime, what can you tell us about your brother?'

'Had you met him?'

'Not that I can remember, and I've been in Salisbury a long time.'

'Richard was or is, if he's still alive, a remarkable person. Highly intelligent, much more than me. He went to Oxford University, did well, but never completed. "Too easy, too boring", his only comment if asked.'

'Schooled in Salisbury?' Clare asked. She had chosen a more uncomfortable chair to sit on, as the room was too warm for her. She didn't want to leave, couldn't as her presence was vital, yet she did not feel at ease.

'Briefly, but for large parts of our childhood we were both boarded, only coming home at the weekends and holidays. Always the best, of course. Our parents weren't stingy, and financially we were very secure, but our mother wasn't the maternal type and our father was a humourless man who showed little affection. Not cruel, though, not to us at least or our mother. Not the sort of man to like, but then nobody hated him, not that I can remember.'

'Is there any reason why it could be your brother's body that was discovered near Stonehenge?' Clare asked. She was struggling with the change in Clive Grantley's manner. When they had arrived at the house, the man had been terse, almost dismissive, but now in the house, confronted with the possibility of his brother's death, he was magnanimous, generous of spirit, affable. And one thing Clare knew about Clive Grantley, the mayor of Salisbury, was that affability was not a trademark that many would have associated with him. Competent, financially astute, a great ambassador for the cathedral city, but a man who maintained a distance, who kept his cards close to his chest, a man that few, if any, knew with any intimacy.

'The last time that I saw my brother was in London.'

'The reason for meeting with him?' Tremayne asked. Clare could see that he was savouring his brandy, enjoying the smoke-filled setting, but she also knew that he was focussed, attempting to gently probe, knowing full well that Grantley was nobody's fool.

'As I said before, Richard was or is – not that I can believe he's dead, although apparently both of you think he is – a brilliant, academically-gifted man. IQ off the scale, so it was reckoned, not that he was ever checked; a possible savant, never forgot anything, and what to you and I would seem impossible to understand, he could see the answer clearly.'

Grantley stood up and walked over to the drinks cabinet. Even though the room was warm, the stone floor was freezing, no underfloor heating, and as the building was listed, the modifications to make it twenty-first-century comfortable were not always possible. Outside the building, a blue plaque attached to the wall showed that it had been the home of a famous artist of the eighteenth century, although Clare had not heard of the man, and she'd google who he was later that evening.

Grantley returned with two more brandies, one for him, another for Tremayne who accepted it gladly. 'A drink for you?' he asked Clare.

'A small brandy would be good,' her reply. Not for the alcohol, purely to endure the room for a little longer.

'As you were saying,' Tremayne said after all three had a drink.

'Richard passed all his exams at school, top marks most of the time. I used to struggle but not him. He was trouble even then, not serious, but if there was a chance for alcohol or a cigarette, and in his teens to smuggle a female in, or for him to be over the fence and into the local girl's school, well, that was Richard. You see, to Richard, it was all too easy. He didn't have to study, not even bother to turn up for the lessons most of the time, so even the school loved him, as did the girls. He was a charmer, charismatic.

'I'm not, I know that. I was seen as the dullard, the plodder. I'd be there day and night trying to be like him, but it wasn't possible.'

'You're not known for your charisma,' Tremayne said, certain that the man wouldn't take offence.

'A boring old …, isn't that what you'd say if I weren't here? I'll not say the word, ladies present.'

'Probably, but you're a respected man in the city. Coming back to Richard. If it's his body, what can you tell me?'

Clare spoke. 'The more recent body had been placed in a hole that had been cut into the side of the mound. We don't know why that location or if it has any symbolism. At the bottom of the mound an ancient body has been found, and it's possible a site of great significance as the artefacts so far recovered indicate that the deceased, almost certainly a man, was a leader in his community.'

'Symbolism? What does that mean?' Grantley asked.

'Why bury the body there? Why not in a wood, or in the river, weighted down? It would have taken time to bury the body, the risk of discovery was obvious, yet someone or maybe more than one person deemed it important. Was your brother into spiritualism, a druid, a sun worshipper or a member of a cult?'

'The only spiritualism that he would have ascribed to would have come out of a bottle. If there's no more, then I suggest we call it a night, don't you?' Grantley finally said, his original offhandedness returning.

'I would agree,' Tremayne said as he downed his brandy. 'We'll check your DNA and give you a call.'

'If it's my brother, then no doubt you'll have more questions.'

'A lot more. So far, you've given us very little.'

'I've given you plenty. I saw him in London, the exact date eludes me, although I could probably give you a more accurate date with time. As to what he was doing in Salisbury after that date is beyond me, and I certainly hadn't seen him.'

'Would you have?'

'It's probable, but not likely. We weren't close, and he did not hold me in high regard, saw me as intellectually inferior, which I'll freely admit to.'

'Your opinion of him?' Clare asked,

'I admired his easy way with people, his charisma, his brilliance, but I'm here, and he's dead, and I assume you believe it to be murder.'

'You just indicated that you now believe the body is that of your brother?'

'Not as such and don't go putting words into my mouth. Not much left after so many years, just a skeleton, would that be correct?'

'The soil had preserved the body better than others, but yes, nobody you'd recognise. It's the clothing that we have, and we're checking dental records and DNA.'

'After Oxford he travelled a lot, here and there, made some money, labouring, selling his brilliance on occasions, but his visits to Salisbury were not prolonged, a few months at a time. I was always glad when he left.'

'Your parents, relatives?' Tremayne asked.

'Our parents are dead, and there's nobody else in Salisbury. There are some relatives in Dorset, but I don't see them, and I don't think Richard did either. I always thought that he'd gone overseas, and either he was living well or in a shack down by the beach somewhere warm, no doubt a woman keeping him company. If it's him, then I don't know, and I don't believe I can help you any more. Now if you don't mind, please leave me alone.'

Tremayne and Clare left the house and walked out into the cold air. Above them loomed the cathedral spire, the tallest in England.

Chapter 8

The DNA collected by Clare had proved positive: Clive Grantley was the sibling of the body in the mound.

Also, Clive Grantley had given the name of a dentist close to one of the boarding schools they had attended, and the dental records obtained had confirmed that the body was that of Richard Grantley.

Clive Grantley intended to make a statement to the local newspaper and any other interested parties. Not that Tremayne and Clare were necessarily in agreement as Grantley, respected as he was in the city, was, by default, the primary suspect in his brother's death.

With a setting sun and dark clouds in the sky, Tremayne and Clare returned to the crime scene. The activity that had accompanied their previous visits to the site, when the twentieth-century body was still in situ, was replaced by a quiet air of industriousness.

Over to one side of the site, Atterton and Dafydd Evans were bolting together a metal framework, although neither of the two police officers knew what its purpose was. Gerard Horsley could be seen close to the mound, his assistant and presumed lover, Sue Boswell, close by. The personal arrangements of Horsley and Boswell did not concern Tremayne and Clare. Their interest was in the crime scene and if anything further had been discovered. The investigation had transitioned from an unknown body to a body with a name, a name that was certain to raise more questions than answers, a name that was associated with a man who had maintained his respectability over many years, a man who had kept his personal life to himself as much as possible.

Clive Grantley's supposed wife, where was she? What had happened to her? Was she still alive? Was she even important? And more pointedly, what of Clive Grantley himself? Why would a man in his fifties, a not unattractive man, although his manner could be unsettling, maintain a life of celibacy? These were the questions that concerned Tremayne and Clare, and even if the archaeological dig offered no more help, it would do no harm to visit the site.

'It's been a great day,' Horsley said as he came over to where Tremayne and Clare were standing, his assistant two steps behind him.

'More finds?' Clare asked. She had read up on the period when the Bronze Age chieftain had walked the earth. She had even been to the museum to see what had been discovered at Bush Barrow by William Cunnington. Horsley was sure that what he had found was more important, and he was regularly in the news and on the television updating an anxious public on what each day had revealed and its significance.

Tremayne had not expected to see security at the site, but there were two guards in uniform, with a command post, a caravan as it turned out, on twenty-four-hour surveillance.

'We've had sightseers and idiots trying to grab some of the gold for themselves,' Sue said. 'Money's no object on this dig, and Lance and Dafydd have done great work shoring up the entrance to the mound and ensuring that we can get down to where the body and the artefacts are.'

'Any more of interest?' Clare asked. Tremayne looked away and wandered over to where one of the security guards was standing.

'A dagger handle, more gold, although it's not the value of the metal that's important. It's what it tells us about the period. This man would have seen Stonehenge at its peak, probably attended ceremonies there, even seen its construction. What he could have told us is immeasurable.'

'Any more for us? We've got a name for the other body.'

'One up on us,' Horsley said. The first time that Clare had met the man he had not been the most agreeable, but now he was friendly and easy to talk to. 'No name for our man. The body at Bush Barrow that Cunnington discovered was given the title of "King of Stonehenge". If he was a king, then ours must be an emperor, not that they had them back then, although that's an assumption yet again. It's remarkable how much we know about the period; how much more there is that remains unknown. Even today, there's still conjecture as to Stonehenge's original purpose.'

'As I asked before,' Clare said, attempting to focus on the police investigation, although she would have been happy to stay and help at the site, 'any more of interest for us?'

'We get regular visits from the crime scene team, but nothing new. We purposely keep away from where that body was recovered, as much as we can, but you didn't expect much more, did you?'

The conversation continued for some minutes before Clare left and went over to where Lance Atterton and Dafydd Evans were working. The two men were pleased to see her, especially Evans, who Clare could see obviously fancied himself as a Ladies Man, not that he appealed to her, not that any man, young or old, did either. She had to admit concern that in her thirties she was on the way to spinsterhood, and it did not excite her. There had been a few dates in the last year, most disastrous, including one where she had liked the man and had slept with him, but he proved very soon after to be a lothario and not 'settling-down' material.

'We're bringing out the body today,' Atterton said.

To their rear, a tunnel had been constructed in the side of the mound at ground level. It was clear from what little Clare understood of mining techniques that the two engineers had shored the entrance and the tunnel with a metal framework and sheeting. It was still low, with only space to crawl through.

'It's larger inside, large enough for two people. Horsley and Sue are in there most of the time.'

'What's with the security?'

'The usual. The ghoulish, the idiots, the ne'er-do-wells, and the plain stupid. I caught one of them myself, gave him a good hiding.'

'Don't get charged with assault. They've still got their rights even if they're trespassing.'

'I let the security guards deal with it now,' Atterton said as he went back to work.

Over at the security caravan, Tremayne spoke to the two guards. With electricity on the site courtesy of a temporary connection organised by the local council, a kettle was on the boil. One of the guards was standing outside, smoking. Tremayne looked at the cigarette longingly, realising that if he took one for himself, his sergeant would report it to his wife. And besides, the need for the cigarette was outweighed by his last encounter with a health scare, his enforced overnight stay in the hospital and two days in bed at home. Even he took note of his mortality, although the smoke blowing in his face did not help.

'It's not the best at night,' Hector Warburton said. He was a big man, Tremayne noticed, and not the fittest man he'd ever seen, but then who would want to be out on an exposed landscape at night, temperatures close to freezing.

'What's your story?' Tremayne asked. He couldn't see much to be gained by conversing with the guards, but he had not wanted to hear any more about an ancient warrior or chieftain or whatever he was. The dead were just that, dead and buried, not to be dragged out from their resting place, and whether the man had met his death quietly in his bed or violently made no difference. It was a cold case, cold by thousands of years, and no one was going to be charged with his death, no one would ever come forward with evidence, and there would be no name on any charge sheet.

'Ex-Army. Did my time in Iraq and Afghanistan. Good with a gun and hand-to-hand, no skills for anything else.'

'There's always the police,' Tremayne said.

'Forty-three, a troublemaker in my youth, smashed a few heads together, spent time in the police cells after a few too many drinks. I don't think you'd want me, and besides, they talk about having a degree, and there's no way I'd get through university, not even if I studied part-time, and I wasted my time at school. A family to feed, three children, another on the way now; they're my priority.'

'Pay good as a security guard?'

'If you're willing to freeze your proverbials off of a night time, it is.'

69

The other guard came out of the caravan with four mugs on a tray. 'One for your colleague,' he said to Tremayne, looking over at Clare as she approached.

'They're taking the body out today,' she said as she took one of the mugs of tea. It was too milky for her, but she was not complaining, only thankful for the man's courtesy.

'The end of your time up here,' Tremayne said to Warburton and the other guard.

'Not likely. According to Horsley, there are another three weeks on this burial mound, and the idiots we're dealing with are attempting to get close to the other mounds nearby. If we're not here, they'll have heavy machinery. It's the valuables they're after, no interest in ancient history.'

'It doesn't do much for me. We've got a more recent history, the last two decades, dead and lying on a slab at the mortuary.'

With nothing more to be gained, Tremayne and Clare left the site. Gerard Horsley and Sue Boswell were up at the mound, both kitted out, both wearing hard hats, both down on their knees preparing to crawl in through the tunnel. Atterton and Evans stood nearby, supervising them, checking for safety. Also, a few more people had arrived, two obviously a TV crew as the chieftain inside was big news and Horsley now a minor celebrity. Clare wondered what Horsley's wife would think when she watched the television that night and saw her husband and his assistant sneak a brief kiss.

***

Clive Grantley, a man who had an image to protect, was at home when Tremayne had phoned from the crime scene. Twenty minutes later, a young woman opened the door to his house.

'Hi, I'm Kim Fairweather, Clive's personal assistant.'

'This is Sergeant Yarwood, and I'm Inspector Tremayne.'

'Clare, good to see you,' Kim said.

'We know each other from yoga classes,' Clare said to Tremayne.

'Mr Grantley at home?' Tremayne asked. He wasn't about to say it, but he wondered how such a dull man with such a dull house could have someone as bright and attractive, and clearly personable, working for him. But then he supposed he was a dullard to some, and he had Yarwood. The analogy was not lost on him.

'Please come in. As you can imagine, he's distressed with the confirmation that the body is that of his brother. I'll get you both something warm to drink, and then Clive will join us in the main room.'

After Kim Fairweather had left and Tremayne and Clare were sitting down, Tremayne quizzed Clare on her friendship with Grantley's PA. 'Have you known her long?'

'Nine months, ever since I took up yoga. And no, I didn't know she was his PA,' Clare replied. 'I knew she worked for the council, and I told her I was a police officer, but apart from that, our conversations were trivial. No one goes to yoga to recount their daily stresses. It's all about letting go, calming the inner demons, cleaning the mind of unnecessary baggage.'

'Maybe I could do with some of that,' Tremayne said as Kim re-entered the room with the tea. Not an old metal tray with well-worn and grimy mugs like the security team up near Stonehenge. This time it was bone-china, a silver tray and a selection of biscuits.

Grantley entered the room and sat close to the fireplace again. He was flustered, red in the face. 'I can't say that I cared much for my brother when he was alive, but now…'

'It's an understandable reaction,' Tremayne said. 'Reliving the good times, minimising the bad. We're sorry that our suspicion proved positive.'

'Don't be. Richard was either going to fly high or crash spectacularly. It's obvious which one proved to be true.'

'Then we need to understand your state of mind at this time, also what you intend to do.'

'Am I a suspect?'

'So far, we've no proof of murder. Only that your brother's body was buried in the side of the burial mound. There must be foul play, but proving murder is another thing. But yes, you must be a suspect, but there's no proof, very little of anything.'

'What do you want from me?' Grantley asked. Kim Fairweather had given him a cup of tea. His hand was shaking perceptibly, spilling the tea onto one trouser leg. No one said anything. Kim handed him a tissue.

'No doubt the media will want to interview you and then you'll need to address the council. We'd only ask that you keep it factual, no mention of murder as that's a variable at this time.'

'I'll need to take legal advice.'

'That's your prerogative,' Tremayne said. 'One issue. It may be a long shot here, but whoever was responsible for burying your brother's body, murder or otherwise, and I'm assuming it's not you, may have a vendetta against the Grantley family. One member dead,

72

another one prominent, it brings forward the premise that you may be a target of retribution or death.'

'I don't see why,' Grantley said. 'I saw my brother infrequently, sometimes here, sometimes in London, and we never discussed what he did, not in detail anyway. Sometimes he needed money, other times he was staying at five-star hotels, a chauffeur-driven limousine waiting for him.'

'Why didn't you question him?'

'I suspected that some of his money-making activities were, if not illegal, probably sailing close to the wind. I preferred not to know, although he was still my brother. I didn't like him particularly, but I couldn't detach myself from him totally.'

'There are more personal questions. Are you okay with Miss Fairweather being here?' Clare asked.

'If you don't mind, Kim,' Grantley said. 'I know what's coming. It may be best if you head back to the office, field whoever's calling, set up interviews if you must and draft a statement for me. We'll go through it later.'

With the PA out of the house – Clare checked to make sure – Tremayne recommenced his interview of Grantley. 'There is, or was, a wife, a Mrs Clive Grantley. Is that correct?'

'Briefly, but that was before I last saw my brother. We married young, and she was a good woman, wanted more than I could give. The marriage floundered, and we divorced. No more to it than that. I've not seen or heard from her in years. A brief meeting once, a hope of a reconciliation, but it came to nothing. I'm not a social person, she was. She wanted to party, I wanted to stay at home.'

'We will need to interview her.'

'If you can find her, that is, and how is she relevant?'

'Your point is taken,' Tremayne said, knowing that he could be talking to a murderer. 'However, what is relevant? We have nothing to go on, only the fact that your brother did not bury himself in that mound and pack the soil around him. A criminal act has been committed. Now, whether it's murder or manslaughter or he died during some bizarre sexual activity, we don't know. We can't leave the case open when the guilty parties are still alive, whatever the crime is. We owe it to your brother, we owe it to the community to give the man justice.'

'Allowing for that fact, I'll accede to your concern, but I'm afraid that you might be opening a can of worms, raising the spectre of intrigue and violence, and no doubt severe embarrassment for some, for people whose reactions may be unfortunate.'

'Are you intimating yourself?' Clare asked.

'Believe me,' Grantley said, 'I'm an innocent in this matter, but Richard went around with some shady characters from time to time. People that you would rather not mess with.'

'Criminals?'

'Gangsters, some government sanctioned.'

'Espionage?'

'I'm hypothesising. Richard's moral compass would not have drawn the line as clearly as you and I about what was right or wrong.'

'Just one thing before we go,' Tremayne said. 'A list of where you met your brother, the times he was in Salisbury, your wife's last known address, and anything unusual that you can remember from back around the time when your brother died.'

'I'll be in the office with Kim. I'll draft a document with her and email it to you within the next twelve hours. And yes, I'll be granting interviews to a few select media outlets and addressing the local council of which I'm the mayor. I will be careful about what I say. Whatever the reason for my brother being in that mound, I want to know the truth as much as you do.'

Chapter 9

'Sitting there staring into space isn't going to help,' Clare said. She had seen Tremayne in his office, weighing up what they had, what they didn't have. She knew that her boss wasn't the man to sit still for long, and a sarcastic comment never went amiss.

'It's a confusing case, this one,' Tremayne's reply.

'It's murder, it must be.'

'I'd agree, but who and why? And why was Richard Grantley in Salisbury, one time at the gentlemen's outfitters, another time having his body stuffed into the side of a burial mound, and more importantly, how come I can't ever remember meeting him?'

'If he didn't frequent the local pubs or the horse races, or even more pertinently the police station, then you and he may have gone separate ways. There are still people you don't know in Salisbury, aren't there?'

'Some, but the Grantley family held some sway here. I can vaguely remember the father, an upright man with an ex-fighter-pilot moustache.'

'Was he?'

'He was active on the council, involved with the cathedral. Apart from that, I can't remember talking to him, although I was only a lowly beat officer, and then a sergeant. It was always the moustache that people remembered, as well as the fact that he had a brush with the law at one stage.'

'Serious?'

'You can check it out. He wanted to develop some land out at Harnham. According to the local conservationists, there were some rare ducks. One day there was a protest and George Grantley, that was the father's name, came out to it and ripped down one of the banners. One of the conservationists, an avowed pacifist, hit Grantley square in the face with a clenched fist, broke the man's nose.'

'Then what?'

'Grantley pummelled the man, laid him out cold. It came up in court that Grantley was ex-military, not a fighter pilot, an army officer and former army middleweight boxing champion.'

'What was the result of the court case?'

'A caution for the protester and George Grantley. It was the most excitement the city had had for some while.'

'The ducks?'

'They either flew away, or they ended up on someone's plate, wrapped in bacon.'

'That's dreadful,' Clare said.

'That's life.'

'But Clive Grantley portrays himself as an honest man.'

'And no doubt he is, mostly. George Grantley was a man easily driven to violence. His son, Clive that is, may be of the same ilk, although personally I don't think he's involved here.'

'Think or know?'

'You're right, Yarwood. I don't know, and that's a concern. If we take Clive at face value, and accept that he didn't kill his brother, then who do we have?'

'Nobody, and have we considered how the body was placed in the burial mound and by who? Not yet, we haven't. Could it be tied in with pagan religion, somehow signifying a fertility rite or a sacrifice to a god for a good harvest?'

'Yarwood, no more of that nonsense. We had enough of that when Harry Holchester died. Sorry about that,' Tremayne said, remembering that in spite of the years since the death of Clare's fiancé, the emotional hurt still remained.

'Time heals. Don't worry about it.'

Tremayne could see in his sergeant's face that neither of the sentences she had spoken was true. He felt a pang of regret at his insensitivity.

'Clive Grantley's wife, any luck?' Tremayne said. Activity was best to divert his sergeant away from reminiscing about the past. 'What do we know of her?'

'Married at twenty-three, the same age as Clive. They lived in London for several years before separating and then divorcing. That information wasn't too difficult to find out, although where the woman is now is unknown.'

'Was a reason given for the divorce?'

'They divorced in 1995 after eight years of marriage, although separated for three. The divorce was uncontested by both parties. The Matrimonial Causes Act 1973 decreed that "no-fault" divorce was allowed.'

'Did they divorce before or after Richard Grantley's death?'

'A long time before.'

'No ménage à trois, then?'

'Inspector, I think you're getting carried away there,' Clare said.

'It's a possibility, even so. Where is she?'

'I'm still checking. But I'd agree that she needs to be interviewed and soon.'

'Anyone else? What about the report that Grantley was preparing with the lovely Kim?'

'She's too young, too pretty for you. And besides, you've got Jean.'

'Just baiting you, knowing full well that you'd react.'

'They must have stayed up all night working on this,' Clare said, waving the document in her hand. 'According to Clive, he last saw his brother at a hotel in Westminster on the 30th or the 31st March 2004. If that's correct, then that tightens the year of death to somewhere between April 2004 and 2009, if we maintain that the body had been there for at least ten years. Except that three days later on the 3rd April 2004, Richard was in Salisbury trying on a jacket.'

'So why did Richard go to London? Why not meet him in Salisbury, save himself the time and effort?'

'The Right Worshipful Mayor of the City of Salisbury still has questions to answer.'

'Curiouser and curiouser,' Tremayne said, quoting Lewis Carroll's Alice.

***

The removal of the Bronze Age chieftain once more came to a grinding halt. Not because of problems with the entrance to his final resting place at the bottom of the burial mound, but because the second body had intervened yet again.

'It can only be animal activity,' Horsley said. He was standing outside the mound, the air temperature just above freezing, and Jim Hughes, the senior crime scene examiner, was not prepared for the cold of the place.

'We have to thank you for contacting us. Judging by the excitement around here, the curious onlookers, the media, you've found something of great significance,' Hughes said. He was pacing up and down on the spot, attempting to keep warm.

'Often, it's badgers that destroy these sites, but there are other creatures, and the compacted soil either collapses from their tunnelling or is weakened sufficiently that a major downfall of rain causes the integrity of the burial to be destroyed. It was only as we were finally removing the soil around our skeleton that we saw it.'

'We thought we had completed our investigation up here, but that doesn't appear to be the case.'

'It's what we agreed. You'd not disturbed the chieftain, and if we found anything, we'd call you immediately, which is what we've done.'

Over to one side, the security guards were conversing with the additional uniformed police brought in to re-establish the crime scene, to move the onlookers further back, to ensure the media did not intrude. Horsley, as did Hughes, knew that the removal of the ancient man now had another complication. A weapon had been found underneath a previously unmoved area of soil, and it wasn't old.

'One of my people will need to go in with you. Is that acceptable?' Hughes asked, out of courtesy. It was a crime scene, and one of the crime scene team was going in regardless.

Horsley realised that a reply in the negative would serve no purpose and besides he was a civically-minded person, although he was sporting a black eye, the result of his wife paying an unscheduled visit to the site after seeing the cosy exchange between the man and his assistant via television footage from the site.

'Someone small, light if possible,' Horsley said.

Forty minutes later, long enough for Tremayne and Clare to cut short their meeting with Grantley and get out to the crime scene, Sue Boswell and Maggie Carswell, a diminutive crime scene examiner, entered the burial chamber.

Maggie carefully eased herself around the small area, Sue watching her every move, careful to ensure that the site was not compromised. Maggie took out an evidence bag and put the weapon inside. With little more to do, she passed the bag outside to another examiner. She then returned inside and helped Sue to gently ease the skeleton of the chieftain onto a metal sheet, attempting to maintain it in one piece, an impossibility given the condition of what remained after so many years.

Once the skeleton was outside of the tunnel, the two women remained, one to look for ancient artefacts, the other for more modern.

Outside there was a sense of excitement, with Horsley fussing over what had been recovered and the police officers and the crime scene team examining a dirt-encrusted metal object inside a plastic bag. It was clear what it was. It was a knife, a possible murder weapon, a clue.

***

The visit to Clive Grantley, abruptly halted, was on hold for the foreseeable future. Tremayne thought back to the 'curiouser and curiouser' comment that he had uttered before, not sure why. He was not a literary man, and as Clare often reminded him, his only reading was the local racing guide, and even that gave him difficulties in that he rarely picked a winner. His wife who had joined him in the occasional flutter made her choices based on the animal's name, how it stood, even if she liked the look of the jockey. Much to Tremayne's consternation, as a man who studied the subject, it was his wife who often had the most success. Not that she rubbed it in, or not too often, although Clare was not averse to making the occasional gibe.

'It seems we have substance now,' Tremayne said.

The two police officers had chosen a pub not far from Stonehenge to have lunch. A steak and kidney pie for him, chicken for her. Tremayne in line with his new enforced health regime ordered a half-pint of beer, Clare, an orange juice.

'Pathology found no evidence of a knife wound,' Clare reminded him.

'Not unexpected. If the knife had entered between the ribs, it could have inflicted a fatal wound. The only entry sign would be a wound on the skin and to the man's innards, a possible tear in his clothes.'

'The condition of the clothing is so poor neither Forensics nor Pathology could be expected to find proof of that. No point asking them to recheck.'

'No point, but we will anyway. Now, what about this knife?'

'It's with Forensics, or it soon will be. They'll not hurry this, so no point annoying them for twenty-four hours.'

'No harm in running past their place on the way back, show enthusiasm.'

'They'll need to clean it first, attempt to get DNA from the blade, possible fingerprints.'

'Not much chance of either,' Tremayne said, but he knew they would try. 'What we need is an indication of the type of knife, the places where it could be purchased, an approximate age.'

Tremayne looked at his half-pint of beer, realised that he should not have drunk it in one gulp. He looked over at the bar, attempted to raise one hand to gain the man's attention.

'Don't bother,' Clare said. She was not smiling.

'What with you and Jean, you'll be the death of me.'

'The opposite and you know it. Look how much healthier you look and feel after you stopped smoking and cut back on the alcohol.'

'If this is healthy living, I'll take the alternative.'

'No, you wouldn't, and you know it. You've got Jean at home for you, and even Superintendent Moulton's given you a reprieve on the compulsory retirement. With any luck, you and I will be solving murders for years to come.'

'It doesn't alter the fact the mind is still young, it's only the body that's getting away from me. Let's get out of here. I've had my daily lecture from you today.'

'Forensics?'

'First port of call, and then we'll interview someone. Clive Grantley probably, or else the mysterious ex-wife once we find her.'

'Nothing mysterious about her, not yet. She's probably married somewhere, a few children, possibly grandchildren.'

'The knife is important.'

'It still doesn't explain the burial mound. There must be a reason, and Clive Grantley doesn't appear to be the sort of man to harbour strange beliefs and bizarre practices.'

'Appearances are deceptive.'

'Harry was a regular person, and he ended up a murdering paganist,' Clare said, remembering her lost love.

Tremayne could see the sadness washing over her again. He stood up abruptly. 'Time to go, people to see, places to visit.'

Louise Regan sighed, rolled her eyes when Tremayne and Clare walked into Forensics. 'I expected you thirty minutes ago, what kept you?'

'You know I like to give you time to do your job,' Tremayne's reply. Clare knew that the relationship between the taciturn police inspector and the head of Forensics was based on mutual respect.

'It's a knife, good enough?'

'We know that. What else?'

'Give us a couple of hours. Go and annoy someone else and I'll give you a preliminary as soon as I can.'

'Anything to be going on with?'

'Eleven-inch blade, thin-bladed.'

'Stiletto?'

'Probably. The blade and the handle may reveal a maker's name, but we'll not know yet.'

'Easy to purchase?' Clare asked.

'You're the police officers, you should know. But yes, the restrictions on knives are not that strict and if what we have is over ten years old, then minimal checks, probably none, would have been carried out on the purchaser. It's unlikely that you'll be able to trace it back to a person.'

Satisfied that they had shown the importance of further details about the knife, Tremayne and Clare drove down to the Guildhall in the centre of the city. Grantley was found at his desk, reading through some documents.

Kim Fairweather sat outside his office, busy with paperwork, typing away on her laptop.

'Will he be long?' Clare asked as she and Tremayne sat opposite Kim.

'Not long. He wants to see you both, anyway.'

Tremayne felt inside his jacket pocket for the cigarette packet that wasn't there. Clare sat passively, checking her mobile phone for messages and emails.

'They're conducting a post mortem on the body,' she said.

'Which one?' Tremayne's irritable reply. The nicotine deprivation hit him most when he was idle, with time on his hands, and when he was feeling impatient. To him, Grantley had questions to answer, and the police investigation took precedence over the mayor's delaying actions.

'The Bronze Age man. It looks as though they intend to ask Stuart Collins to assist; also, Forensics to see if they can find DNA.'

'Our pathologist and Louise Regan's people?'

'Good PR for the police. Superintendent Moulton will agree.'

'I can't see a problem, but we should be in with Grantley, not sitting here.'

The door to Clive Grantley's office opened, and the man came out. He shook Clare's hand first, Tremayne's second. 'Come in, please. It's been a busy day, and I'm just starting to come to terms with my brother's death.'

'We've found a weapon,' Tremayne said. 'Subject to further investigation, it's a proven murder.' He looked over at Kim Fairweather who was still at her desk. 'That's confidential, by the way. We'd appreciate it if you'd keep that to yourself for the time being.'

'Don't worry about me,' the young woman replied. 'I won't tell anyone.'

Inside Grantley's office, the man became serious and looked Tremayne straight in the eye. 'If it's murder, then you suspect me, don't you?'

'We've no one else,' Tremayne said honestly. 'Not that we have any proof or any motive, but it's invariably the nearest and the dearest.'

'This intrusion into my personal life is something I've always avoided.'

'Have you prepared a statement for the media, the council?' Clare asked.

'I've already spoken to the other councillors. They've expressed complete faith in me, and I will remain as mayor. I've agreed to an interview with the local newspaper later today, and a television crew will be here in one or two hours. I will give a short statement, no questions.'

'They'll be persistent,' Tremayne said.

'They may be, but I will say what I have to, no more. I am taking legal advice as to how I proceed with you and the general public.'

'Your legal advisor, what does he say about us?' Clare asked.

'He has advised transparency on certain matters.'

'Such as?'

'My wife, my brother.'

'Anyone else? What about your personal assistant?' Clare asked. 'You seem to have a close relationship with her. She's only young, but you place a great deal of trust in her.'

'I have spoken to her mother before your coming here.'

'That's understood.'

'Very well. There are two items of interest that I will reveal to you now. One of them is damning. If there is other information that I'm not telling you, I will decide when or whether I should inform you.' Grantley sat back on his chair; he had stated the conditions under which he would help the police and hopefully had allayed their suspicion of him.

'Withholding vital evidence is a criminal offence, more so when the crime is murder,' Tremayne said. Clare said nothing, not sure how to respond to a man who should have been more open but wasn't. Whatever was to come of Grantley's speech it boded ill for him and for the police.

'I understand that. If you come to me with other information which points to me and others, I will then consider what more I can say. Is that understood?'

'Understood? No. We have no option to do any more at this time, but we will be back. I only hope it is not to arrest you for murder or withholding evidence, or perverting the course of justice. All three are indictable offences, the first one is a mandatory prison sentence, the other two will almost certainly ensure that you spend time behind bars, your reputation shattered.'

'That is as may be. Let us focus on my brother and I. We were of a similar age, two years between us, I the older of the two. He liked to gloat at my ordinariness and to belittle me.

'You can understand why I did not like him very much when we were younger.'

'And now?' Clare asked. She had to admit a reluctant liking of the man. A man who represented good values, the values that led to him being the mayor of the city, a well-respected person, a person who kept himself to himself, not criticising, not aggrandising.

'My life is complete, as you will soon understand. I am ambivalent about my brother.'

'Is there more about your brother?' Tremayne, tired of Grantley's procrastinating, asked.

Grantley passed over a sheet of paper to Clare. 'On there is the phone number of my ex-wife. Kim found it for you. I have not spoken to her or made any contact.'

'Is that it?' Tremayne said.

'When I married my wife, Richard was not in the country. Five years later he turned up at our door. He was broke, supposedly some investment venture in the Middle East had gone wrong. I don't know if it was true or not, but I let him in, and he stayed with my wife and myself for two months. By that time, he was on his feet again and flush with money. I did not see him for another eleven months, not until I found out that he had worked his charm on my wife. He had seduced her.'

'What did you do?'

'At first, I was indignant, angry. But we worked it out, my wife and I, or, at least, I thought we had. Another four months, a repeat occurrence. I confronted my brother. He laughed in my face. To him, it was the same as when we were children, him stealing my Christmas presents, taking them or breaking them, always blaming me for a broken pot or a broken window at school or at home. I hated him with a vengeance. I could have killed him.'

'Did you?'

'No. I left the matrimonial home, filed eventually for divorce. I do not harbour hatred or anger for long, both of them are wasted emotions. I saw my wife once more before the divorce was finalised and once after, a weekend in Paris attempting to rekindle dead emotions. It was a disaster, and I have not seen my wife since.'

'Your brother?'

'Once, and you have the date. Believe me, I had moved on that last time we met, and I felt nothing other than pity for him. I had a complete life by then, he did not. What is life without love and a sense of belonging?'

'But you were alone,' Clare said.

'I was never alone. After the divorce, I met another woman. We were together for five or six months, and in that time she became pregnant. She was a strong-willed woman who had suffered when she was younger. She did not want marriage, and neither did I.'

'The child?'

'I'm coming to that. The romance had weakened by that time, replaced by admiration for her, and her for me. We became the best of friends, my only true friend, but we were never lovers again. She raised the child, never formed another romantic arrangement, no live-in lovers, and every week or two I would go to her house and be a family for the child. She knew from a young age that I was her father and she loved me as dearly as I loved her.

'The child grew up with two parents who never mistreated her, showered her with love and affection. Her mother has not been to Salisbury for over twenty years, her daughter has.'

'Kim?' Clare said.

'Now you can understand why I cannot be angry with my brother, even when he had wronged me so much with my wife. Kim and her mother are my family. I have no need of any other.'

Even Tremayne seemed stunned by the revelation, aware that Grantley had protected that information all his life. 'Does anyone else know?' he asked.

'We tell no one, but it is not the greatest secret. Check Kim's birth certificate, and you will find my name there.'

Clare felt so emotional on leaving Grantley's office that she grabbed hold of Kim and gave her a firm embrace. Even Tremayne felt inclined to touch the young woman's arm as he passed.

Chapter 10

The former Mrs Clive Grantley came as a surprise. The photo that Grantley had shown Tremayne and Clare had been taken a long time before, and although it was pre-digital, it was a clear photo taken on a beach in the south of France, the beaming Clive with his arms wrapped tightly around a slim and pretty young woman. She was a stunner then, but the woman who opened the door to the modest semi-detached house on the outskirts of Manchester was no longer slim or pretty. She was a haggard woman in her mid-fifties, the once long hair now cropped and grey.

'Yes, what do you want?' she said. In one hand, a lighted cigarette, its ash ready to drop onto the wooden floor.

'Grace Thornberry?'

'It depends who's asking.'

'Inspector Tremayne and Sergeant Yarwood. We're police officers, from Salisbury.'

'A long time since I've been there.'

'May we come in?' Clare asked.

'If you must. Mind the dog, it doesn't take kindly to strangers.'

Inside, the house was remarkably tidy considering the state of the owner who was dressed in faded jeans and a creased blouse which had not been ironed. On her feet, Grace Thornberry had a pair of slippers, well-worn and clearly old. She slouched as she walked, pulling one leg after another across the floor.

'Now what is it you want?'

'It's about your former husband, Clive Grantley,' Tremayne said. 'Any chance of a cup of tea?'

Clare could see that the woman was disinterested in talking to two police officers.

'I suppose so,' Grace Thornberry said as she attempted to rise from the chair she had slumped into.

'I'll do it,' Clare said. 'Milk in the fridge?'

'The tea's in the first cupboard to the left of the sink, second shelf.'

With Clare in the kitchen, Tremayne continued to interview the woman.

'Can we confirm that you are the former wife of Clive Grantley of Salisbury.'

'I am, but as I told you before, it's a long time since I've been there. The memory's not so good these days.'

'When was the last time you saw Clive?'

'We tried to patch up the relationship once, but it didn't work out. Sometime after the divorce. I'm not sure of the year, although I remember us taking a flight somewhere.'

'Paris?'

'That's it. Until you mentioned his name, I hadn't thought about him for a long time. Is he still alive?'

'Yes, he's alive. We've not come about him.'

Clare returned and gave one cup to Tremayne, another to the lady of the house. Grace Thornberry's hands shook violently, so much so that Clare took hold of the cup from the woman before it spilt.

'I suppose he's not that old,' Grace said, not commenting on her shaking hands, only putting them on her lap and clasping one hand with the other.

'Do you need medical attention?' Clare asked.

'It's what it is. I've got Parkinson's, not too severe yet, but the prognosis is not good. Apart from that, I'm fine, a little forgetful.'

'Your domestic situation?' Tremayne asked.

'My husband is at work, and we're fine enough. Not as comfortably as Clive would be, but money wasn't my reason for marrying him, if that was what you were going to ask.'

'We need to understand why you married Clive and what caused you to subsequently divorce,' Clare said, looking to see if the story told by Clive was corroborated by his former wife.

'Why are you here? You've not told me that.'

'I'm sorry to say that his brother, Richard Grantley, has been killed.'

'I should feel more sorrow than I do, but it was a long time ago.'

'What do you remember of him?'

'Charming, attractive, great company. Nothing like Clive. It was hard to believe that they were brothers.'

'Let us come back to when you met Clive.'

'We met in London. We were both young, and Clive was a decent man. Not that I liked him at first, but I'd had a succession of exciting men, and each of them had disappointed. One had taken off with my best friend, another had hit me, and another had stolen money out of my purse. And then along comes Clive, thoroughly decent, upstanding, good family. The sort of man who pays for the meal at the restaurant, holds the chair while you sit down, insists you go through the door before him. An old-fashioned gentlemanliness about him; it was seductive.'

'You fell in love with him?'

'It wasn't difficult.'

'But then it went wrong?'

'Somewhat. With Clive and his good characteristics also came a stodgy, stay-at-home nature. He'd prefer a good book and to be in the house, and whereas that was fine for most of the time, sometimes I'd like to get out, kick up my heels, get drunk, make a fool of myself. Clive couldn't understand that sort of behaviour.'

'You were still young,' Clare said.

'So was he, but he acted twenty years older. How does he look now?'

'His age, but still the same as you describe him, not that we know him that well.'

'Did he make a success of his life, other than what his parents left him?'

'You met them?'

'Yes. I liked his father, and his mother was sweet, always fussing around the house.'

'And you've had no contact or knowledge of Clive for a long time?'

'Not at all. I'm not the curious type, and I was here, two children to look after, a husband. No time really, and I have been content. Of course, I missed the lifestyle that Clive could have given me, not him, but the money. Times have been tough for us. I'm not that materialistic anyway, and I've accepted what I have for better or worse, and mostly it's been better.'

'Richard Grantley?' Tremayne interrupted what he thought was going to become a rambling monologue. Clare, if she had known what he was thinking, would not have called it rambling or a monologue. Purely the conversation of a woman who was in her fifties but looked much older, a woman whose life was slowly ebbing away.

'We'd been married for some years, Clive and I, and I was bored. And then, Richard was at the door, down on his luck, looking for somewhere to stay. He was a revelation after Clive. The man was alive, flirtatious, always acting inappropriately when Clive wasn't looking. I was still young, still had the energy and the passion of youth. Regrettably, I fell for him, not love you must understand. Three weeks after he moved in, he was sharing my bed whenever Clive was out of the house. I suppose that makes me sound cheap, but it wasn't like that. I didn't want to hurt Clive, but I couldn't resist Richard.'

'And Clive found out?'

'He came home early one day, caught us together. The one time that I saw Clive angry, and he struck Richard. But Clive couldn't maintain the anger, and thirty minutes later we're all downstairs discussing the situation. The upshot of it was that Clive left the house, as did Richard.'

'Did you see Clive again?'

'We reconciled, tried to make a go of it, and for a time, Clive was more attentive, more demonstrative, more loving, but that wasn't the way the man was made. Soon enough, Richard's back in my life. All the good characteristics that Clive had, Richard had none of them. He mistreated me, no violence, but he'd stand me up, cadge money off me, expect me to pay if we found a pub in the country for a one-night fling. Clive and I agreed on a divorce, although neither of us was happy about it. Although with Clive you could never be sure what he was thinking. He rarely smiled, never laughed, never truly loved.'

Clare remembered the last conversation with Clive Grantley, the love he had for his daughter, the joy she brought him. Grace Thornberry was incorrect in one aspect; the man knew the meaning of love.

'Richard is dead,' Tremayne said. He sat forward on his chair to emphasise what he was saying.

'I'm sorry about that. You said he had been killed, I remember that. It's strange, lost memories flooding back.'

'We now believe he was murdered, not far from Salisbury.'

'And you suspect Clive?'

'Your reaction is surprising,' Clare said. 'We would have thought you would be more concerned with Richard's death than with Clive.'

'Clive couldn't harm anyone. He was the most decent man I ever knew, my one regret.'

'Murderers come in all shapes and sizes, some clearly violent, others ardent pacifists.'

'Clive loved his brother. Why, I don't know, considering how badly he treated him.'

'Clive loved you, but you let him go.'

'Who knows, he may still feel a fondness for me in his own way. Not that we'll ever know, will we? I'll never see him again.'

'You don't surf the internet, look up old friends? Most people do.'

'I never do. Should I?'

'Clive is the mayor of Salisbury. He's on the Salisbury City Council website.'

'Show Mrs Thornberry,' Tremayne said.

Clare took out her smartphone, entered 'Clive Grantley' into the search engine. The council website came up, a picture of Clive in his mayoral robes, the chain of office around his neck.

Claire handed the phone over to Grace
Thornberry who looked at it for over a minute. 'He looks
well,' she said when she handed the phone back to Clare.
'Did he remarry, children?'

'Never.' Clare did not intend to mention Kim
Fairweather, partly because it would serve no purpose,
but mainly because the beauty of the relationship
between father and daughter would be soured in the
presence of Grace Thornberry, a woman who although
obviously ill, did not engender strong feelings of
compassion in either of the two police officers. A woman
who by her own admission, had turned a good man away
for his rogue brother.

***

Clive Grantley remained a conundrum. On the one hand,
he appeared to be the least likely person to have
murdered his brother; on the other, he clearly had a love-
hate relationship with Richard, and from what they had
gathered from Grace Thornberry, former wife of Clive,
former lover of Richard, the dead man had few
redeeming characteristics.

'Who else can help?' Tremayne asked Clare as
they drove back from Manchester, a four-hour trip; Clare
as usual in the driving seat.

'Did Kim Fairweather's mother ever meet Richard
or even Grace? Clive Grantley never mentioned that she
did.'

'He wants to keep her out of it. Understandable,
and any other time, we could respect his wishes, but we
need to know the truth.'

'What are you suggesting?'

'We visit her.'

'It'll have to be tomorrow. We need to check on the murder weapon, talk to Kim about what we intend to do.'

'Have it your way. You talk to Kim, heart-to-heart, woman-to-woman. Just let her know that we need to talk to her mother, either at her place or a neutral location, keep it low-key, conversational.'

Clare dialled Kim Fairweather on hands-free. 'Kim, Clare Yarwood, can we meet tonight for a talk, nothing formal, just your perspective.'

'Clive told you?'

'He did in confidence.'

'That's Clive. Sorry, I don't call him Dad for obvious reasons, and besides, I never did, not even when I was young.'

'We'll respect that confidence as much as possible, but it's still a murder investigation. It may come out at some stage.'

'Sometimes I wish it would, but that's Clive, always reticent, a closed book to everyone except my mother and me. Seven o'clock, the Pheasant Inn?'

'See you at seven.'

'Clive's ex-wife?'

'We've seen her, but that's in confidence. It's a police matter so I can't say much.'

'He still keeps a photo of her next to his bed. Still carries a flame, although he loved my mother as well.'

'She doesn't look the same now. Don't ask any more, Kim, please. I don't want to tell you that it's not your concern, not now.'

'Seven o'clock. First drinks on me.'

The phone line went dead.

'I like her,' Tremayne said. 'She's like you in many ways.'

'The first compliment of the month,' Clare said cheekily.

'Watch it, Yarwood, any more smart-arse remarks from you and you'll be on a disciplinary.'

'Yes, sir,' Clare's reply, both enjoying the repartee.

The final report on the retrieved knife was waiting at Forensics on Tremayne and Clare's return to Salisbury. Louise Regan handed it over to Tremayne with due ceremony, a slight tipping of the head, as if he was bestowing honour on her by his presence.

'It's interesting reading,' she said. 'The knife is an Italian Godfather Mafia Stiletto Pocket Knife. An 11-inch blade as I told you before, an acrylic handle. They sell it as a camping and hunting knife. They can be purchased in Salisbury, even today.'

'Its age?'

'The model went out of production twelve years ago. Recent examples have a slight design change. It was also produced in quantity. Why anyone would want such a weapon for camping is beyond me, but there you are. It's also foldable, in that the blade folds into a recess in the handle. It is capable of killing a man.'

'Yarwood, get some people on to it. A long shot, but a sporting shop may remember or have kept records of knife sales,' Tremayne said, although he realised that although they may have the murder weapon, putting a person's name to it would be unlikely.

Clare left Tremayne and Louise Regan and went back to Homicide. She entered the day's events into her report, checked her emails, passed on the knife details to those charged with seeing if they could find out who could have purchased it, and then jotted some notes for the next day's activities. She briefly went home to freshen up, a change of clothes, before meeting Kim Fairweather.

She found Kim sitting in the far corner of the pub, two glasses of wine in front of her. 'I saw you parking your car, assumed you were a wine person.'

'I am. Tremayne's into beer, but he's cutting down.'

'I like him,' Kim said. 'Gruff, plays it cool, uncaring, but I don't think he is.'

'He's not, but don't tell him. He works hard on his image. It wouldn't help for you to destroy it for him.'

'You've tried?'

'As often as I dare.'

The two women laughed. Clare had to admit that Tremayne's statement that the two women were very similar was true.

'I take it that our meeting here is not strictly social,' Kim said.

'We need to meet your mother.'

'She can't help you.' Kim visibly tensed, distanced herself slightly from Clare.

'I can understand your reluctance, but it's a murder investigation. We need to meet with all the people who may be involved or on the periphery. We've met with your father's ex-wife.'

'Clive, please.'

'Why the reluctance to tell people about the two of you? There must be strange looks at you two from others, misreading the signals.'

'There are, but Clive's intensely private. He does not want attention focussed on him at this time, and he told you about me to abate your curiosity and to show that he was attempting to be as honest as he could.'

'But he also indicated that he knew more, but he wasn't willing to tell us.'

'We do not discuss his past, and definitely not his brother's. In fact, until you phoned to say you were coming to the office, I didn't know about a brother. Sorry, that's not altogether true. I had seen references at Clive's house to his family, a mention of Richard, but I never spoke to him about it.'

'Why?'

'It wasn't my business. He has been a great father to me, and while he wasn't there all the time, he was there when it mattered. If I had a problem, I would phone him up, and he would never let me down. I won't let him down now by telling you more than he would be comfortable with.'

'It's an unusual relationship,' Clare said, remembering that her father and mother were there all the time, and while her father could be distant, her mother could be intrusive and always matchmaking, which explained why mother and daughter rarely spoke and met only on special occasions: Christmas, birthdays, anniversaries.

'It was a wonderful childhood. My mother is a remarkable person, a university professor. You would like her.'

'Do you live with Clive?'

'I have a small place in town, not far away, although I'm at his house most days, mainly on business, and we sometimes have a meal together. He's a great cook, and he's got a great wine cellar. Sometimes I drink more than I should, and I spend the night at the house. No doubt the local gossips have a field day, the staid and tired mayor and his personal assistant.'

'Questions must have been raised.'

'The truth of our relationship would only set more tongues wagging.'

'You're remarkably well-balanced for your age,' Clare said.

'My parents always included me in their conversations. I learnt from their wisdom, but I'm still young, still inclined to fall into foolish love, to drink more than I should if given a chance.'

'A boyfriend?'

'Not recently. One day, I hope to find someone, but Clive has set the bar high. Can anyone reach that far?'

'You will find someone eventually, but they're rare and far apart. Another glass?'

'Of course. At least I won't be done for drunken driving, not with you here.'

'You won't be driving if you're over the limit. I'll make sure of that.'

'Are you married?'

'My bar was set high. No one has come close since then.'

'Do you want to talk about it?'

'One day in the future if you want, and I'm drunk enough, I will tell you about it. But not now, and not today.' Clare took out her tissue and held it to her eyes.

Kim put her arm around her. 'It's not only Clive who keeps secrets, is it?' she said.

'Sorry about that. Sometimes the past is best left unspoken, even forgotten.'

'Not so easy, not always.'

'We need to meet your mother tomorrow. You will need to explain to her that it's a formality. Will she understand?'

'She will. But remember, for many years our family secret has remained just that, a secret. She will be as reticent as Clive has, possibly more so. Can you go on your own, not take Inspector Tremayne?'

102

'I can.'

'Good. Then please do. My mother will be open with you, especially if I tell her that you're my friend and I trust you.'

'Two glasses are your limit if you're driving. Another one if we stay another hour or two and have something to eat,' Clare said.

'I insist on paying,' Kim said, as she asked for a menu to be brought over.

Chapter 11

Clare couldn't help but notice the smell of old books in Liz Fairweather's office. It was incongruous given the modern decor and the view from the window overlooking a quadrangle and the modern buildings of one of the newer Cambridge University colleges. The early morning drive from Salisbury had taken just over three hours, and she had enjoyed the tranquillity of not having her senior with her. He had understood the need for her to go on her own, trusting her to ask the pertinent questions, to dig deep if needed, to apply pressure if required. Clare hoped that she would not have to revert to bullying tactics, although she knew that both Clive Grantley and his daughter were skilled at not answering certain questions.

Withholding evidence was an issue with both of them, and Clare was sure that it was going to be no different with Liz Fairweather, a Professor of Ancient History.

'Ancient Greek mainly, although other members of the academic staff focus on Ancient Rome.'

'Bronze Age Britain?' Clare asked. She was glad that Tremayne was not there with her, not because Liz Fairweather would be less open and subjective when dealing with anyone involved with the Grantleys, but because an academic's lair, surrounded by old books, was not the kind of place where he would have felt comfortable.

Kim Fairweather's mother was elegantly dressed, her hair cut short, but stylish, not with the severity of

Clive Grantley's ex-wife. Clare noticed the high-heel shoes that she wore and which Clare had wanted to purchase in Salisbury, but had deemed the price just too much for a police sergeant.

'You do know why I'm here, don't you?' Clare said.

'Kim told me, and apparently our little secret is out in the open.'

'Inspector Tremayne and I know. So far, we've had no reason to divulge it to others.'

'You will, I'm sure. All part of the investigative process and now you want me to open up, tell you secrets about the three of us and his delinquent brother.'

'Delinquent?'

'Reputedly. I never met him, although what little I know of the man, he was trouble with a capital T.'

'That appears to be the consensus. Our knowledge of him is minimal, only through people who knew him, or, in your case, what Clive has told you.'

'Which is not very much. You know Clive well enough to know that he is intensely private.'

'Strange that he should be the mayor of Salisbury, wouldn't you think?'

'Not at all. Clive regards his giving to the community as important. He takes these sorts of things seriously. What do you think he'd do if he weren't involved with the council in Salisbury?'

'Reclusively hiding away in his house, counting his money.'

'Reclusive, I'd agree. The money is not his driving force, and he's given a lot to charity.'

'He never mentioned that.'

'And he never will. I've met men of note: Nobel Prize winners, brilliant academics, political leaders and many others. None are of the character and the substance of Clive.'

'You make him out to be a saint,' Clare said, a little tired of hearing of the great and beneficent Clive Grantley. The man must have some vices, a dark secret too shameful to reveal. Everyone else does, and there's always a skeleton in the cupboard, something never revealed, not even to Liz and Kim Fairweather, the two closest to him.

'Kim asked me to be open with you. I will tell you what I know, but I'm afraid it will only be a character reference for Clive. I never met Richard, so I can't help you there.'

'Then please, from the beginning. How you met Clive. The relationship between you two now and Kim.'

'I had just graduated, a PhD in Ancient Greek. I'd been to Greece on several occasions, but armed with my knowledge of the culture, as well as being able to read Ancient Greek, I had travelled to Athens to test out my skills. I was there, not far from the Parthenon, close to where Socrates had died. I was reading some inscriptions, jotting them down in a notebook that I always carried, when Clive, not that I knew who he was then, came up behind me and read them in English to me from a book in his hand. He thought I was just a tourist attempting to soak up the history of the place, not aware that I knew more about the history of the country than most Greeks.'

'Clive is not the sort of person to approach anyone,' Clare said.

'He was clumsy in how he did it, gave me quite a start, and if it had been anywhere else, then maybe I would have told him to clear off, not in those words though. I may have been able to converse in Ancient and Modern Greek, but I could swear like a trooper.'

'But you didn't.'

'His apology was so articulate it startled me.'

'Why?'

'I had spent a long time at university, a hotbed of ferment, political extremism, ardent feminism. Even I in my earlier years was involved. We may have been smart, most of us, but we couldn't see the world as it really is, its foibles, its injustices, its beauty, its malevolence. I thought that student revolt, indignation and protesting about everything wrong was the way forward.'

'And now?'

'Intelligent debate, rational and constructive action, not that the youth of today believe that. Socrates, if you've ever read him, or, more correctly, what others wrote about him. There is no written word from Socrates' hand, plenty from others. He was the great orator, the great debater, the man who showed the validity of discussion and clear thought.'

'I've read Plato's account of his death,' Clare said. She did not mention that she had attempted other works by the man but with little success due to the complexity of the text.

'That's in your favour. I can see why Kim likes you. Anyway, Clive and I start talking, and before either of us realise it, it's late at night, and we're sitting in a small restaurant drinking and eating and enjoying ourselves. After that, for the next five days, we were inseparable, although at night, separate rooms, his choice not mine.'

'Why his choice?'

'At the time, I didn't understand it, although it was another of his endearing characteristics. At university, the men assumed that if they had bought you a drink, the women were expected to offer themselves by way of thanks.'

'Did you?'

'Too often, I'm afraid. And here's Clive, educated, articulate, polite, asking nothing in return except my company. You can't believe what an aphrodisiac all of it was. Excuse my bluntness.'

'It's refreshingly honest. Does Kim know this story?'

'She does, and she also knows why we never lived together, never married.'

'Then you have more to tell me.'

'I'll open the window first. The air's not good here, old manuscripts, no doubt a few too many dust mites. If you feel itchy afterwards, blame them.'

Clare was not feeling uncomfortable sitting in the office, because the conversation was engrossing and she had to keep reminding herself that she was there for a murder enquiry, not a social occasion.

Retaking her seat, Liz Fairweather continued. 'We returned to England, and I didn't hear from him for a couple of weeks. I was smitten by then. The former communist, the former ardent 'burn your bra' feminist, the former believer in the rights of the individual over the fat cats controlling the country. I wasn't any of what I just said when I met Clive, but I was still in sympathy with some of those views.'

'You were in love?'

'It seemed illogical. Sure, I needed the occasional man, who doesn't, but that was it. No great maternal instincts, no wish to be the housewife waiting dutifully at home for her husband's return. I was destined for academia, and like all occupations, it's flawed, with a degree of male chauvinism.'

'I can understand the strength of the emotion.'

'After Kim gave me your name, I googled you. It seems that life has not always treated you well.'

'It hasn't,' Clare said. With Liz Fairweather, she did not feel the sadness that normally accompanied any mention of Harry Holchester. 'Kim said she wouldn't check and I said that one day, a very drunk day, I would tell her.'

'Then tell her, it always helps. Let's not linger on that. After two weeks, Clive and I met in Cambridge. He told me the story of his wife and his brother. We slept together that night. I was like a giggly adolescent with him; he was verbose, chatting away about this and that. Strange that two people could be so out of character.'

'After that?'

'We were together as often as we could be. I was busy as a professor here, the youngest in my faculty; Clive was in Salisbury working with his father on various projects, investments, real estate developments. We'd meet in Cambridge, sometimes in London, sometimes in Salisbury.'

'You became pregnant?'

'We still loved each other, but I didn't want to commit to marriage, a personal trauma in my earlier life, constantly seeing my parents at each other's throat day and night put me off the concept. Clive didn't want a repeat of his first marriage and her betrayal with his brother. By now, I'd become maternal, desperate for the child, the same as Clive. We talked it through, agreed that I would look after it, and he would be the father, always there, never intruding in how I brought up the child. It was an agreement forged from respect for the other, a genuine belief that neither party would harm the other. And that's how it's been since then.'

'You weren't lovers again?'

'Never. We fumbled around a few times, trying to recreate the ardour, but it wasn't there. Neither of us was overly sexual, and when he visited, he shared my bed, but only for sleep.'

'Kim?'

'You've met her. What do you reckon? Do you think she suffered from the arrangement?'

'Not from what I can see.'

'She's with Clive now, learning about life. One day she may well embrace academia, but I doubt it. She's a more emotional woman than I am, and no doubt she'll find a husband in time. I only hope he's as good as Clive.'

'Not so easy,' Clare said.

'Is there any more? I've got a lecture in fifteen minutes.'

'You lecture on Ancient Greek. Have you at any time lectured on ancient British history?'

'Never. It's not an area I have a great deal of knowledge of. Why?'

'Richard Grantley was found buried in a Bronze Age burial mound. You must have read about it.'

'Are you attempting to make a connection between one of my colleagues or one of my students and his death?'

'It's a thought. We don't understand why the burial mound. If Richard was murdered for a reason, although we don't know that reason yet, then why the burial mound? It makes no sense, but it must have relevance, however obscure.'

'I will put you in touch with someone who can help, but it's a disturbing thought that I may have contributed to his death, met his murderer.'

'You never met Richard?'

'Not to my knowledge. If I had it would have been circumstantial, a chance encounter when I was younger and I tended to drink more than I should. Sometimes I'd wake up the next day not sure of where I'd been.'

'Until we understand the reason for the burial mound, we're floundering with this enquiry.'

'I'll help if I can. I spoke to Clive last night, and he seemed to be holding up well.'

'You don't go to Salisbury?'

'Not for many years, not since Kim was born.'

'Why?'

'Nothing in itself. Clive and his need for privacy, and then after Kim was born, we felt that she should remain here with me, no conflict of two homes, two parents. Our thoughts were always with her. She's the most important person in both our lives.'

***

Clare had returned from Cambridge pleased with herself about the possible connection between the mound and Liz Fairweather's ancient British history faculty members and former students. It was Tremayne who deflated her as they sat in his office.

'Yarwood, I'm appreciative of what you achieved with the woman, but once again you're allowing emotion to cloud your reasoning.'

'You commented that Clive Grantley was not a murderer, if I remember correctly.'

'I said it, not because it's a fact but because of what I, as a police officer of many years standing, believed. That did not obviate the need to investigate the man. He could be as guilty as anyone else of the murder and Liz Fairweather could have been his accomplice, not the perpetrator, as she wouldn't have had the strength to place the body in the mound on her own.'

'Are you intimating she could have been involved? Where's your evidence?'

'Circumstantial, as most of this investigation is at the present moment. As a result of what the woman told you, you believe that a third party somehow had a grudge against Richard Grantley, a man Liz Fairweather claims never to have met. Where's the proof that she never met him? She was, as she admitted, a sabre rattler in her youth, a woman who slept around.'

'She didn't admit to sleeping around, only that the men expected sex in return for a buying her a drink.'

'And you don't believe she did?'

'We never elaborated on that, although she probably did. We all go through that time, the hormones going wild, wanting to be part of the group, and her group were into anarchy or their version of it, and promiscuity would be part of it. Let's grant that she slept around. Where does that lead us?'

'Richard Grantley, a university student, a fellow rebel, a pint of beer in exchange for whatever. It's not beyond the realms of possibility. What do we have on him? University, the member of an anarchist clique, standing on a soapbox in Hyde Park, up in London, sprouting nonsense?'

'Our records of Richard Grantley are incomplete. We know he left school at the age of eighteen and travelled overseas for some years.'

'Clive Grantley mentioned there was more we didn't know. And what about the reference to working for the government? He would have been the age to infiltrate the more radical university elements. Some of them were pervasive, capable of violence, capable of causing trouble.'

'We're heading into intrigue and subversion. Shouldn't we keep to the straight and narrow, look for the more logical rather than heading down rabbit holes without end.'

'And, Yarwood, that's where you're missing the point. You've become emotional about Kim Fairweather and her mother. Is the mother as agreeable as her daughter?'

'So you find Kim agreeable?'

'As you do, don't deny it.'

Clare knew that she was pushing Tremayne, expecting a rebuke, but she knew this was how he liked it, the cut and thrust, the exploration of fanciful ideas and plots, even subplots, the attempt to separate the wheat from the chaff. Of course she was emotional. She couldn't help the soft side to her nature, no more than Tremayne could, although he was better at concealing his.

'I don't. And I like Clive Grantley in his own way, a thoroughly decent man, but that doesn't mean I'm a pushover.'

'Okay, your theory,' Clare said.

'Didn't you consider why Liz Fairweather has not been to Salisbury in twenty years?'

'She said it was because of Kim, not wanting to confuse her.'

'Balderdash, and you know it. The child when she was young wouldn't have had any issues with coming here, and as she grew older, she was well aware of who her father was, his constant presence in her life. She must have had friends where the parents were in the family home, parents who had divorced and kept apart, even hated the other, the child being the meat in the sandwich.

And you're telling me that you believe Liz Fairweather kept away for the child.'

'Your evaluation?'

'What if she was involved with the death of Richard Grantley? What if the reason was that she didn't want to come back to the scene of the crime? If, as she has stated to you, her and Clive Grantley were beside themselves with love and lust for a couple of months, maybe more, either of them could have broken out of the mould, committed a grievous sin.'

'But why?'

'Love knows no bounds, and what if Richard had found out about Liz? He had made an effort to seduce Grace, Clive's wife. Maybe Richard, a despicable character from what we know so far, had taken the challenge up to seduce Liz, been rebuffed, acted violently towards her. She had suffered trauma as a child, warring parents, but what if there's more to it. She had a drunken phase as an undergraduate, promiscuous, slept around, sometimes said no, the man not heeding the refusal from her, assuming it was a yes, the no there as an attempt to maintain her innocence. It happens, and you know it.'

Clare did but had no intention of elaborating. The past, that past at least, belonged to her teenage years in Norfolk, not to her now as a serving police officer.

'She couldn't have done it on her own,' Clare's reply, realising that what Tremayne said had a degree of plausibility; in fact, it was a solid motive and a distinct possibility.

'Clive, after a lifetime of maltreatment from his more charismatic brother, could rationalise what the two of them had done, even rejoice in it. But Liz, gentler, a woman, could not. They've spent a lifetime, the three of them, living a fairy tale existence, but with fairy tales,

114

there's always a villain. Not, in this case, a witch or an evil ogre, but a flesh and bone villain by the name of Richard Grantley.'

'What you say has some logic to it. I hope it's not true.'

'There you go again, allowing emotion to enter into it. We can't ignore the possibility. If Kim Fairweather's parents committed murder, then it's up to us to arrest them. You either accept that fact and do your duty, or you have no place in the police force.'

'I resent your aspersion that I would do anything else.'

'I'm tough for your own good, Yarwood. You're the finest police sergeant in the station, but overt sentimentality can cloud even the most capable investigator. I've been guilty of it in the past, although we've never come across people such as these three. Normally, it's a villain, a known rogue, someone that it's easy to dislike, but I'll grant you, all three this time are admirable people.'

Chapter 12

After Tremayne had given her a dressing down, Clare had to admit that it was for her own good, realising that he had been right. She did see the best in people, and his logic in evaluating the case subsequently had been flawless.

The most likely culprits were Clive Grantley and Liz Fairweather. For the time being, Clare knew that she would have to curtail her friendship with Kim, to delay the drunken lunch where she would tell her about Harry.

Richard Grantley was proving to be more of a mystery than expected. There was a record of him returning from overseas at the age of twenty-one, then a period where he had dropped off the map, the time that Tremayne postulated that he was undercover with one of the more demonstrative and disruptive student or anarchist groups. Clare was concerned that somehow Liz Fairweather had been in the thick of it. Grantley could have been using a false name, possibly had changed his hairstyle, changed his appearance, his manner, the way he walked, the way he talked, but not his ability to seduce women, a possible reason for Clive Grantley and Liz, the love of his life, to plot revenge against him.

It was clear to both Tremayne and Clare that further pressure needed to be put on Clive Grantley and Liz Fairweather. And then there was Grace Thornberry, Clive's ex-wife, and her husband. None of the people identified as the possible murderer or murderers figured high on the list of definites, and certainly not Grace

Thornberry's husband, an overweight, red-faced man when the two police officers met him at the family home.

Clare had driven again, a chance for Tremayne to close his eyes – going through the case in his mind, he would say – but Clare knew that he slept most of the time. And when he was awake on the trip, he'd be there, reading the racing guide, asking Clare's advice about which horse she fancied for the 3.30 at Cheltenham or the next day's races at Ascot. He may as well have asked the horses themselves, as Clare, who had learnt to ride as a child, had no interest in horse racing, and less interest in losing money on a three-legged donkey. At least, that was how Tremayne would refer to his choice after he had lost money on it.

Clare had phoned ahead, told Grace Thornberry that they were coming and the visit was official, to take place either at their home or at the local police station. Grace chose the family home.

The door opened, but not to a tired-looking woman, old for her years, a cigarette dangling precariously from nicotine-stained fingers. The short-cropped hair had been treated, no longer showing grey streaks, and no longer the old slippers, the worn clothes. Grace Thornberry wore a dress, her nails were manicured, makeup had been applied, and the sullen face was replaced with a beaming smile. It all seemed too artificial for Tremayne, but Clare was pleased to see it, able to see an older version of the woman who Clive Grantley had had his arm around all those years before on a beach in the south of France.

'Geoff's here,' Grace said. In the hallway of the house a vase with flowers, a pleasant smell in the air. The unwelcoming modest semi-detached had been transposed into charming and inviting. Clare wondered why the change in the woman and the house. What secrets were they attempting to hide, to deflect from the police.

In the other room, Geoff Thornberry stood. He stretched out his hand and shook Tremayne's formally. With Clare he was more vigorous, clenching her hand firmly, shaking it more than he should.

'Grace has told me all about you. How pleasant you were to her. How much she enjoyed your company.'

If he had been trying to intimate an air of married harmony, the man failed miserably. His attempt was overstated, too ingratiating. It was not a good marriage, and without the presence of two police officers, Clare imagined that the house would either be silent or in uproar, slanging matches, broken pots.

'I'll fetch the tea,' Grace said. 'Make yourselves comfortable.'

It was Tremayne who brought balance to the situation. 'Mr Thornberry, this is not a social visit. A man has been murdered, and your wife is part of the investigation. So, please, let's stop this charade. You don't want us here, and that's understandable. We're raking over old history. How long have you two been married?'

'Twenty-two years this April. Good years let me tell you.'

'Please, Mr Thornberry. I've been a police officer for too many years not to know that you're wasting your time. Now, we don't wish to insult you, far from it, but we are going to ask your wife questions about a past life, a time that she probably wants to forget and you'd rather not hear about.'

'We've nothing to hide, and sure, sometimes Grace and I have our differences, but we're here through thick and thin, good and bad.'

Clare thought the bad probably outweighed the good by a significant margin. She did not like Geoff Thornberry, who gave every indication of being the sort of person who was good at pretending friendship at his place of employment while stabbing someone in the back; the adolescent child who would have been the school bully. Compared to Clive Grantley, Grace's first husband, the man was an obnoxious bore.

Grace returned with the tea, not smiling as much as she had before, and it was clear that she had heard Tremayne's words with her husband.

'Times have been tough,' Geoff said.

'It's not as bad as he paints it, Inspector,' Grace said. 'Geoff's tried to make a go of it, but life doesn't always work out the way you want. And yes, the marriage isn't good, but we don't intend separating, as much for ourselves as the children.'

Clare knew that she didn't want such a relationship, unable to separate for fear of the unknown, willing to stay with someone you either despised or loathed, although which of those emotions was Grace's, she didn't know.

'I had to put the interview on a level plane, no more pretences from you both,' Tremayne said, directing his conversation at Grace. 'Now, let's go back to when you were married to Clive. I'm assuming that your husband knows the story?'

'I know most of it,' Geoff Thornberry said. 'Enough to know that I'd rather not be here.'

'Let's clarify your position,' Clare said, 'before we continue with Grace. How much do you know of the murder investigation? How much do you know of Clive Grantley? Have you met him?'

'We've got the internet. Richard Grantley, the brother, was found dead. According to Grace, she had met him, but it was a long time ago.'

'*Met*!'

'Okay, she made a fool of herself, laid it on a plate for him, had an affair. What else do you want me to say? She screwed around with her husband's brother.'

'It disturbs me raking over the past,' Grace said. 'It's a period of my life that I'd rather forget.

'Excuse my wife,' Geoff Thornberry said. 'I've been a disappointment to her. She married me because I was stable, a steady provider, a person who could offer her a reasonable life. Clive Grantley was and still is a dull and decent man; I know that.'

'How?'

'I'll come to that in a minute. Grace back then was on the rebound from Clive. She'd had the mad fling with Richard Grantley, regretted what she had done, but the man had charisma, according to her, and she succumbed every time to his advances.'

'Not every time,' Grace interjected.

'More times than you should have. Grace saw me as a steady bet; I saw her as a beautiful woman, way out of my league. We met, married, had children, enjoyed ourselves some of the time, argued the rest.'

'Clive Grantley?'

'I'm a construction engineer. I was in Salisbury consulting on a problem with the new bypass. Grantley came to the site. He wasn't the mayor then, just a councillor. I shook his hand, explained the issue to him and the others there. It was a five-minute conversation, nothing more, and I never mentioned who I was, no reason to. I know all about Grace and her earlier life, or most of it. Everyone has secrets, and if Grace hasn't told me all, then it doesn't matter. Water under the bridge as far as I'm concerned.'

'Thanks,' Grace said. Clare could see some affection between husband and wife, not the passion of young love, but enough for the two of them to stay together. It was not how she had seen her future with Harry when he was alive; not how she could foresee it with someone else.

'Is that it?' Tremayne asked. 'Mrs Thornberry, not forsaking your current marriage, let us go back in time. I hope that you have revealed all to your husband as I feel that we need to go deep here. It's clear that one strong man could have placed Richard Grantley in his resting place. You could not have done it on your own. He was killed with a knife which we retrieved at the crime scene. Did you ever see Clive or Richard with a knife? It folds, the blade recessing into the handle, a long thin blade.'

'I don't remember much in the way of possessions with Richard. He knocked on the door that day dressed in a tee shirt and a pair of jeans even though the weather was cold. He had a backpack with him, but no suitcase, nothing else. Clive lent him some clothes, and for a few days, they talked constantly, always reminiscing about old times. I don't think on reflection that much of it was genuine, purely a need with Clive to believe it was.'

'Richard?'

'As I found out later, the man could affect any manner that he wanted. He'd have you believe that you were the love of his life, the friend you had always wanted.'

'So his reminiscing with Clive could have been disingenuous?'

'Clive must have known. He was an educated man, but Richard was smarter. If I think back…easier to do than with more recent events, Richard could have engineered the conversation, spun a tale about what had gone wrong in the Middle East, why he was in England with no money, no belongings, just a passport, not even a driving licence. Not that it took him long to get back on his feet again and there he was outside the house with a decent car, another woman in the passenger seat. I was superfluous, but the damage was done, and Clive was out of the house, out of my life.

'When Clive wasn't there, I missed him, more so than Richard. But Richard could liven up the room, make any woman feel special. It was a Catch-22, and I blew it.'

'Which doesn't absolve you from the murder, does it?'

'I think it does.'

Clare could see that Geoff Thornberry was becoming agitated, shuffling on his seat. His face was red, redder than usual. The man was getting angry, and that anger was directed at Tremayne. She would have preferred to question Grace on her own, but Tremayne had been adamant. 'Conflict, ignite the passions, exacerbate the anger, the hatred, let them show if they're capable of violence.'

'Grace, let's be honest here,' Tremayne said, glancing over at Geoff. 'Clive Grantley is a man of strong beliefs. This we know. If he had married you for better or for worse, richer or poorer, and so on, your marriage would have weathered the storm regardless of his brother. Did you have such strong beliefs?'

'Not that strong. If the marriage had failed, then that was that. I don't believe that Clive was as strong in his views as you say he was, either.'

'I'd disagree on that point, but let's not linger. You've stayed with Geoff through good and bad, and I hope he doesn't mind what I'm going to say, although he probably will.'

Clare could see Tremayne raising the tempo, looking for the bite from one of the Thornberrys. Which one was going to crack first? Geoff, if he did, was a big man, not so easy to hold down.

'Clive came from an affluent family, a generous family, dependable, polite, and was someone who'd not let you down. Has he helped you financially since the divorce?'

'No.'

'Why?'

'Shame on my part for what had occurred. He would have helped, I'm sure of it, but after the divorce I moved north to Manchester. I met Geoff some time after and we married.'

'The same passion that you had with Clive? The same lifestyle?'

'You must understand that times were hard. I refused Clive's money, even at the divorce. Up here, I worked in a factory, lived in a squalid bedsit. I saw it as my punishment for what I had done.'

'Self-imposed?'

'It took several years of counselling before I was stable. Geoff was there with me for most of it.'

'Thanks for your honesty,' Clare said. 'This must be painful for you.'

'It's more painful for Geoff. He knows the truth of our relationship, the same as I do. Unspoken, we can deal with it, but raw emotions are now exposed, emotions which will be difficult to quell. No doubt after you've both left, we will talk late into the night.'

'The outcome?'

'We'll weather the storm; we always do.'

The red-faced Geoff Thornberry was on his feet. His fists were clenched. 'Are you accusing my wife of murder?'

'I'm accusing no one,' Tremayne said calmly. 'Either you sit down, or we'll reconvene at the local police station.'

'My wife is not guilty of murder.'

'I don't think that Mr Thornberry can remain calm,' Clare said to Tremayne.

'He will,' Tremayne replied. Thornberry may fume, but he was sure the man had had his moment of revolt at the line of questioning. From here on in, he would be mute, biting his tongue, saying nothing, just exhaling loudly, puffing out his chest, and getting redder.

'I didn't kill him. Clive could have killed him, I suppose,' Grace said.

'So far the dates don't match; you would have been married to Geoff by then and living in Manchester. Although, Richard could have found out where you were, made a play for you.'

'Is that it?' Geoff Thornberry said. 'You come in here, upset my wife, accuse her of being a tart, a murderer, and God knows what else? Is that how you conduct a police investigation?'

'It's a murder enquiry. No stone must be left unturned, no person excused from the investigation purely because they are a good person or they're ill, even if they're dying. I apologise. We will leave you now.'

Outside the house, Clare spoke. 'You were rough in there.'

'What option did I have?' Tremayne replied. He had instinctively put his hand in his jacket pocket to pull out a cigarette packet. 'Damn you and Jean. I could do with a cigarette right now.'

'It's for your own good, Jean will tell you that. You didn't like doing that in there, I know, but it had to be done. There's only one problem. The burial mound. What's its significance?'

'Clive Grantley's the glue between the two women and the burial. He's not off the hook yet. Focus on Richard Grantley: aliases, business dealings, bank accounts, residential addresses.'

'That's what we have a team for. They're busy finding out what they can, but there's not a lot.'

'Find more, and you'll need to follow up on Liz Fairweather's colleagues. Did she have a love affair with someone before Clive or after? Did she somehow meet Richard?'

'Any possibility of anyone else dying or dead?'

'Check, but there often is,' Tremayne said. 'I need a pint of beer.'

'After that, you can have two,' Clare said. She wouldn't tell Jean that he had broken his alcohol limit, not this time.

Chapter 13

The chieftain that Gerard Horsley and his team had recovered from the burial mound had a more complete history than Richard Grantley. DNA had been extracted, and oxygen isotope analysis of his tooth enamel found he was a native of the region, not like the 'King of Stonehenge' who was shown to have come from what is now modern Switzerland. Radiocarbon dating of the grave confirmed that he was laid to rest circa 2300 BC, which gave the number of years to the present time as approximately four thousand three hundred years. His age was ascertained to be between thirty-five and forty-five years old, and he had been in reasonably good health for the period. That was not an assessment that would be given to a modern man as Horsley's chieftain was shown to have one arm weaker than the other, and probably of minimal use. His dentition showed a good set of teeth and one abscess which would have caused him pain. There was no sign of trauma to explain his death, and failing further information, he was believed to have died of natural causes. The items recovered with the man were still being collated, and a permanent display, with Horsley's name prominent as the archaeologist responsible for the find, was in preparation, a date two months later for the unveiling of the prize exhibit.

The irony of the work done on the ancient body and how much was known about him was not lost on Tremayne. It had been a long day, mainly in the office, as the leads had dried up.

Clare was still following through on Richard
Grantley, trying to find out more about him. Clive had
opened up with more about his brother's return from
overseas to the family home at the age of twenty-one. It
had lasted for three months, enough time for him to
detox, and then one night he had left again, a note on the
kitchen table telling his parents not to worry about him
and that another adventure beckoned.

Clare spent time with Kim Fairweather, believing
that the young woman had more sway with her parents
than anyone else, and Kim had shown that she wasn't as
reticent as they were. Clare was full of admiration for
how the woman conducted herself, but not for what Kim
had said: 'I'll not say anything without their permission. I
believe in their innocence unreservedly, and in time the
truth will come from another direction.'

Neither Tremayne nor Clare could break through
the barrier, and the interviewing techniques which
Tremayne had honed, and Clare was continually
improving on, whereby the pressure was maintained and
the questioning became faster, shotgun staccato, trying to
bewilder the interviewee and to confuse them, wasn't
going to work with these three.

Clare had broached Liz Fairweather's radicalism
when she was younger with Kim, the possibility that she
had mixed with unsavoury elements, possibly committed
illegal activities.

'My parents were extremely conservative as I was
growing up. If either of them had acted unwisely when
they were younger, then I have no knowledge of it. My
mother always ensured that I was home at a reasonable
time, ensured that I didn't skimp on chores around the
house and that I did my homework on time. Sometimes,
especially in my early teens, that irritated me, but that was

my mother, and when my father was there, we'd have long talks about it. They kept me from making a complete fool of myself. I can't believe that my parents have dubious pasts, not the two people that I know.'

'They're determined to have us charge them,' Tremayne said as he wandered over to Clare's desk. The day was drawing to a close when additional information came in about Richard Grantley.

It was Liz Fairweather on the phone. 'Kim's phoned me,' she said to Clare. 'There's a side to my history that I'd prefer forgotten, but you're not going to let this rest until you've solved Richard's death, are you?'

'We can't. If you or Clive are guilty, we'll find out in time, and you'll be charged. You do understand that?'

'There was a period in my student days. How much have you researched about me?'

'Grade A student, rebellious, took part in a few demonstrations, mildly promiscuous from all accounts, even while you were burning your bra. Does Kim know all this?'

'There are no secrets between us. What she doesn't know are the names of some of the men I may have been involved with.'

'May? What does that mean?'

'We experimented with mind-enhancing drugs, a higher level of consciousness. Mild by the standards of today: magic mushrooms, LSD, some others. Sometimes I'd know who it was I slept with, sometimes I didn't, not until the drugs had worn off.'

'Do we need to come up and see you?'

'I'll give you two names. Check them out and give me a call. I've spoken to Clive. He's not comfortable with my doing this, but he understands.'

'I've got pen and paper in front of me,' Clare said. Tremayne stood to one side, the phone on speaker.

'Des Wetherell. You've heard of him, no doubt.'

'The firebrand union leader and professional agitator.'

'He was a polite young man back then, more extreme in his views than most of us were, but not the person he's become. We had a bit of a fling, nothing too serious, but he did become fixated on me, became a nuisance later on. No violence, just persistent phone calls, hanging around where I was. In the end, I told him that it was over, firmly the last time. He never came near me again.'

'He spent time in jail for manslaughter, the sentence overturned on appeal,' Tremayne whispered into Clare's ear.

'Don't worry. I can hear your senior alongside you. It pains me to mention his name. And there's one other. Monty Yatton. He's a professor at Dundee University now. He specialises in ancient British history. He was a vain, mildly eccentric student back then. Always dressed bizarrely, a dandy he would have once been called. He went around in a top hat and tails, a pair of jeans and a faded Ban the Bomb tee shirt. You know the type, with the CND symbol on it.'

'Why didn't you tell us about them before?'

'I'm after a promotion here as well as a grant to conduct a dig on a location outside of Athens. It shouldn't matter that I'm indirectly implicated in a murder. Of course, those making the decisions about my future will say it doesn't, but we all know the reality. Recounting my past, having it opened up to scrutiny, is not what I wanted. And besides, I'd prefer Kim not to know of some of the sordid details, what a cheap lay her mother was once.'

***

The revelation about Des Wetherell and Monty Yatton understandably put new impetus into the murder investigation. One was well known to the general public, the other wasn't.

Clare spent time in the office checking up on Wetherell, a man with a fearsome reputation, a man who had maintained his strong socialist convictions, his belief in the power of the trade unions, his commitment to the working man. He was a man that many regarded as out of touch with modern-day reality, and whereas many had suffered under the onslaught of Margaret Thatcher and her emasculation of the trade unions, others had prospered, and the twenty-first century was not like the eighties of the previous century. Most people were more prosperous, and the politically ideological differences of the left-wing and right-wing political parties in Westminster were not so obvious. But Clare knew, as did others, that change was inevitable, and the recent waves of migration, the separation from Europe, the threats to the prosperity of the individual were all combining to give Wetherell a platform on which to debate – and debate the man did.

Wetherell was no cloth-capped working man from a coal mine nor a steelworker who had risen up through the ranks of unionism, starting as a shop steward calling the workers out on strike for whatever petty grievance could be levelled against the corrupt bosses. Nor had he spent time as a regional organiser, swapping the cap for a suit. He had instead taken a position with the Public

Services Union, with a membership of over eighty thousand. At that time, he was involved in setting up a credit union for the members, shaping union policy, drafting submissions to the left-wing Labour Party in power at that time. With the change in government, a reflection of more prosperous times, he had become more ardent, taking part in panel shows on the television, banging his fist on the table occasionally for effect, but always, behind the persona of strident socialism, the well-spoken, immaculately dressed and urbane Wetherell.

His detractors, and there were plenty, referred to him as a 'Champagne Socialist' on account of his wealth – he lived in a five-bedroom house in Surrey – the Jaguar he drove, the fact that he preferred wine from his extensive cellar to a pint of beer at the local pub with his fellow comrades. He was an anachronism; Clare could see as she compiled a dossier on him. He was also, according to Liz Fairweather, a former lover of hers. A man who could be involved in the death of Richard Grantley, a man who had been known to revert to violence in his younger days at university, once spending three months in jail for assaulting a policeman by knocking him to the ground. And then sentenced to two years, out after six months, for manslaughter after he had thrown a rock during a demonstration, inadvertently hitting an opposing protester on the other side of the road, causing the woman to fall to the ground, smashing her head against a kerbstone as she did so, eventually dying as a result.

The trial had been flawed from the start. The evidence presented showed that the rock had caused the woman's death. The defence team on appeal had ordered another post mortem where it was shown that the rock had not been responsible for rendering the woman unconscious; it had been the kerb, the impact with it enhanced by the milling mob around her accidentally pushing her as she fell down, increasing the impact pressure.

The verdict was tossed aside, an enquiry was ordered into the travesty of justice, the results of which were brushed under the table. Some said it was a cover-up by the government of the time; others said the legal system was prejudiced against a firebrand and political agitator who spoke a lot of sense and could argue against the inconsistencies in their treatment of the more disruptive in society, the good people as Des Wetherell would see them.

Tremayne perused the report that Clare had prepared on Wetherell. He wasn't a man given to studying written documents in detail, and it was still up to Clare to give him a verbal précis.

'He's no fool,' Clare said. 'Violent in his youth, that's proven by the two police cases against him.'

'Liz Fairweather, what about her? She's fooling around with Wetherell and others, not the saint that you might want to portray her as. If Wetherell is at the demonstrations, what about her? Where was she? Holding the placard, throwing rocks?'

'There are no convictions against her name, and yes, she would have been at some. Mostly protests against one or another government policy, the compulsory purchase of low-cost housing for an airport runway or a new road, train line, whatever.'

'Is that it?'

'Not totally. They were radical back then, and Liz Fairweather's indicated that she was one of the more extreme, not that you'd know it now. We were all a bit silly in our youth,' Clare said.

'I didn't go around throwing rocks, protesting against the government. So much nonsense, if you ask me.'

Clare had to agree with her senior. She couldn't imagine him wasting energy on causes, no matter how relevant. Tremayne, she knew, was a plodder, a decent man who did his job and was ruthlessly honest. That was what she liked about him, an open book.

'We still come back to the burial mound and how Richard Grantley is involved with Liz Fairweather and by default Wetherell and Yatton. What's the deal with Yatton?' Tremayne asked. The man interested him more, an academic who would know about Bronze Age burial mounds and their significance.

'He studied with Liz Fairweather, a similar area of interest. Wetherell studied politics. Yatton was involved with the student union, as were Wetherell and Liz.'

'Liz is it now?'

'I'm focussing on my job. What do you want me to call her? Ms or Miss or Professor?'

'As long as you don't get emotional. My money's still on Clive Grantley and *Ms* Fairweather,' Tremayne said, emphasising the 'Ms', knowing that it would irritate his sergeant.

'My money isn't. We've got no tie-in with Richard Grantley for any of the three university anarchists. Grace Thornberry's the only one who had any meaningful contact with him.'

'She couldn't have done it, and her husband isn't the sort to get off his backside unless it's for a McDonald's cheeseburger with fries.'

'He may have when he was hungry, although he doesn't look the sort to get excited about anything much.

As long as life rolls along in a more or less pleasant manner, then he's no threat to anyone.'

'After we left the Thornberrys, did you check with the wife?'

'A flaming row, a slammed door as he sulked off to the pub. He came home in the early hours of the morning smelling like a brewery and ended up sleeping downstairs.'

'Life washes over those two. It's hard to believe she was a knockout when she was younger.'

'We all get old, even you, *Inspector Tremayne*,' Clare said. Her turn for emphasis after the earlier '*Ms*' from Tremayne.

'Getting back to Yatton, what can you tell us about him?'

'Montgomery Yatton, although he uses Monty. A similar academic path to Liz Fairweather. No convictions, although he did take part in some of the protests. I managed to find a few newspaper clippings from the period, and he's there, as are Liz and Wetherell. Yatton's a slight man, not tall, and compared to Wetherell, over six feet tall and strong, he looks vaguely effeminate.'

'At the protests?'

'His picture is on the University of Dundee's website. A balding man, gaunt, and he doesn't look well. I can't be certain on that, though.'

'Have you made contact with either of the two men?'

'Not yet. I thought that I should run it past you first. We can then decide on our course of action. Personally, I'm inclined to go with Yatton, try and understand the reason for the burial mound.'

'Was Liz Fairweather keen on either of these two men or were they just drunken flings, fellow Bolsheviks sharing bodily fluids?'

'Casual, according to her. As she's said, she was just going with the flow, living the life of the committed socialist and sleeping around was expected.'

'So why did she choose those two to reveal to you?'

'A question that's not been fully answered yet. I have to agree with you that Clive Grantley and Liz Fairweather are still the most likely candidates for a conviction.'

'Don't say it for me. Say it because as a police officer you believe it.'

'As a police officer, who else could have been responsible?'

'No one else, not until we make the tie-in between Richard Grantley and others.'

'I'm still following through with Richard Grantley being undercover, an operative for the security services in this country.'

'It'll be hard to find out the truth, Official Secrets Act.'

Chapter 14

Superintendent Moulton approved the travel request, Clare booked the tickets. Monty Yatton had been contacted and told firmly – he had protested fervently to Clare on the phone – that he would need to be available from midday until 6 p.m. the next day.

'I've got lectures to prepare, research to conduct, and besides, it was a long time ago. You can't expect me to remember back then. I've never heard of a Richard Grantley. Sure, I read about it, a burial mound, a great deal of treasure. I know Gerard Horsley; I've arranged to come down at some stage and meet him.'

'Liz Fairweather?'

'I know her, but what's it got to do with me?'

Regardless of the man's protestations, he would be available.

Early next morning Clare and Tremayne drove down to Southampton Airport. She parked in the long-stay parking, as an overnight stay in Dundee was required. She could see that Tremayne was salivating at the opportunity of drinking more than he should, maybe even smoking a cigarette.

On arrival in Edinburgh, the nearest direct flight from Southampton, Clare handed over a credit card to the rental car company, and got a blue Toyota Corolla in return. It was just after ten-thirty in the morning when they drove up to the university, time enough for them to find a place for lunch, a chance to compare notes, and to check in at the Premier Inn on Riverside Drive. It was close enough to the university to walk, but Tremayne declined the opportunity for some much-needed exercise. He didn't mention to Clare that his left knee was troubling him, knowing full well that she would tell Jean who'd fuss on his return to Salisbury. And then he'd be seeing the doctor and then the specialist, both probing, x-rays, bone density tests, whatever else, a possible knee joint replacement, early retirement. For now, he would keep quiet.

Monty Yatton arrived at his office five minutes after the agreed time. 'Sorry about that. The lecture went over time.'

He was a gaunt man, as his photo on the university website had shown, although he was older by five to ten years. The balding crown of his head was still there, but the wispy growth on the sides was gone, and he was cleanly shaven. Clare could see that he was not a bad-looking man, though nothing remarkable, with a slightly beaked nose on which perched a pair of frameless spectacles. He no longer wore a tattered Ban the Bomb tee shirt and jeans, preferring now to wear a roll neck sweater and a tweed jacket. The top hat was gone too.

'Inspector Tremayne and Sergeant Yarwood,' Tremayne said as he shook the man's hand.

Yatton declined to shake Clare's hand. 'I've got a germ phobia. The inspector caught me by surprise. I hope you'll excuse me.'

'Of course,' Clare said, although she couldn't understand why the man who had a phobia wore a sweater that smelt from the lack of a good wash, and he worked in an office surrounded by dirt and decay.

***

Des Wetherell, aware of the complication of his past history intervening in the present, sat in his office. An attractive man, tall and not overweight, even though life had been good to him, better than most of his union members he would admit, sat back in the expensive leather chair. Across from him, his two lawyers, one paid by the union, the other paid by him.

'I'm expecting the police to contact me soon, to come here and conduct an official interview,' Wetherell said.

'Do you have anything to hide?' Justin Ruxton said. He was a fresh-faced man in his mid-thirties. Four years with the union. He still had a degree of naivety, as well as respect for the man opposite who had brought him on board.

Wetherell knew he was a good judge of people, but he would never have said it. To the rank and file unionist, he was a self-effacing man, capable of espousing their cause when required, which had been increasingly often in the last seven months. The position of Deputy General Secretary of the Trades Union Congress, the TUC, the federation of the majority of the trade unions in England and Wales, with a membership of over 5.6 million, had become vacant, and it was a position he wanted. The last thing he needed was the diversion of a murder enquiry, even though he knew he was innocent. And as for that rock-throwing incident, the woman's death, he wanted it kept quiet, and that needed sharp lawyers, the subtle threat of legal action if anyone or any organisation attempted to raise it.

Why Liz Fairweather had mentioned his and Yatton's names, he wasn't sure. He had never given her much credence at university, not that he could remember her much. Sure, he had slept with her on more than a few occasions, but so had others, including the wimpish Yatton, so she couldn't have been that fussy.

'Why worry? Your position's unassailable,' said Nigel Nicholson, the more senior of the two lawyers, and the one that Wetherell trusted above the other.

'Mud sticks and you know it.'

'What do you want us to do?' Ruxton asked. He had known the man for some years, and he had never seen him as concerned before. He wondered if there was more to the story of a long-dead man than Wetherell was telling them. Even if there was, Wetherell had been the man who had mentored him, the man who had trusted him with a senior position in the union's hierarchy. He wouldn't let him down, he knew that.

'Don't let the mud be seen. Squash any rumours, dissent, anyone who threatens my aspirations. In short, do what you've always done.'

'Then level with us. Your conviction for manslaughter, overturned on appeal, is on the public record. Your membership of the communist party as a radical university student is known. What else is there?' Nicholson asked. He had known Wetherell for a long time, having met the man after both of them had finished university. Diverse backgrounds, but a shared friendship forged over many years.

'There's no more to tell,' Wetherell replied. Nicholson knew there was. He was curious about whether the bombing of a polling station to the north of London during Wetherell's university days had anything to do with his friend and most important client. No one had been hurt, and it had been put down to an anarchist group opposing the primary candidate, a man of dubious right-wing views. If it had involved Wetherell, then he, even with all his legal expertise, wouldn't be able to prevent the mud sticking.

***

Monty Yatton was a nervous man, not used to being questioned by the police. His nervousness translated itself into talking excessively, diverging from the subject, rattling on at a breakneck speed about the lectures he took, the students – bone idle, half of them, in his estimation – and how they cheated at exam time if they could, shirked their workload on group activities, and that it wasn't the same in his days at university. Clare knew that the man's estimation of those in his charge was incorrect, and she had worked hard, as had the others in her time at university. The man appeared to have a down on people, on life in general.

'Mr Yatton,' Clare said, impatient with the man's verbosity. 'Richard Grantley was murdered. Does that name have any significance to you?'

'Only from what's on the internet. You mentioned Liz Fairweather before. I do remember her and our time at university.'

'Ms Fairweather mentioned that you may be able to help us.'

'With what? I haven't seen her since, not often that is; university functions only. We were all a bit wild back then, and I used to go around in some strange clothes.'

'Radical?'

'Some of us were. Liz was definitely. I thought it was a bit of a lark, a chance to experiment with drugs.'

'And get laid,' Tremayne interjected.

'I didn't want to say it, not in front of a lady.'

'Liz mentioned it to me. There's no need to be polite in my presence,' Clare said indignantly. She had had this deference to her sex on several occasions before. The police badge should have obviated her from such discrimination. 'You screwed Liz as well as others?'

'We were on heat, like rabbits, and if you've ever smoked what we had, you'd understand.'

Tremayne didn't, his drug of choice was cigarettes, and sitting in that dusty office he could have quite happily lit up. Clare had had a brief encounter with marijuana as a teenager, but had not had any great fondness for it, and had never smoked.

'Do you still take drugs?' Tremayne asked. Clare could tell that her senior had not warmed to the man.

'Some weed at the weekend, nothing like I used to.'

'Are you married?'

'I was once, but it didn't last.'

Clare was sure that the man was a latent homosexual and that his promiscuity at university, his sleeping with Liz, his short-lived marriage, had been attempts to conceal the fact. Not that she had any opinions about someone being gay or not. It didn't concern her either way, and she would have thought that academia was tolerant of all people – as long as they didn't murder someone and bury them in a Bronze Age burial mound, that is.

'What's Liz got to do with a murdered man?' Yatton asked.

It was a fair question. So far Tremayne and Clare had managed to skate around revealing too much, but Yatton had a right to know, a probable area of investigation missed if the right questions weren't asked.

141

'We're concerned that Richard Grantley, a man adept at concealing himself, may, as a result of anarchist activities by you and others at university, have infiltrated your group.'

'We weren't anarchists; just university students attempting to right the wrongs of the world.'

'You were determined to overthrow the government, to install a new order.'

'Big Brother, 1984, that sort of thing,' Clare said.

'You know your classics,' Yatton said. 'It's good to see someone who does. Most of my students could give you an essay on the lives of vacuous celebrities, their idealised lives, their multiple lovers, but ask them if they've read Orwell or Huxley or Charles Dickens, and most of them will look at you as though you're talking a foreign language. And before we go further, the world defined in Orwell's 1984 was not the world that we envisaged. That book was a satire. And, no, I don't love Big Brother. Never did really, but it was fun for a while, Liz was fun.'

'Any other women?' Tremayne asked. He had not followed the previous intellectual conversation between two people better educated than him. He did not intend for them to continue into areas that did not assist the interview.

'Some. The names are vague now. I'm not sure if I can remember more than three or four of the group.'

'Des Wetherell?'

'You couldn't forget Wetherell. The man was full-on, even back then. He's quite a celebrity these days. He had a fling with Liz.'

'Wetherell's an agitator, always baiting the government, denouncing the more foolish of their decisions,' Tremayne said. 'Was he capable of coercive action?'

'Violence, causing physical harm, damaging property?'

'Was he?'

'He was certainly more ardent than me. I didn't mind marching up and down waving a banner. Ban the Bomb was a bit before my time even if I had the tee shirt. But we would make the banners, take the train to London and march up Whitehall, down past the Houses of Parliament. Gay rights were one of our causes, although I don't think Wetherell took that too seriously.'

'But you did,' Clare said.

'It had more relevance to me. I was suppressing it back then, but today, who cares?'

'What else?'

'There was a campaign to bring back capital punishment, but a few people had been executed in the past who were innocent. You must know that. Some of it was through not having DNA, some as a result of the police looking for a conviction.'

'Before my time,' Tremayne said. 'The last execution in England was in 1964.'

'One politician was keen to bring it back, so were some of the police. There had been an upsurge in violent crime, the murder statistics were up. We were against hanging, even considered positive action.'

'Bombing of a polling station?'

'It wasn't us, and besides, we were high as kites most of the time. Wetherell breezed through university, passed with honours. The rest of us gave thirty, maybe forty per cent to studying, the rest to getting drunk, getting laid and proselytising.'

'Was the man guilty of the bombing of the polling station, other acts of anarchy? Was Richard Grantley one of your group?'

'Who knows with Wetherell? The man always came up smelling of roses, always smarter than anyone else. He could have belonged to other subversive elements, but we wouldn't have known. We were just university students, full of hormones, full of a belief in our intelligence, our capabilities, our determination for a better world.'

'Did you find it?'

'Dundee University, yes, I believe so.'

'Your life now?'

'Mundane, the opportunity for study, for research.'

'Ancient history?'

'That's correct. I've followed Horsley's success with great interest. We've attended conferences together. I can't say I remember him, but he says that he knows me. Not surprising as I've often presented papers. Now he's the star, the one spoken of in hallowed archaeological circles. A great find, credit to him.'

'Bronze Age England, a burial mound. What's the significance?' Tremayne asked.

'The more important the person laid to rest inside, the larger the mound, the choicer the location.'

'And close to Stonehenge?'

'Highly significant. Not all the mounds have been opened, and some are not visible after millennia, some have faded into the surrounding area.'

'Why would someone bury Richard Grantley in one?'

'If it weren't murder, I'd say it was a mark of respect, an honour accorded to few.'

'Or a form of sarcasm.'

'It could be, but why bother? If the body's not discovered, what's the point?'

'Psychopathic, deranged, a distorted view of reality, an attempt at self-justification for killing the man?'

'Someone with an intimate knowledge of Bronze Age England, more likely.'

The day with Monty Yatton was concluded; interviewing the man was not. Based on what he had said, there was the need to delve further into Des Wetherell's life, to find out if he had, in fact, belonged to other groups; whether he had been an anarchist committed to action, not words, as it appeared that Yatton was.

Chapter 15

Liz Fairweather was not pleased about Clare phoning late at night.

'We've just spent the day with Monty Yatton,' Clare said. She had returned to the hotel at six in the evening, had a meal with Tremayne, and then had spent three hours researching anarchy groups of England and their actions, violent or peaceful. The majority appeared to have been strong on rhetoric, weak on action.

'I gave you his name. I didn't expect you to contact me about him.'

'Why did you give me the names of Des Wetherell and Monty Yatton? You must have realised that they'd know it was you and that they'd start asking questions as to why you had involved them.'

'Did you tell them?'

'Not directly. Yatton was curious, but we brushed over it. He told us that you had had a fling with him, but he wasn't the only one. A bit of a tart, he said.' Clare knew that Yatton hadn't said that, but she was looking for a reaction from the previously unflappable Liz.

'I gave you their names because they were more serious than us. Des was capable of going to the next stage, and Monty was smart enough to rig a bomb or a remote-control detonator.'

'You have proof they committed criminal acts?'

'No.'

Clare did not believe her. The woman was digging herself in deeper, about to fall into a hole from which there was no escape.

'Des Wetherell?' Liz asked.

'Not yet. After we leave Dundee, we'll probably meet with him. He's aware of our interest in him, a letter from his lawyer informing us that Mr Wetherell resents any aspersion that he's involved in the death of a man he has never met, never heard of.'

'Does Des know that I gave you his name?'

'Not from us, he doesn't.'

'But he will.'

'How can we prevent him? He'll have legal advisors with him, and they'll not let us hide the truth, even if we want to. You must have known this. Why did you give us those two names, not others?'

'I just told you. Des was capable of violent action, Monty would have been his able lieutenant, scared to act himself, willing to assist someone else, and in this case, Des.'

'Liz, you're holding back. This is not looking good for you and Clive Grantley, and what about Kim? Have you considered where this is heading? How she'll feel when we arrest the two of you.'

'We are innocent of all crimes.'

'Not from where I'm sitting. I've gone out of my way to go easy on you. Inspector Tremayne thinks I've gone soft, and he's right, but I can't let you keep hiding information from me out of misguided loyalty to Clive.'

'When you get back to Salisbury, we will meet with him, thrash it out, come to a decision and hopefully a solution to the murder of his brother.'

Clare ended the phone conversation and lay on her bed. Sleep was not going to come soon, not that night.

***

Clive Grantley paced around the living room at his house; Kim sat to one side, trying to read a book. In the weeks since the discovery of Richard Grantley's body, she had spent increasing amounts of time with her father, although she had never called him that. To her, he had always been the man that her mother had loved with a passion in her youth, the man who had given her a child. To Kim, he was the most important man in her life, and she was troubled. Not because he was guilty of a crime; she knew that could never be the case, as he was the most decent man she had ever known, one of the two rocks in her life, her mother being the other. It was because the privacy that he regarded as paramount was under threat. Secrets were being revealed, people were pointing fingers, casting sly gazes as he walked in the street, speaking in whispers if he was with her.

'It's too much,' Clive said as he finally sat down. 'The police are asking questions of your mother, revealing her earlier life.'

Kim had not known of the past in detail before, but did now, as she had paid a visit to her mother, spent the night at her house. Over a bottle of red wine, Liz had laid out her earlier years in detail, told Kim about her fascination with communism, the protests, the men she had known, carnally and otherwise.

Kim had been shocked at the mention of Des Wetherell, not the number of lovers. After all, she knew that her mother shared the same bed with Clive when he visited, although it came as a surprise when her mother told her that nothing ever happened. A goodnight kiss, maybe, but no more. But Des Wetherell was unexpected.

'You've seen him on the television, you know all about him,' Liz had said.

148

Yes, Kim did know about him. She had studied politics at university, spent time at Westminster, a junior aide to an up and coming politician by the name of Hazel Waverley. The politician, in her forties with the voice of a foghorn, her hair piled high, her clothes only the best designer labels, had a fearsome reputation in the parliamentary chamber, a defender of the poor, an advocate for the rights of the minorities and better treatment for the immigrants flooding into the country.

Kim had liked the woman without reservation, although the raucous bellowing voice was annoying. It was there during that time that Kim had met Wetherell.

'And he didn't say anything?' Liz asked. 'Fairweather's not a common name. He must have put two and two together, come up with four.'

'It was strange. He was all over the other women, but he kept his distance from me. Always addressed me as Miss Fairweather. One of the other women in the office, a few years older than me, had been swayed by the man's eloquence. I'm sure they spent the night together.'

'Hazel Waverley?'

'He wasn't interested in her; I'm sure with her it was strictly business, although she was gushing whenever he was around. Any other man, she'd give him a verbal ear bashing, the man cowering, desperate to get out of the room, but with Wetherell, all smiles and laughs.'

'A charming man,' Liz said, reminiscing.

'And you and he?'

'We were young and foolish and high on alcohol and other things.'

'It's what Clare said. You got around.'

'You've always known this, not the details though. And not since I became pregnant with you, not once.'

'But you were still young.'

149

'I had a child; I had my professorship, my research. I had academia.'

'It's not enough. Everyone needs love.'

'I had you. I had Clive.'

'You still love him?'

'Neither of us is interested in close personal relationships, not that kind. He wants to be alone, and so do I. You were the glue that kept us together. In his own way, he still loves me, I know that, but it wasn't the enduring passion that you look for.

'I made mistakes in my earlier life, became involved in causes that on reflection were silly and unrealistic. I never wanted you to fool around the way I had, stray men, names I couldn't always remember.'

'You've remembered Wetherell well enough.'

'What with the man being in the public eye all the time, he's hard to forget.'

'Why am I here?' Kim asked; another bottle of red uncorked.

'Because I don't remember all of the men that I might have slept with.'

'Mother, don't use such a benign word. Say it as it is, men you had sex with. Why so coy? We've accepted that you were a tart in your youth, a lot of women are, a lot of my generation. I'm not condemning you, nor is Clive.'

'What if one of those men was Clive's brother? How would I know? If he was a believer or he had infiltrated us, it could have been him.'

'Infiltrate a group of drug-addled university students? Why would they do that?'

'Des Wetherell may have taken the cause forward, committed acts of anarchy.'

'Did you?'

'Never. I was comfortable with protesting, issuing manifestos denouncing capitalism and the aristocracy and so on, but a violent act, I couldn't.'

'The two names you gave to Clare?'

'I had to give her something to deflect them away from Clive. Des was up to something, so was Monty Yatton, dear sweet Monty. He was gay back then, but he wouldn't admit to it, kept trying to prove that he was all-man.'

'Did he succeed?' Kim asked. Her friends at school as she was growing up were always intrigued by the openness that mother and daughter enjoyed. It was to the young Kim that they would come for advice on matters of the heart, the first tentative intimate encounter with someone of the opposite sex. Kim was their agony aunt, a position she appreciated.

'He succeeded. Hardly the most satisfying of experiences, but he managed.'

'Des Wetherell had no such problem, I assume. I remember the other woman in Hazel Waverley's office the next day, a smile from ear to ear. She waddled as well.'

'That'd be Des,' Liz said. Both women laughed hysterically, tears rolling down their cheeks. It was the first time that the mother had relaxed that night.

'What if it had been Clive's brother that you slept with? Does it matter if you can't remember?'

'Des was more strident than us, determined to have positive action rather than debating and waving a few banners. Monty was enamoured of Des and his manly ways, wanting to emulate him, sucking up to him all the time.'

'You suspected that they committed a criminal act?'

'Suspected, never proved. There was a polling station, a general election. We had our sights set on the politician who would be there at some stage. He was all for bringing back capital punishment: "No time for leniency. If these people can't live within a civilised society, then they have no place in it", he'd say, or words to that effect.'

'You protested?'

'We had the banners, but it was Des who said that it was off. We never went, and then there was an explosion. Luckily no one was around at the time, no one was hurt.'

'And you suspect Wetherell?'

'Never proven, and until recently I've never given it any more thought. But now, with Richard and the possibility that I may have slept with the man…'

'That doesn't explain why he's dead,' Kim said. She had drunk more than she should have, so had her mother.

'But it does. Don't you see it? Richard bragged to Clive about how he had seduced his wife. What if later on, when I'm with Clive, Richard realises who I am?'

'But you never met Richard?'

'No, but Richard could have been bragging about the women he had seduced, mentioned a protester by the name of Liz, smart, interested in history, an easy lay. Clive could have probed, found out who I was, and then…'

'You think that Clive could have killed his brother, don't you?'

'I hope not, but it's plausible. If the police knew what I had just told you, they could arrest him on suspicion.'

'Clive would admit guilt if it were true, we both know that. Why didn't he admit it at the time?

'He would have regarded his duty to you and me as more important. He could have been nursing this guilt for all these years, fearful that the truth would be revealed. He'll not allow your life to be destroyed by letting it be known that you are the daughter of a murderer, a man guilty of fratricide.'

***

Monty Yatton, although he believed that he had handled himself well with the police, remained nervous.

He thought back to Des Wetherell, to Liz Fairweather, to their left-wing group. It was a time when he had felt that he belonged, a time when others saw him in a better light. Now he was a university professor and content with life, but his sexual orientation confused him.

For a brief period in his life, the confusion had not concerned him, and with Liz, he had forgotten. She had made him whole, and then she had rejected him for Des Wetherell, the man he admired and envied, the man he wanted to hate, but couldn't.

His recollection of that day at the polling station was vague. He had been there with Wetherell, observing from across the road, discussing the plan, agreeing who was going to be responsible for affirmative action, and then, the explosion, the panic in the street, the two of them hurrying away, trying not to run, unable not to. Even to this day, the memory of it was confused. He couldn't remember planting the bomb; he wasn't even sure if it would work, and afterwards, Wetherell stood there shouting at him, blaming him for what he had done.

But it wasn't him, he was sure of it. He had never wanted to hurt anyone; he only wanted to be Wetherell's friend, and the man had chastised him, called him a mincing little faggot who could only get it up when he was drugged and then only with Liz. 'She reckoned you were a lousy screw,' Wetherell had said, half-laughing, half-angry.

It was then in his small flat that Monty Yatton wished the man dead, himself dead, everyone and anyone who had ever laughed at him or ignored him or criticised. But mainly, it was Liz Fairweather that his anger was directed at.

Suppressed anger and hatred welled in Monty Yatton as he sat in the living room of his small one-bedroom flat. In one hand he held a glass of whisky, in his mouth a cannabis joint. If he were taking note of the situation – not possible after the alcohol and several joints – he would have realised that the feelings he felt, transmuted from the initial euphoria to confusion and anxiety and paranoia, were a clear sign that it was time to stop. But Monty Yatton was beyond such comprehension, as he was most nights of the week. He coughed as he attempted to stand up. He fell back into his chair, barely able to focus, not sure where he was; the room swirled around him. He picked up the phone that was lying on the table beside his chair and made a phone call, the number entered into its memory earlier that day.

'Wetherell,' the voice answered at the other end.

'It's Monty Yatton, do you remember me?'

'What do you want?' Wetherell's angry response. He had no time for or interest in a silly little man who belonged in the past.

'You blew up that polling station, didn't you?' a slurred voice said.

'You weasely little man, what are you talking about, and where did you get my phone number from?'

'Man of the people, always available. Isn't that your catchphrase?'

'Not to you, I'm not. What we did at university was a long time ago, long enough to have been forgotten.'

'Attempted murder isn't. You would have killed that man that day.'

'No one was killed and what are you talking about? Still taking drugs to cover your inadequacy, are you?'

'Medicinal,' Yatton's reply.

'What do you want? Tell me now or go to hell.'

'The police have been here, asking me about Richard Grantley. Do you know who he was?'

'They're coming to see me, but I won't be high on drugs, scared out of my wits, and I never killed anyone, not even this Richard Grantley, whoever he is.'

'Liz gave our names. She knew.'

'Knew what?'

'About the polling station.'

'She never did, not from me. Did you tell her? Are you the one causing trouble? Whatever Liz has done by telling the police, I will deal with her in time. You, Yatton, better find yourself a hole to climb into and hope that I never find you.'

Wetherell slammed down the phone and made a call. 'Nigel, a name for you. Monty Yatton, University of Dundee. He's a lecturer there, ancient history.'

'What do you want me to do?' Nigel Nicholson, Wetherell's senior lawyer and confidante, asked.

'He's an effeminate little man from my university days. He just phoned, out of his mind on some drug or other. He's raking the coals, not that he's right, but I don't need this now. Shut him up.'

'Permanently?'

155

'Either get him out of sight, at least until I've secured the Deputy Secretary General's position with the TUC, or stop him talking. The police have been with Yatton, trying to find out who murdered a Richard Grantley.'

'Did you?'

'I've never met the man. Sure, I've met some rogues over the years, but the name means nothing to me. I've laid a few out flat, dragged some others through the courts for libelling me in their newspapers, but not murder, no percentage in that.'

Chapter 16

It was to be another long day, and both Tremayne and Clare intended to take advantage of the full English breakfast on the plates in front of them at the Premier Inn on Riverside Drive. Outside, the Firth of Tay where the River Tay, Scotland's largest river in terms of flow, emptied into the North Sea.

'Inspector Tremayne?' A tall man with a strong Scottish brogue approached their table. He was dressed in a suit, white shirt, a blue tie and black shoes. Clare knew instantly who he was, although Tremayne who had drunk more than he should have the last night did not – he was a police officer.

'Yes. Can I help you?'

'I found your card at a crime scene, your address at the Premier Inn written on it. Your mobile's not answering.'

Clare knew why not. He had switched it off to stop Jean phoning to check on him. She would have known by his slurred voice that he had been drinking.

'We're here to interview a Monty Yatton, a lecturer at the university,' Clare said.

'Mind if I take a seat. The name's Inspector Roddy Wallace. I'm afraid you'll not be interviewing Mr Yatton today.'

'Why's that, Inspector?'

'Roddy's the name. Your Mr Yatton had an unfortunate accident last night at his flat. He's dead.'

'We saw him yesterday at the university,' Tremayne said, his breath still stale from the previous night's imbibing. Clare thought that Roddy Wallace wouldn't mind, as she suspected from the ruddy complexion, the bulbous nose, that he and Tremayne were a matched pair – old-style policemen, heavy drinkers, smokers, not too keen on office paperwork and suspicious of computers.

'We weren't informed.'

'It's a murder enquiry in Wiltshire, not far from Stonehenge, a Richard Grantley.'

'We keep abreast of what goes on around the country. I've heard of it. Was Yatton a suspect?'

'No proof and probably not involved. It was a line of enquiry we were following through with him. We intended to meet him one more time, see what else he could tell us and then catch a flight from Edinburgh later tonight.'

'We've got an airport here.'

'The connections are difficult, better for us to drive to Edinburgh. Now, what's this with Yatton, an accident?'

'Clepinton Road, a good area, not more than five minutes' drive from the university. His flat went up in flames last night. We found a bottle of whisky and the man had been smoking cannabis.'

'Can you prove it was an accident?'

'I can't, the crime scene team can. They're there now. After you've finished, we can go up there, and you can tell me more. Whether we should regard his death as suspicious, or just a middle-aged space cadet who should have known better.'

Clare followed Roddy Wallace's car to the crime scene. Tremayne made a phone call to Jean to tell her that he was fine, his voice no longer slurring, and then another phone call to Superintendent Moulton to update him on the latest development. Moulton did not hold Tremayne long, only asking him to make a full report on his return.

On Clepinton Road, the signs of last night's drama; excess water from the fire hoses still sitting on the pathway and round the drain at the side of the road. From outside the flat, the upper floor of a converted terrace house, the burnt curtains were visible, as was the shattered glass from the windows. The glass had probably been broken by the fire brigade as they hurried up a ladder, the fire hose at the ready. A police officer stood outside, the crime scene tape running along the front garden fence, the obligatory onlookers confined to the other side of the street.

'You know the drill,' Wallace said as he handed over the coveralls, the overshoes, the gloves.

An elderly woman was vigorously complaining to a police sergeant about the damage to her flat. Clare could sympathise as the fire brigade would have been concerned with protecting lives, putting out the fire, not with the damage caused to property. She hoped the woman had adequate insurance.

Inside the flat, space tight on account of the number of people, was the body of Monty Yatton.

'Smoke inhalation, more than likely,' one of the crime scene team said.

Apart from charring around the body's left leg and burn marks on one side of the chair, the immediate area where Yatton sat was unscathed. Over towards the kitchen, the damage was extensive.

'The smoke detector would have been connected directly to the fire station,' Wallace said. 'They would have been here within five to ten minutes.'

'Foul play?' Tremayne asked the crime scene examiner.

'Initially, it was considered, but he'd been cooking, probably forgot about the frying pan and the oil in it, died of smoke inhalation when the kitchen caught alight. He was lucky he wasn't burnt alive.'

'Not so lucky,' Clare said. 'He's still dead.'

Outside the flat, the three police officers stood on the street. Roddy Wallace had lit up a cigarette, offered one to Tremayne who had declined, knowing full well that his sergeant would see him, and that she would be reporting back to base, back to Jean.

'Accidental death,' Wallace said, hopeful that it was, and that the paperwork could be quickly dealt with.

'Keep us up to date on the post mortem and forensics,' Tremayne's reply. He could understand Wallace wanting the death wrapped up clean and easy. However, Tremayne wasn't so sure. To him, it was too convenient.

***

Liz Fairweather was devastated on learning about Monty Yatton's death. 'I could have been responsible,' she said on the phone to Clare.

Clare knew that if the man's death was foul play, then she probably had been. Not that any of this mattered at the present time. Emotions were raw, people were dying, intentionally or otherwise, and if Yatton had been targeted, then the person who had focussed attention on him was also under threat.

Tremayne saw it as the time when the pressure is raised, when people make mistakes, when hidden truths are revealed. His money was still on Clive Grantley and Liz Fairweather, the diversionary tactic of Liz Fairweather just that.

'She's drawing us away from the truth. The three of them, the compact modern-day family, expecting nobody to question them too much, never wanting to reveal the inner turmoil in their lives, the skeletons that lie hidden, and expecting us to respect their wishes. Yatton was the first; he's not the last, and Clive and *dear* Liz are in the thick of it.'

Clare wasn't sure if Tremayne was serious or he was taking the war to her, expecting her to pressure Liz and her daughter, Kim. Or whether he was going to sit Clive down in an interview room and sweat a confession out of him.

Not that Tremayne had to worry for too long. It was Clive Grantley who appeared downstairs at Bemerton Road Police Station at four in the afternoon the next day. 'I want to make a confession,' he said to the constable at the desk.

Clare brought the man up to Homicide, settled him in the interview room.

Tremayne came into the room, took one look at him and said, 'Grantley, what's this all about?'

The police inspector was surprised, not because the man wasn't guilty, but because he was confessing. He had held on to the secret for a long time, and now when there was no proof, and other potential murderers were being lined up for further investigation, he had in a moment of contrition and remorse decided to come forward.

'I'm guilty. Read me my rights, lock me up.'

Tremayne had no option but to follow through, explain the procedure. Grantley declined legal representation.

'Let us go back to the murder,' Tremayne said.

'We'd had a row, Richard and me.'

161

'What about?'

Clive Grantley sat solemn-faced, answering when asked, keeping quiet when not. Clare sat to one side of Tremayne, observing Grantley's face, his body language.

'He was belittling me, pointing out my faults.'

'You were a grown man by then, not a child around the Christmas tree, playing in the garden. What could he say that would bring you to violence?'

'There is more than one way to raise a man to violence, you must know that.'

'We do, but you're the mayor of Salisbury, a respected citizen, not a worthless drunk. Tell us how and what was said.'

'He accused me of taking the family home from him, of altering the will.'

'We've checked the will. It's on the public record. Your parents had given you the house, and left a substantial bequest to Richard. He was not ignored in the will, and he could have purchased a similar house with what he had been given.'

'He wanted the family home, to maintain the legacy.'

'We've not seen any evidence that Richard was interested in such matters,' Clare said. 'On the contrary, he was an adventurer, and as long as he could indulge his fancy, go where he liked, seduce any woman including your ex-wife, Grace, then what did he care?'

'Was it about Grace?' Tremayne asked bluntly.

'Not this time, but I had never forgiven him.'

'Was it about Liz? Had he made a play for her, threatening to weave his magic, take her away from you, the same as he had with your other women? Is that it? What's the truth? This is about Liz, isn't it?'

'She never knew him; never knew what an insufferable lecherous waster he was. If he had known of her, he would have felt the need to take the challenge, to show her how much better he was than me.'

'You're protecting her,' Clare said. 'You disagreed with her telling us about Des Wetherell and Monty Yatton, and now one of them is dead. The other's a powerful man. You suspect Liz's past is catching up with her, and that she was involved in criminal activities, activities that Wetherell wants to stay hidden.'

Clive Grantley said nothing, only looked away and up at the ceiling.

'You believe that Wetherell had Yatton killed, don't you?' Tremayne asked.

Yet again, no response from Grantley.

'Please, Mr Grantley,' Clare said, 'you've come here to deflect focus away from Liz, but it's already there. She knows more than she's telling us, and if Yatton was murdered, a possibility we'd have to agree, then she's the next target.'

'Not if I'm here charged with the murder of my brother, she isn't.'

'Do you want to confess to blowing up a polling station while you're here?' Tremayne said.

'Whatever it takes to save Liz.'

'Nothing will save her or you, even Kim. If Yatton was murdered and your brother was placed in that burial mound by who knows who, they're not going to back off now just because you've offered yourself up as the sacrificial lamb. Okay, we can lock you up, hold you for twenty-four hours, longer if needs be, but then what? We've got a half-baked confession from you, while Liz is up in Cambridge, alone and vulnerable, and Kim is here in Salisbury. People who kill witnesses while two police officers are sleeping are not the sort of people to fall for your cheap trick. Admit you're hoaxing us, telling lies to protect those you love.'

'This is not helpful,' Clare said. 'If you were honest with us, it would be productive.'

'I've said all I'm going to say. Type up my confession, and I'll sign.'

If Clive Grantley weren't such a prominent and upstanding man in the community, Tremayne would have said he was mad. To him, Grantley's action was illogical. The belief that murderers are deterred by someone else making a false confession made no sense. Not that Tremayne believed that Grantley was innocent of Richard's murder. It was just that Clive had given no new facts, no satisfactory evidence, no clear understanding of why the burial mound was significant.

It was a confession from a man who could be a murderer, but it wasn't an honest confession. Yet Tremayne knew that he had no option but to charge the man. He knew that trouble was afoot, the sixth sense again, the twitch in his knee, not just from the increasing pain, but from a feeling that something was wrong with the murder investigation, something he couldn't get around, something that was in plain view, yet he was still missing it.

Clare left the interview room twenty-five minutes later, Clive Grantley duly charged and in the holding cells at the police station. A statement would be issued by Tremayne, another one from the Salisbury Council expressing their belief in the innocence of Mayor Clive Grantley and their wishes for a speedy resolution and his return to his mayoral duties at the earliest opportunity. One statement was factual, the other was not. Factions and dissent would soon rise amongst the remaining councillors; the chance to wear the robes of office, the opportunity to enjoy the perks foremost in their minds.

***

Questions started to be asked about Des Wetherell's suitability for the high office of Deputy Secretary General of the Trades Union Congress. A newspaper article mentioned his dubious past, the manslaughter conviction later quashed on appeal, his possible links to anarchist groups that had openly railed against the ruling elite of the United Kingdom.

'How and why?' Wetherell asked. 'You were meant to slap restraints on anyone hostile, threaten them with libel.'

'The newspaper is favourable to you; the editor's a personal friend,' Nigel Nicholson said. It was late, Wetherell's favourite time. He looked out at the River Thames from his penthouse, a large glass of brandy in one hand.

'It appears his control on content is not as strong as it was.'

'You can't deny the past. It's on the public record, and everyone knows about it, even the TUC.'

'Know is one thing, but if it goes too far, they'll not be able to ignore it. Where do we go from here?'

'We need to stop your past causing you more problems. Is there more than I know? I can't halt a police investigation.'

'What do we know about the officers looking into the death of Richard Grantley?'

'Inspector Tremayne, crusty, determined, honest, not in good health. His offsider, Sergeant Clare Yarwood, thirty-four. Bright, articulate, and as determined as Tremayne.'

'Any chance of waylaying their enthusiasm until I'm elected?'

'North of the border is a possibility. Inspector Roddy Wallace is the investigating officer into Yatton's death. He's an alcoholic, mildly competent, likes a gamble.'

'Successful?'

'He's in debt to the tune of ten thousand pounds.'

'Make it twenty,' Wetherell said.

'It was pure luck about Yatton,' Nicholson said.

Wetherell did not respond. He didn't know if what had happened to Yatton was a coincidence or something else; the truth was best left unspoken.

'What about Liz Fairweather?' Nicholson asked.

'What's the dirt on her? Why did she mention Yatton and me?'

'She has a daughter. Richard Grantley's brother is the father.'

Wetherell knew that Nigel Nicholson's web spread far and wide. He might be a prominent lawyer, but he was also a networker, a man who had the dirt on a few, could find out about the rest. And he knew people who knew people. None of it linked back to him, but he could fix anything, even death. Wetherell did not need to know the details of Nicholson's activities, only that he was on his side, primarily out of friendship, but equally important to the lawyer, his own benefit. The two men complemented each other admirably.

'Did he do it?'

'Clive Grantley's confessed to the murder, although the evidence is flimsy. He's being held for twenty-four hours, but the police don't believe he's telling the truth.'

'Then what's he doing?'

'What he's always done. He's protecting his privacy and that of others.'

'It's a diversionary tactic, to lead the police away from Liz Fairweather, to lead us away from her,' Wetherell said. 'Are we leaving Liz alone?'

'What do you want? Her wellbeing, or your position with the TUC, your political aspirations?'

'Nigel, what do you think?'

'You don't care about anyone if they get in your way. Liz Fairweather's a tricky situation. She's very visible, and her daughter is sharp. Also, Sergeant Yarwood is sticking close to her.'

'Act if necessary,' Wetherell said. He held up a cigar box and offered Nicholson one of its contents. The man took the cigar, rolled it in his fingers. Wetherell followed suit. The two men lit up, poured themselves another brandy each.

Yatton's death had been fortunate, both men knew that. It would never be mentioned again by either of them.

Chapter 17

The concern was that Liz Fairweather had become inexorably linked to the death of Richard Grantley. Either she and Clive had killed him, or Wetherell had with or without the assistance of Monty Yatton.

Whichever way the investigation turned, Liz Fairweather sat fair and square in the middle.

Clive Grantley bided his time in the cells, hopeful that Liz would survive, angry with his brother yet again after so many years. As he had said to Tremayne, who visited him in the cells, 'The man was bad news when he was alive. In death, his legacy lingers on.'

'I'm letting you go after twenty-four hours whether you like it or not. If you think this was all worth it, then fine. Sergeant Yarwood's up in Cambridge with Liz and her mother, aiming to get to the bottom of this quagmire that you've created.'

Tremayne could see that Clive Grantley was the type of man who'd go over the top on a battlefield, risk his life for his fellow soldiers, show bravery that few could muster. How the man rationalised his actions, he couldn't say, but Tremayne thought that somewhere, somehow, the man was probably right. He was buying time, taking the emphasis away from Liz Fairweather. But time wasn't bought forever. There was to be a reckoning, and it was hours away, possibly days, but no more. Either someone else would die, or he, Inspector Tremayne, would solve the murder of Richard Grantley.

In Cambridge, the spectre of what had happened, what could occur, weighed heavily on Liz Fairweather's mind. With her were Clare and Kim, both were equally disturbed. Kim, on account of her mother and what she could have set in motion, her father languishing in a cell, rapidly being ostracised by the people of Salisbury and those who had feigned friendship over the years; Clare because she realised that Monty Yatton's death was too suspicious to be regarded as just an accident.

Inspector Roddy Wallace had been on the phone, calling Clare before Tremayne, but she had become used to that by now. Somehow the overweight, red-faced man thought in his arrogance, his incompetence as well, that he was attractive to female police officers.

Clare was not impressed when he phoned. 'Pathology states that the man died of smoke inhalation, and he had consumed a large quantity of alcohol, and had been smoking cannabis,' he had said.

'We knew that already from the crime scene,' Clare replied. 'Any more?'

'That's about it,' Wallace said. He had wanted to talk; Clare had not. She had ended the phone call and then phoned Tremayne to update him. He could get the official case report sent down by email; she had more pressing issues to deal with.

'I killed him,' Liz said. She was sitting in the kitchen of her small house. Kim was at her side, an arm around her.

'It was an accident, Mum,' Kim said.

The closeness of mother and daughter was apparent, something that Clare could not say about her relationship with her own mother. Two nights previously, she had been on the phone. 'It's time you found yourself a nice man and settled down. You're too fussy and running with that old man isn't going to help your prospects, and now you're ferreting around for the

169

murderer of someone who died years ago. What kind of life is that?'

A great life, Clare had wanted to say but didn't. Contradicting her mother when she was on a roll was counter-productive and only led to one or the other slamming the phone down. Best just to let her go on for ten minutes, and then politely say that duty called. And as to the reference to the old man, Tremayne had more life in him than her mother.

The 'nice man' had not been appreciated either. She had had a nice man, a doctor at Salisbury Hospital, the type of man her mother would have approved of. However, it had become evident that his idea of the happy family was him at work, the wife at home looking after the house and the children, ensuring that the evening meal was prepared when he came home.

Idyllic apart from being stranded in the home. Clare was determined to remain in the police force. And if there were a child, then she'd devote the time necessary, take advantage of the generous maternity leave offered. Of course, with a baby, there would be constant intrusion by her mother, something she would deal with when the time came.

Kim could see that her mother was not faring well. Clare could see the hounds of hell unleashed if Wetherell decided to act.

With Des Wetherell mentioned by Liz and what Clare found out when researching him, it was clear that he had had a chequered career. A man sentenced for manslaughter, even if he had been cleared on appeal, was still the man who had thrown the rock. It would have been enough to thwart the career of a lesser individual, but Wetherell was still riding high.

Such men, Clare knew, do not leave things to chance. Wetherell was a man who made things happen, criticism vanish, people cease to have relevance. Not necessarily by murder, but by destroying their credibility, ensuring they are thrown on the scrapheap of life.

Liz Fairweather was in for a fall, yet she and Clive Grantley acted as though they were naïve in such matters.

'Why did you bring Wetherell and Yatton into the investigation?' Clare asked.

'Have you spoken to Des Wetherell?' Liz asked, ignoring Clare's question.

'Not yet. We're meeting him tomorrow. In the meantime, you need to tell me more. What about the acts of anarchy? What about Richard Grantley? Had you ever met him or someone similar? Is there a doubt in your mind?'

'Doubt, regret, yes.'

'Then tell me. We can't leave Clive where he is, we can't have him carrying the guilt. We need the murderer of his brother, and somehow you're the key.'

'I don't see how.'

'Mother!' Kim interjected. 'Tell Clare about the other men.'

'Very well. There were men I can't remember, men at some march or other, a demonstration here and there. I was a tart, Kim knows that, and one of those men could have been Richard. I wouldn't know.'

'And he may have bragged to Clive that he had slept with you, given him personal details, insulted you. Do you believe that Clive murdered his brother?'

'I don't want to,' Liz reluctantly said.

'Proof? Where's the proof?'

'When we met, Clive and I, he mentioned his brother on a couple of occasions. How much he disliked him.'

'Wished him dead?' Clare asked.

'Not in those words, but yes. To me, Richard sounded fine, but then I never met him.'

'Did you ever meet Grace Thornberry, Clive's ex-wife?'

'Clive came with me to Manchester once to a presentation by a scholar on Greek philosophers. It was before I became pregnant. We were sitting in a restaurant when a woman came and sat down with us. She shook my hand, smiled at me. She leant over to Clive and whispered in his ear. She then left. Afterwards, I asked him who she was. He told me. It put a dampener on that weekend, I can tell you.'

'Have you seen her since?'

'Never, and I don't think Clive has. He would have told me if he had.'

***

Des Wetherell weighed his options very carefully. Nigel Nicholson told him that there was nothing to worry about, all loose ends had been taken care of.

Outside, waiting to enter the plush office, Inspector Keith Tremayne and Sergeant Clare Yarwood.

Wetherell was not so confident that Nicholson was right in this instance. 'What do you have on the two outside,' he asked.

'I gave you a summation before. Tremayne, crusty, heading to retirement, old school policeman.'

'The type that doesn't listen to their seniors when they tell them to back off, incorruptible, never taken a backhander in his life?'

'That's our Inspector Tremayne. He likes to have a flutter on the horses, not very successfully, though. He's not in good physical condition, either. A health scare sometime back, and he's currently off the cigarettes, cut back on beer.'

'Life's pretty miserable for him,' Wetherell said. He could sympathise with Tremayne on the cutting back. His prostate was giving him trouble, his libido was down, and he was missing out on his ego-boosting escapades.

'Sergeant Clare Yarwood, competent, admires Tremayne, friendly with his wife. Attractive, I've just seen her outside.'

'Tremayne, gambling on the horses, compulsive?'

'A moderate loser, a few pounds each way, nothing to hold the man with.'

'Inspector Wallace?'

'He's under control. Anything of concern, he'll keep us updated.'

'No connection back to me.'

'Of course not. I'm not a fool. How are you going to handle our visitors?'

'Lay it on thick. A friend of the police, a fine job they're doing. Good old Liz, I haven't seen her for a long time.'

'I hope you don't,' Nicholson said. 'Tremayne will see through that in a flash.'

'I'll play it straight and professional. What about Liz Fairweather?'

'She's trying to protect Clive Grantley, maybe even herself. Why she mentioned you and Yatton still makes no sense.'

'A tactical error?'

'I doubt if she knows much about tactics.'

'She knew about other things when I knew her.'

'Don't mention that to the police, don't ridicule her.'

Wetherell pressed a button on his desk, it was answered from the other room. 'Would you please ask Inspector Tremayne and Sergeant Yarwood to come in?'

Inside Wetherell's office, the man stood to greet Tremayne and Clare. He shook Tremayne's hand first, placing his free hand on Tremayne's shoulder, an approach Clare had seen him do before on the television.

'Pleased to meet you, Sergeant Yarwood,' Wetherell said as he shook Clare's hand, no hand on the shoulder, no broaching the invisible barrier between respect and intimidation.

Wetherell looked over at Nicholson, a brief handshake from him. The man did not smile although he maintained a pleasant demeanour.

'What can I do for you?' Wetherell asked. Clare looked around the office, the luxury of it.

'We're investigating the murder of Richard Grantley,' Tremayne said.

'I heard about it, not sure why I'm of interest.'

'We follow up on every lead, no matter how remote. Your name has been mentioned as someone from the time when the man died.'

'My client is not going to answer questions for which he has no answers,' Nicholson said calmly. 'He is an important man, well-respected in the community, influential.'

Clare knew that Nicholson had erred. If the words 'influential' or 'friends in high places' were ever mouthed, it meant something was hiding in the shadows.

Tremayne ignored Nicholson's statement.

'Mr Wetherell, you were a university student along with Liz Fairweather and Monty Yatton, is that correct?'

'A tragic loss, Monty. I read about it, burnt to death, they said.'

'Smoke inhalation. At this time, we're treating his death as accidental, although we may revise that to murder subject to our investigations.'

'We're not here about Mr Yatton,' Clare said. 'Your association with a radical element at the university, your subsequent membership of an anarchist group, concerns us more.'

'We were all idealistic back then. It was Liz who mentioned my name. I don't know why.'

'Are you denying that you belonged to an anarchist group determined to overthrow the legitimate, democratically elected government?'

'Sergeant Yarwood, may I remind you that Mr Wetherell is not on trial here,' Nicholson said. 'He's not been accused of any crimes, apart from foolishness in his youth. If your belligerent questioning of a man who has done a lot for the working man in this country continues, then I will be forced to end this meeting.'

'My apologies,' Clare said. She looked over at Tremayne, knew that he'd be pleased she had rattled the chains.

'I'll forgive your outburst,' Wetherell said. 'I was involved with a radical group at university. We saw communism as a better option for this country. Mostly we theorised, debated, made banners, drank, smoked. Not a lot more than that.'

'And got laid.'

'As you say, got laid. Why has Liz mentioned my name? She's a respected university professor now, an

175

expert on Ancient Greek history. Back then, she was not the same person.'

'We are aware of her past, her involvement with you, with Monty Yatton.'

'And a few more besides. Has she been candid with you?' Wetherell was gently taking down Liz Fairweather's credibility, an approach postulated by Nicholson. It was not going to work.

'She slept around. Sometimes with men she knew, you and Monty Yatton, sometimes with men she didn't. She has told us that she was promiscuous, and she has no regrets from that period.'

'Then why myself and Yatton? You've not explained your reason for being here.'

'Richard Grantley remains a mysterious character. We believe that for some years he was involved in undercover work, infiltrating anarchist groups, radical university elements. He may have come into contact with you and Yatton, as well as Liz Fairweather,' Tremayne said.

'If he were undercover, he wouldn't have used his real name, so how would I know?'

Clare pushed a photo across the desk. 'This is what he looked like in his twenties.'

Wetherell looked at the photo and then pushed it back. 'I can't say I recognise the man, but it was a long time ago. I can't remember anyone suspicious.'

'A polling station was blown up, no loss of life. It was around the time that you were at your most radical.'

'My client is not here to discuss anything other than the death of Richard Grantley,' Nicholson said. He had risen from his chair to emphasise the point. 'He has made it clear that he never knew the man, that he's not involved, and this assertion that he was involved in an act of violence is not acceptable.' Nicholson sat down again, a look of disdain on his face.

'We believe that Monty Yatton was involved,' Tremayne said. 'We also know that the intended target was a man with extreme right-wing views.'

'Half the country was against him. He wanted to bring back capital punishment,' Wetherell said. 'There were demonstrations, banner-waving up and down the country, a few in support, most against.'

'Someone went further than sounding off, someone made a statement, exploded a bomb.'

'And Liz thinks it was that silly little man and me.'

'You didn't like Yatton?' Clare asked.

'Not at all. Not enough gumption to stand up for himself and to tell the world he was gay. It's not as if society was too condemning back then, and it wasn't illegal. Sure, he would have received a few comments, a few offers probably. Why hide it?'

'He still slept with Liz Fairweather.'

'He was always trying to blend in, appear more macho than he was. If you pop enough pills, you can manage anything. That's what it was with Yatton. He was game for anything.'

'Addicted?'

'He couldn't keep away from them. Not totally addicted, not like heroin. The great philosophical debates we had when we were high.'

'Richard Grantley, are you sure you never met him?' Tremayne asked one more time.

After the two police officers had left, Nicholson came close to Wetherell. 'Don't give me any more nonsense about how you were a harmless bystander. You recognised that photo, didn't you?'

'It could have been the man who sold us the explosives. But I'll state it again. We didn't explode our bomb, someone else did it before us. I'm innocent of the crime, not the intent.'

Chapter 18

Clive Grantley was released from his cell at Bemerton Road Police Station. He had protested vehemently to Tremayne, yet was not willing to confide more if there was more to be told. Tremayne was not sure on that point. He knew one thing, he wasn't going to hold a man in a cell when he had offered no proof of how he had killed his brother. Not even a where and when, nor how he had managed to dig a hole into a burial mound at night unseen, and to have concealed it in such a way that none of the hikers who regularly traversed the area had seen anything suspicious.

'I'm guilty,' Grantley protested as he was removed from the police station. Outside Kim sat in the driving seat of her small Audi; in the rear, Liz Fairweather. It was her first time in Salisbury for over twenty years, the first time that she publicly acknowledged the relationship with Grantley.

It had happened late the previous day, the revelation that Clive Grantley was indeed the father of Kim, his personal assistant.

Tremayne was sure it was the handiwork of Nigel Nicholson, Wetherell's lawyer. He had met his sort before, the man who could fall into a pigsty and come up smelling of roses. Wetherell was guilty of crimes, Tremayne knew that, although which ones he couldn't be sure. But the man was connected, and he'd make sure to keep his distance, not say anything out of turn in case it was misinterpreted and to discredit those who could throw stones at him, such as Liz Fairweather and Monty Yatton.

Yatton was dead, and the erstwhile Inspector Roddy Wallace was holding to the story that death was accidental, and the case would be wrapped up tight soon enough and filed away.

Liz Fairweather, if not discredited, was a person with a history, a probable anarchist, the mother of a child born out of wedlock, a secret lover. None of these individually was condemning, but seen as a whole they would weaken any story she wished to weave against Wetherell and anyone else.

A media crew were at the police station, their microphone and camera thrust into Clive Grantley's face, another crew were shouting through the closed windows of Kim's car, scratching the paintwork, annoying Kim, frightening Liz.

A uniformed constable came over and moved the crews away. Clive Grantley got in the front passenger seat; Kim drove off. Clare was one car behind as the vehicle headed towards Grantley's house in the Cathedral Close.

Grantley said little on the short trip, occasionally glancing around at Liz, not speaking, attempting a smile.

At the house and with the door closed, he was more vocal. 'Liz, you exposed yourself to danger to protect me. Why?'

'I had to, you know that. If the police were looking elsewhere, they wouldn't be focussing on you.'

Kim Fairweather stood to one side. At any other time, she would have been glad to see them both in the house, the acknowledgement, now public knowledge, that she was indeed their daughter, but she could not feel any pleasure in the situation, the calmness that such a revelation should engender. In short, she was frightened for them both. Two people that she loved dearly.

'We've got to be united,' Kim said. 'One of you can't do something without telling the other. And how are we going to handle the television crew outside? You both need to make a statement.'

'Why?' Clive said. 'Our lives are private. They belong to us.'

'Father,' Kim said, the first time that she could ever remember saying the word, 'our lives are public property now. The privacy you relish can only be restored by an acknowledgement of the facts, being open with the police, an arrest of someone else for Richard's murder. You must see that now.'

Kim could see that her father – the only word she would use from now on to refer to him – was wrestling with the concept. Her mother, more open, could see that it was the only way forward.'

'One time only,' Grantley said. 'I will speak for all of us.'

'You shouldn't have mentioned Yatton and Wetherell,' Kim said.

'Your mother had my best interests at heart,' Grantley said.

'I will speak as well. As the daughter, it is important that I am portrayed as a sensible and well-brought-up woman.'

Kim set to work with her laptop. She sent an email to the television stations, the major newspapers in the country, as well as the local paper, the *Salisbury Journal*. She also phoned Clare to advise her of what was intended.

Tremayne did not like the idea; press conferences invariably got out of hand, and the media were masters at asking intrusive questions, not allowing those presenting a chance to catch their breath, to clear their mind, to come up with a reasoned response.

Regardless, at three in the afternoon the next day, the throng assembled at the Grantley residence. Outside the house, two uniforms ensured that the vehicles were parked far enough away; those that didn't comply would receive a fine.

Inside the house, the sunroom at the back had been prepared. Clive, Liz and Kim stood behind a table at one end of the room; the media had plastic chairs to sit on, recently delivered by a hire company. Clare stood to one side of the room; Tremayne was not present.

Clive stood to speak, to a clamour from the assembled reporters. He chose to ignore them, having dealt with rowdy council meetings in the past, when a local environmental group, a disgruntled ratepayer, someone who felt the need to protest whatever the cause, would get up and interject at every opportunity, not willing to let the democratic process unfold.

'Thank you for coming. My family,' Grantley said – with the emphasis on 'my family', Clare noticed – 'has asked you here to make a statement.' Further clamouring from those in the front row, wanting to be the first to ask a question.

'I have come under intense scrutiny recently due to the discovery of my brother Richard's body. I have not seen him for fifteen years and the last time was in London. His whereabouts have been unknown to me since then, not due to a disagreement, but because he and I were fundamentally different. Richard was a gregarious, extroverted man, an adventurer, a person who was high on life or laid low by it. I am, however, intensely private and my personal life is not for general view.

'I have always fulfilled my civic duties with due diligence, similarly my personal affairs. However, Richard's death had exposed me and those I hold near and dear to intrusive scrutiny, something I do not want for myself or for those who are important to me. It is necessary for me to outline the chain of events that have brought us here today.'

'Is Kim going to speak?' a voice from the back.

'Kim will speak, but unfortunately, you will need to hear me first. These are unusual circumstances that have caused me to act unwisely; circumstances which I deeply regret. Richard was, to use a term often used in error, the black sheep of the family. Our father was a serious man, and his wife, our mother, a devoted and loving mistress of the house, this house.'

'Kim,' another voice shouted out. Clare knew that press conferences, especially the more contentious ones, invariably degenerated into mob rule, the crowd waiting for the tumbrel to pass on the way to the guillotine. She wondered if Grantley was cutting his neck as well.

'Why did you admit to the murder of your brother?'

'To focus attention away from Liz and Kim.'

'The sign of a madman,' another voice howled out.

'Pray, let me continue.' Grantley said, his voice elevated over the hubbub in the room. 'It is now known that Kim is our daughter, Liz's and mine. It has not been revealed before as neither Liz nor I wanted what to many is the ideal. Liz wanted academia, I wanted solitude, to be by myself. During the intervening years, Kim has been an integral part of my life, as I have of hers. There had never been any intent to hide the fact, and every week or

183

two I would be at Liz's house. I am also on Kim's birth certificate as the father.

'Whatever people may make of our relationship, the three of us, we are a loving family who only wishes the best for each other. I have stood aside as the mayor of this fine city until the investigation into the death of my brother is concluded. After that, I hope to return to the city council. I have no more to say.'

'Kim,' the voices came in unison.

Kim stood, remarkably calm, Clare thought. The first time she had had to speak at a press conference at Bemerton Road, her legs were like jelly, and she had stuttered her way through the event. But with Kim, nothing was going to phase her.

'My speech will be short. My parents have always been there for me; I will always be there for them. I hope that the good people of Salisbury will respect our wish for privacy, our wish to see this current situation through to its conclusion, and for my uncle, who I never knew, the desire to see his killer brought to justice.'

With that, the Grantleys left the room. Clare wasn't sure that anything had been achieved. Later that day, Tremayne told her that it had been a waste of time. Des Wetherell, who sat with Nigel Nicholson to watch the press conference on the nightly news, smiled. Nicholson was sure that his work was not finished.

***

A week passed by. The murder investigation had ground to a halt; the leads, weak at best, had petered out. Superintendent Moulton had informed Tremayne that he had received a phone call; Des Wetherell had registered a complaint.

184

Tremayne didn't know what for as he and Clare hadn't harassed the man, had been polite with him. It wasn't the first time someone had used connections to make it known that they were off limits. Moulton told him not to take any notice and to do his job. An arrest for murder was more important than a powerful man taking umbrage.

Tremayne had to admit that he had more respect for his superintendent now that the man had stopped asking for his early retirement, although it was still a possibility. The left knee was still causing trouble; he hadn't told Jean yet, but he would have to soon.

Clare continued with the Grantleys – strictly speaking the Grantley and the Fairweathers. Liz Fairweather had returned to Cambridge confident that all was well in Salisbury. Clive Grantley rarely left the house, and whenever he did, it was to the acknowledgement by those that he met of what a fine fellow he was. The most vocal in their accolades would have been the most critical before, he knew that, but he remained courteous, hopeful that the curiosity would wither soon. Kim, out and about more than her father, had achieved minor celebrity status, something she had enjoyed at first but was now starting to tire of. She could see reclusive traits in her own personality, the result of her parents. Her peers wanted to be out and about, down the pub of a night, falling in love, falling out. Yet she could spend long periods of her time alone, with a book to read, a documentary on YouTube to watch.

The research into Richard Grantley continued. Two aliases had been found for him. At one stage he had been Raymond Alston, an entrepreneur in Singapore setting up financial deals, tax avoidance schemes for those who could pay enough. That had lasted for just over five years before he had left the country eight hours in advance of the police arriving at his twentieth-floor office. The man had lived well, paid his bills when he could and then had left three hundred thousand dollars in cash in the office safe, another nine hundred thousand dollars in unpaid debts. The police officer that Tremayne had spoken to in a long-distance call reckoned that Alston, or Grantley, or whatever he called himself, had left enough cash to pay the more immediate local debts, and those that had lost nine hundred thousand weren't likely to say anything. How much the man had smuggled out of the country, hidden in offshore bank accounts and safety deposit boxes, was unknown, but it was thought to have been in the millions.

Richard Grantley had then popped up in Sydney, Australia, this time using a different name, and had promptly checked into the best hotel in town, a BMW in the parking lot underneath. Six months later he was gone, the car in its parking spot.

After that, Richard Grantley's whereabouts were unknown for six months until he reappeared in England. A brief sojourn in Salisbury when he had bought the clothes for his burial, not that he would have known that at the time.

The period from when he had left the family home at the age of twenty-one, detoxed and fit, and his reappearance in Singapore remained a blank. No one had any information that could point to his activities during that time. It was as if the man had disappeared, which is what would have happened if he was an undercover operative. And if that was the case, Tremayne knew that the records would remain hidden, whether the man was dead or not.

The situation in Singapore brought into play another line of enquiry. If Richard Grantley had absconded with money that belonged to high rollers with plenty of cash and a wish to keep it hidden, then those same people could either be corrupt politicians or criminals.

Richard Grantley, it appeared, was not just an adventurer, he was a risk taker, and such people fly close to the sun, only to get their wings burnt.

Superintendent Moulton had argued that as much could be achieved with video conferencing and emails as could by travelling to Singapore. Tremayne, never much of a traveller, argued to the contrary. 'I need to see the place, his office, where he lived. Find out who he could have cheated. I can't do that glued to this police station.'

Two days later, Tremayne, the envy of the police station, and in the face of Jean's ire – she was not going – boarded a Singapore Airlines A380 at Heathrow Airport.

Chapter 19

Des Wetherell seemed to be constantly on the television. Every time that Clare switched it on, there he was: at his most obsequious, his most gushing, his most sensible.

Clare had to admit that the man was good and the charisma that she had encountered when she and Tremayne had met him that one time was apparent. It did not, however, regardless of the public perception of the man as someone who had made mistakes in his youth, absolve him from the polling station bombing nor the death of Monty Yatton.

Clare had driven Tremayne to London Heathrow; his instruction to her to focus on Monty Yatton's death. As he had said, 'I've met a few bent coppers in my time. Roddy Wallace fits the stereotype. As long as he's got the easy life, he's not worried if the man was murdered or not.'

It matched Clare's opinion of the man. Wallace had been on the phone twice to her; once to relay the findings from the crime scene investigators, and that he was sending down the reports from Pathology and Forensics and the second time to find out how she was, whether she was coming back up to Dundee in the near future, and how about a night out together.

Clare had remained polite, not out of deference to his rank, nor on account of the wedding ring on his left hand, but because a return to his city was very possible.

It was Jim Hughes, Salisbury's senior crime scene investigator, who had spotted it; Stuart Collins, the forensic pathologist, who concurred.

'Judging by the amount of alcohol in the man's system and the cannabis, the question remains, did he or did he not have the ability to walk to the kitchen, put the frying pan on the stove, pour in some oil, and light the gas flame,' Collins said. 'Professionally, I'm not disputing their findings up north, but it's a question that should have been asked by the investigating officer. What was his name?' Collins asked.

'Inspector Roddy Wallace,' Clare's reply.

'Yatton's death is important to you, is it?'

'It's a possible link to the death of Richard Grantley.'

'Then you'll need to ask the question.'

'That's what I intend to do.'

'The surf and sun for Tremayne; the rain and cold for you,' Jim Hughes said. 'It doesn't seem to be a fair trade.'

'There's no surf in Singapore, and he'll hate the heat. An old raincoat, the chance to complain about the weather suits him more.'

Wallace took the phone call from Clare badly. When she had returned to Homicide and made the call he had initially been his smarmy self, but when the reason for the call was explained, his attitude changed.

'We're professionals up here.' Wallace's defence of his position. Clare imagined that his ruddy complexion was getting ruddier by the second.

'It's a line of enquiry, not a comment on your professional competency,' Clare said diplomatically. She didn't need a battle royal on her arrival in Dundee. 'There's a possibility that Yatton couldn't make it to the kitchen and that he was comatose before that. If that's the case, then it's not death by misadventure. It's an open conclusion, the possibility of an intentional act concealed as an accident.'

'They'll not take kindly to your disputing their findings.'

'That's as may be. I'll be there tomorrow in the afternoon. I've booked into the Premier Inn again.'

The phone call ended badly, with Clare breathing a sigh of relief afterwards and helping herself to a cup of coffee from the machine in the corner.

A text message from Tremayne: *hot as hell, wish you were here instead of me*.

Clare had to agree with him. Where she was heading was another kind of hell. No serving police officer, no pathologist or forensic scientist, appreciates their professionalism being questioned. Superintendent Moulton had advised taking a more senior officer from another department to Scotland with her, but she declined. She was going to do this on her own, Wallace or no Wallace intruding. And if the man made an inappropriate comment or gesture, she knew where her knee was going.

***

Tremayne, his body clock out of sync with the time difference from the UK, couldn't sleep. It was evening where he was, and Clare was preparing to leave for the airport.

The text message from Tremayne earlier had been unexpected; in fact, it was the first time he had ever sent one. The phone call was not.

Clare would have used Skype or Viber for the call, but her senior was not computer savvy. For him, it was a phone call.

'How are you?' Clare asked.

'Fine, now,' Tremayne shouted back. Clare felt like telling him that he didn't need to shout; the line was clear.

'We've had developments.'

'When I'm not there. What kind of developments?'

'Jim Hughes and Stuart Collins reckon the final report on Yatton's death is not robust. It's a possibility that Yatton wasn't in the kitchen; too far out of it to have started the fire.'

'Proven?'

'Not proven and probably can't be, but the report needs to be changed. I'm on my way back to Dundee.'

'Wallace?'

'I don't think he'll be there with a bouquet of flowers for me, not this time.'

'Watch him. He's the sort that causes trouble, and if he tries any fancy footwork, get on to Moulton.'

'And you? How's Singapore?'

'At Changi Airport you could have fried eggs on the pavement, and the humidity is intense.'

'Jean?'

'She's fine now, upset that she couldn't come.'

'The local police?'

'I've been assigned an Inspector Ong. He picked me up at the airport. Everyone speaks English.'

'You need to travel more. Of course they do. What's the plan?'

'We'll check out where Grantley's been, who he may have cheated. Inspector Ong reckons if some of those he cheated had found him, then his life wouldn't have been worth living.'

'Criminal elements?'

'Drug money, gangsters, corrupt politicians. The sort of people you and I thankfully don't meet too often.'

After the brief phone conversation, Clare left her house and drove to Southampton Airport, this time without having to deviate to pick up Tremayne.

Upon arrival in Edinburgh, she picked up a rental and drove to Dundee, not needing the GPS this time to find the Premier Inn. Wallace, who had known of her arrival time, was not at the hotel; she found him thirty-five minutes later in his office at Dundee Police Station on West Bell Street.

'You made it, I see,' Wallace's first words. He shook Clare's hand, begrudgingly she thought.

'I'm not here to dispute the findings, just to ask for them to be re-evaluated.'

'Yarwood,' no longer Clare or Sergeant, 'we pride ourselves on our professionalism. Your coming here from down south has upset a few. Don't expect to find too many smiling faces around here.'

Clare looked Wallace in the face. 'I'm not here for a good time. I'm here because a man, possibly two, have been killed, and Yatton indirectly may or may not be involved. We need to explore all possibilities, and if you or anyone else thinks they're going to find me a pushover, a piece of fluff, then they'll be severely disappointed. Do I make myself clear?'

'You can't talk to a superior officer like that,' said Wallace, his face red, his hands sweaty.

'I have said nothing wrong, nothing that Inspector Tremayne wouldn't agree with. Now, are we clear? Are you going to assist me or do I need to find someone else?'

'Don't worry, I'll do my job.'

'Very good. First the report. Why wasn't the possibility of a third party in that flat considered?'

'No evidence from the crime scene investigators,' Wallace replied. He was calmer now, careful what he said. Clare knew that by the evening he'd be back to his usual obnoxious self, trying to get her to have a drink with him, to ignore the wedding ring which he was no longer wearing, the imprint on his finger still visible.

'No evidence of that fact is still not a reason not to mention the possibility.'

Wallace said no more and raised himself from his chair. 'You'll want to talk to the pathologist,' he said. He brushed against Clare as he left the office. His actions were hostile, his manner dismissive, his anger palpable. Tremayne had warned her to be careful with the man, treat him with kid gloves, let him shoot himself in the foot.

Superintendent Moulton, unbeknown to Clare and Tremayne, had already been onto his counterpart in Dundee and found out that Inspector Roddy Wallace was a sloppy police officer. More than one villain walked the streets due to a failure of the prosecution to prove their case; the testimony of Wallace under oath devalued by the defence.

Moulton chose not to tell Clare what he had found out. He still intended her to reach inspector rank within the next year, Homicide the best place for someone of her capabilities, someone who had been mentored by Tremayne. If she could handle the situation in Dundee on her own, then he was sure she was the right person to put forward on Tremayne's retirement. He had seen the inspector dragging his leg, and although he'd also seen the curtailing of smoking, the healthier look in the man's face, it was an aberration, Moulton knew. Tremayne was on the way out, Clare Yarwood's star was in the elevation.

***

Tremayne raised himself from his bed. Although the air conditioning in his room had kept him cool, he had slept no more than three hours, and he still felt exhausted. Outside the sun was blazing, not a cloud in the sky. On the television – it had the BBC on cable – the temperature was showing as 35 degrees centigrade outside.

After a shower to refresh him, Tremayne dressed in the suit he had brought from England. He left the room and headed down for breakfast. Inspector Ong, a man in his late forties, was waiting for him.

'It's a long time since your Richard Grantley left Singapore. It's an old case to us, and he didn't murder anyone, just cheated a few,' Ong said.

'A few?' Tremayne said as he sat down for his breakfast. It was either local or English. He chose English. The night before he had eaten in the restaurant, local Chinese food. It had come with chopsticks, which he had rejected in favour of a fork and spoon.

'I'm not sure we're going to be of much help to you. We closed the investigation into the man a long time ago. We can visit where he lived and worked, check our files, but that's about it.'

'Does anyone remember his disappearance?'

'I was with Fraud back then. I was new in the police force, still in uniform. We investigated the man,

194

found out that he was playing a tricky game. He took advantage of changing tax laws around the world, shifted the money from one to another as a situation presented itself, hid it in various bank accounts in dubious jurisdictions, played the markets with other people's money, win on some, lose on others.'

'How much money had people deposited with him?' Tremayne asked. Even with the air conditioning blasting in the dining room, the heat was starting to get to him again.

'It's difficult to be accurate, but we reckon he had control of upwards of fifteen million dollars.'

'How much was found afterwards?'

'The three hundred thousand dollars in cash, nine hundred thousand dollars in local debt. Eventually, the local creditors accepted what was on offer.'

'Does a criminal offence stand against Grantley?'

'Legally, yes. But if the man's dead it's unimportant. And even if he were still alive, we'd not bother with extradition. He's not the first swindler we've had to deal with.'

The two men left the hotel, Tremayne momentarily pulling back as the first direct blast of the heat hit him. In the car, Ong driving, its air conditioner pumping out steam, they moved through the traffic with ease. Tremayne had to admit to the beauty of the place, the cleanliness, the people going about their business, the general calm of a bustling city. He knew that Jean would love it.

Access had been granted to Grantley's former apartment, a three-bedroom fifteenth-floor place of exquisite beauty, a view out to Sentosa Island.

'He lived well,' Tremayne said.

'The villains always do.'

'His office?'

'A ten-minute drive.'

Tremayne had dispensed with his jacket, loosened his tie. He felt marginally better, and he could feel that his knee responded to the heat. The pain that it had been giving him had reduced enough for him able to apply equal weight on it as his other leg. He had to admit to enjoying himself, the chance to do a little sightseeing, buy a gift for Jean, something silly for Clare.

Tremayne entered the former offices of Richard Grantley, now the premises of an insurance broker. The view, like at the apartment was outstanding, although the offices, luxurious though they were, were functional. At the reception desk, a young Chinese woman, a Singaporean national, asked why they were there, responding politely when told the reason.

Tremayne and Ong sat down, the woman bringing them both a cold drink.

'Anything yet?' Ong asked. He was a similar height to Tremayne, sixteen years in the force, hopeful of promotion in the next six months. Tremayne liked the man: helpful, knowledgeable, interested in his wellbeing. He knew that Clare would not be having such a pleasant experience. He intended to phone her, knowing that it would be late at night where she was, but an older woman came out from the offices to the rear of reception.

'Please come in,' she said. 'I'm the manager.'

In the woman's office, Tremayne explained to her why they were there, what they were looking for; a needle in a haystack was increasingly his thought, but not what he said.

Back outside the manager's office, the three of them stood, looking around. Tremayne moved away, looking here and there, not sure if he would find anything.

'Over here,' he shouted to Ong. 'On the wall.'

'It was here when we moved in,' the manager said. 'We left it where it was. I've been there myself.'

Tremayne took out his phone, took a photo, attempted to send it to Clare.

'Let me,' the manager said. 'I'll do it for you.'

Clare, roused from her sleep, took one look and phoned. 'It's Stonehenge in the background,' she said.

'Grantley left it when he took off,' Tremayne said. 'You've seen the burial mound in the foreground?'

'You can't miss it. Does this mean that it's not Clive and Liz, not Des Wetherell?'

'It means I need to spend more time here with Inspector Ong. How about you? Any luck?'

'Luck is not a word I'd use. Let me deal with here, you deal with what you've found,' Clare said. She tried to go back to sleep, but could not. She opened her laptop and entered the events of the previous day into it.

Chapter 20

Clare had not wanted to elucidate on her day with Inspector Roddy Wallace – 'call me Inspector' in his office in the morning, 'Roddy' by the time Clare had returned to the hotel at seven in the evening. The man insisted on the two of them sharing a bottle of wine, a meal, no doubt hoping for whatever else he could conjure up. His behaviour before she had given him the final brush off was verging on disciplinary, but she would not be making a complaint. He had, however, taken the hint and he had walked out of the hotel, not crawled, Clare's knee not finding the target that he deserved.

The pathologist in Dundee was not pleased to have his professionalism questioned.

'I stated that the man died of smoke inhalation, which is correct. I had been told that he had a history of substance abuse, he lived alone, an unusual character by all accounts. Whether he was unconscious before the fire started is not easy to determine.'

'It was never mentioned in the report,' Clare said. Wallace had stood to one side, sheepishly looking away, avoiding eye contact.

'I gave the facts, the time of death estimated by the condition of the body. The fire brigade's time of arrival and the crime scene team's report had some bearing on giving a more exact time, but that's it. No one suggested that the man's death was suspicious, no one at all. As far as I was concerned, it was death by misadventure, an unfortunate set of circumstances set in motion by a man who should have known better.'

'You weren't aware of my presence and of Inspector Tremayne in the city? The fact that we had interviewed him the day before, and we intended to interview him again about his student days, his possible involvement in a violent act.'

'It was never mentioned. Now if you don't mind, I have work to do.'

Clare duly noted the man's comments, Wallace saying nothing. The conversation between the two of them was strained for some time after that as they went to meet the senior crime scene investigator.

Nicola Byrne – Clare had met her briefly at Yatton's – proved to be the exception of the day. Conservatively dressed, she impressed Clare with her manner and her professionalism. She definitely didn't like Roddy Wallace, a plus in her favour. She quickly moved Wallace out of her office, poured Clare a cup of tea. In one corner of the office, an electric kettle stood on a small refrigerator; in the other, an old hat stand.

'Garage sale,' Nicola Byrne said when Clare looked up at it.

'I'm not satisfied with the report that Inspector Wallace submitted,' Clare said as she sipped her tea.

'My people were thorough. What's your concern?'

'There is the possibility that Monty Yatton's death was not accidental.'

'We found no evidence to the contrary.'

'No sign of other persons having been in the flat?'

'Our function was to conduct a thorough examination. We found no evidence of anyone else than the dead man. From what we could see he led a solitary life.'

'We know of his earlier history, and there remains the possibility that he was privy to information of a damning nature, information that certain people would not want to be revealed. Could someone else have been in there?'

'Certainly not an amateur. A professional might have been able to conceal their presence if they had taken certain precautions. It's highly unlikely, not impossible.'

'Will anything be served by re-examining your findings?'

'The report stands. I can't write up what wasn't there.'

Clare had confidence in Nicola Byrne. She was also satisfied that the pathologist had conducted his post mortem with due diligence. The only concern was that Wallace had not pursued the possibility that the man's death had been murder, and if the fire brigade had not arrived in time, Monty Yatton would have been reduced to a burnt cinder, the old woman downstairs as well.

If Yatton had been killed on orders, then those orders had come from someone known, from Des Wetherell, from Nigel Nicholson. The thought of the callousness of such men made her feel physically sick. She was concerned about where it was all heading, and whether Liz Fairweather on her own in Cambridge was safe.

***

Tremayne anticipated the weather the next day and had purchased a lightweight pair of trousers, a short-sleeve shirt. Whereas the dress was formal at police headquarters out on Irrawaddy Road, he thought that for the one day he would be forgiven for not wearing a jacket.

Inspector Ong made no comment on Tremayne's attire, although he was dressed in a suit and tie. The man's office was on the second floor of the building, a file of papers on his desk.

'I've put together what we have,' Ong said. He was drinking green tea. He offered a cup to Tremayne, who declined. His tea came with milk. He had tried the local tea, found it wanting. The food in the country was excellent, but he was missing Jean's cooking, the potatoes, the steak, the sausages, not that she gave him them too often anymore, part of the healthy eating routine that she had imposed. Mostly, he missed Jean.

'We need to know who could have seen that picture.'

'Not so easy. Most of the communication that Grantley would have had would have been by phone or email, probably fax back then. We've no way of knowing for sure.'

'You must have names.'

'I remember the case, but not the details. And I was only new, not involved in the details. Most of the time I was collating information, looking through files, doing the jobs the others didn't want to do. It wasn't the greatest time of my life.'

'Okay, let's go back to the beginning. Grantley's done a runner; he's out of your jurisdiction. No doubt you put out an all-points for him, checked the airport, ships leaving the harbour.'

'We did that. We know he took a flight in the name of Raymond Alston to Kuala Lumpur. After there, the trail went cold. We didn't know at that time that his name was Richard Grantley.'

'The man's taken off. There must have been people around at his office.'

201

'There would have been. It wasn't a crime scene, just a place of interest.'

'Which raises the question of how you found out about him; how he found out about you.'

'Not so difficult. He would have been subject to regular checks, any business is in Singapore. He had been acting as an investment advisor, not breaking any laws. The tax avoidance schemes he had been promoting were not necessarily illegal, not all of them. He came to our notice three months before he absconded. The schemes were starting to concern us, some of the high-income individuals were disturbing.'

'Any names, anyone that could have killed him if he had cheated on them?'

'I'm coming to that. The files that I've given you list all the clients that he had records of; the more dubious will probably not be there, or else they're hidden behind a false name. There are about forty names which seem to be genuine. As I was saying, the man, on the whole, was legitimate. He was running close to the wind, but whether he would have faced charges in Singapore is still open to speculation.'

'If he had stayed?'

'His passport would have been taken, and he would have had to answer to the courts as to what he was doing and whether it was illegal or not. A sharp lawyer would have probably got him off.'

'But he would have been visible, and if he had been playing both ends, skimming off some of the money in his care, then those people would have been knocking on the door,' Tremayne said.

'Which, we believe, is why he got out of the country. Easier to disappear, change his name, distance himself from Singapore and those who wouldn't have used an interview room to get answers.'

'Tied to a chair, beaten out of him?'

'Probably. You'll not find the names of those individuals in the files I've given you, but then, those sorts of people don't get involved in violence personally.'

Tremayne visited Richard Grantley's former office one more time. The manager of the insurance broker had no problem with him taking the picture from the wall. 'I've never liked it much, really. We just left it there, barely looked at it.'

The picture of the burial mound with Stonehenge in the background would be going back to Salisbury with him.

That night, at Inspector Ong's insistence, Tremayne gave the chopsticks one more try. He managed better than he thought he would, downed more local beer than he should have. At ten the next morning he was on a flight back to London. Jean would meet him on arrival.

***

Clare woke to a dull day in Dundee, a day she was not looking forward to. Monty Yatton's death was now playing a less critical role in the investigation, and she wondered whether the animosity she had encountered, the unfriendliness, being made to feel like a pariah, was worth it. But she would prevail, she knew that. One more piece in the puzzle, a minor piece now, but there was still the unknown element of Inspector Roddy Wallace. Why had he not been thorough in his investigation? Why had he not informed the pathologist that Yatton was indirectly involved in a murder enquiry? If Yatton had been killed, then why?

Questions that had no answers. Her first call of the morning was to the pathologist. The man was welcoming on her arrival; the day before he had been terse, but now he shook her hand and offered her tea, which she accepted.

'No Inspector Wallace,' he said.

'He's got another case to deal with.'

'I'm sure he has. As I said before, I wasn't aware of the victim's significance. I'm willing to change the report, not sure how to word it though. I gave you the pathologist's report. The man died of smoke inhalation between the times stated. He could have been asleep or in a drug-filled alcohol-laden stupor before or after the frying pan was put on the cooker. I can't tell you that with any certainty. It's still up to you to speak to Wallace for him to change what he's written.'

'I don't think that's likely to occur.'

Clare phoned Superintendent Moulton; Tremayne was still in the air, somewhere over the Middle East.

Moulton agreed to Clare's suggestion. He then phoned his counterpart who agreed to conduct an internal enquiry into Wallace's lack of diligence.

She then drove to Edinburgh Airport; her time in Scotland was at an end.

***

Events started to move fast. By the time Clare landed at Southampton Airport, Superintendent Moulton was on the phone. 'Good work,' he said. 'Wallace has been in contact with one of Wetherell's team, a Justin Ruxton. Have you heard of him?'

'We never met him, only Nigel Nicholson. Ruxton is more junior.'

'It seems foolish on their part to allow us to trace back from Wallace to Wetherell. It seems suspicious.'

'Wallace?'

'He's on suspension pending further enquiries. They're checking his bank accounts as well. The Dundee police are re-examining the death of Yatton, expect there to be fireworks. The pathologist, the crime scene team, forensics?'

'They're professional. I don't think you'll find fault with them. Whatever happens, my name will be mud up there.'

'That's why you're staying in Salisbury. Find Grantley's killer. If Des Wetherell is involved with Yatton's death, then the man will be working overtime to protect his image, to distance himself.'

One phone call ended, another started.

'Yarwood, you've been causing havoc up in Dundee,' Tremayne said.

'Is Jean with you?'

'She met me. We're on our way back to Salisbury on the train. Pick us up at the station. 7.20 p.m.'

'Wallace is on suspension,' Clare said.

'Moulton phoned me earlier. He's impressed, so am I.'

Clare did not comment on Tremayne's compliment. She had to admit to feeling pleased with herself.

***

Des Wetherell was elected unopposed to the position of Deputy Secretary General of the TUC. A safe Labour seat would be his if he waited for two more years, a cabinet post assured when the people of England voted his party of choice into government.

Wetherell knew that a chequered history, even criminal actions, were not unknown in Westminster, but those that had erred had ensured that what could cause friction and aggravation were dealt with in advance.

Nigel Nicholson had been one of the first to congratulate him. The two men stood in Wetherell's office; each had a glass of brandy; each smoked a Cuban cigar of the best quality.

'We have a problem,' Nicholson said. His client's euphoria abated slightly.

'The solution?' Wetherell asked. Worrying served no purpose, an adage that had always guided him well.

'The solution has become complicated,' Nicholson said. 'Our Inspector Roddy Wallace, Dundee's finest, has got himself suspended.'

'Our concern?'

'He will be subjected to an internal enquiry.'

'Can he be traced back to us?'

'Ruxton phoned him. His mobile number will be found and traced back to here.'

'The solution?'

'There is none, not yet. Sergeant Yarwood has been up in Dundee again. Wallace failed to ensure the robustness of the police report into the death of Monty Yatton. She has been up there ruffling feathers, making herself unpopular.'

'Can it be traced back to you?'

'Trace what?'

'Yatton's death,' Wetherell said.

'The man died as a result of his own stupidity,' Nicholson said brusquely.

Wetherell had no idea if what his friend had said was true or not; it did not concern him either way.

'What else?'

'Liz Fairweather. She's still a loose cannon.'

'Can the cannon be silenced?'

'It depends on the truth, doesn't it? Whether she can prove a criminal act by you or not.'

'There is nothing to prove. Someone else exploded a bomb. Why and who, I don't know.' This time it was Nicholson who did not know whether he had been told the truth or not.

Chapter 21

Tremayne sat in his office, still jet-lagged after the long flight from Singapore, the change in time zones. Clare could see his head drooping, his eyes closing. She thought that notwithstanding his tiredness, he looked better for the sun and heat.

Clare's problems, however, were more than a sleeping police inspector. A drunken phone call from Wallace late the previous night had upset her.

'You've done me, you bitch,' the slurred voice had said.

It should not have concerned her, but it did. It was one of those nights in her small house in Stratford sub Castle – a moonless night, the wind rustling the leaves in the trees, an owl hooting in the distance. It was the type of night when she thought back to Harry, and the night he had died saving her.

It had been six years since then, but she had not moved on, not sufficiently to commit to another man, and Wallace had not helped. Any other time she would have slammed the phone down, but he had caught her in a weakened state. She felt the need to defend her position.

'Inspector Wallace, your phoning me will not help you,' she said. At the bottom of her bed, her one remaining cat. On the dressing table, a photo of her and Harry in happier times.

'All those years, my pension, all gone, because a snotty-nosed degree-educated woman feels the need to belittle every man. No wonder you're on your own.'

It was later the next day as she had watched Tremayne dozing that she remembered Wallace's, 'no wonder you're on your own'.

She had never mentioned her personal life to Wallace, nor had Tremayne. Someone was checking on her, and it was very suspicious. Her marital status would be on police records, so that wasn't the issue, but the sneering way that he said it showed that he knew more than he should. Googling her on the internet would have revealed the history of the events that night in Avon Hill, the terrible storm, the deaths in Cuthbert's Wood. There would have been no reference to her inability to let go and to move on with her life. That would only have come by intrusive inquiry; by Des Wetherell or one of his cohorts.

And now, Liz Fairweather was on the phone, and she was frightened. 'A woman has been watching me,' she said to Clare, her voice nervous.

'Stay there, I'll get someone around to your house,' Clare's response. She did not phone Liz's daughter, Kim.

Tremayne woke from his slumber, saw his sergeant at her desk. He came over and pulled a chair from a desk behind her and sat down. 'We've got plenty to be going on with,' he said.

'Liz Fairweather is frightened.'

'No wonder. If Wetherell was involved in Yatton's death, it shows the arrogance of the man, his dismissive attitude towards the police.'

'He's an important man, not so easy to take down.'

'He will be if we can find anything in the files I brought back.'

209

'You suspect that Wetherell may be tied into Richard Grantley's death?'

'We're suspicious of him anyway. Could he have been in Singapore, could he have seen that picture?'

To Clare, it seemed unlikely. Wetherell was wealthy now, but in his thirties when Richard Grantley had died, he had not been so prosperous, not with so much money that he would have needed to hide away vast quantities. A small flat, a late-model car, nothing more.

Clare resumed her phone call with Liz. 'I'll get someone over from the local police station. Stay where you are.'

'I'm heading to Salisbury. I'm in the car now.'

'Call me when you get here.'

Clare returned to Tremayne. 'What have you brought back, anything of interest?'

'Names, addresses, financial details. Most of what Grantley was doing was legitimate; most of it will be no use to us.'

Two hours later, as Tremayne and Clare went through the files, a phone call on Clare's mobile: a distraught Kim.

'It's my mother, she's been in an accident.'

Clare left Tremayne's office and picked up her handbag, barely having time to speak to Tremayne, instead garbling out, 'Liz, she's crashed her car.'

'Dead?' Tremayne's response.

Kim, overhearing his comment, responded, 'Not yet. She's in Salisbury Hospital. It appears that they waited until she was near Salisbury before they ran her off the road.'

'Where are you?'

'On my way to the hospital. Father is with me. She could die.' Kim burst into tears.

It took Clare fifteen minutes to get to the hospital. Dr Steve Warner, Clare's former paramour, the man who had wanted to marry her, was talking to Kim and her father.

Clare shook the doctor's hand; it felt strange, considering that they had been lovers, but that was before she had rejected him and he had found another.

'Why would they do this?' Kim asked as she flung her arms around Clare.

'Your mother's condition?'

'A broken leg, a pierced lung, concussion,' Warner said. 'She'll be fine in time. Two days in here for observation and then she can be looked after at home.'

'She has a home, mine,' Clive Grantley said.

Clare walked over to the two police officers who had been summoned to the crash site. 'What happened? An accident or intentional?'

'It's a treacherous section of road. It's not the first accident there, won't be the last,' the more senior of the two officers said.

'I'll need the crime investigation team out there.'

'Apparently, you know the woman. Miss Fairweather said you did.'

'A former student friend of Liz Fairweather has recently died under unusual circumstances, and Mr Grantley's brother's body has been discovered. One is clearly murder, the other is highly suspect. So is this accident.'

Clare phoned Jim Hughes; his team would be at the site within the hour.

At the hospital, Liz, semi-conscious, asked for Kim.

The three, Kim, Clive and Clare, entered the room. Liz was heavily bandaged, a nurse standing by.

'It was her,' Liz said. 'I'm sure of it.'

'We're checking the accident scene. Can you remember any details, the car, a registration number?' Clare asked.

'It was red, or maybe it was blue. I can't remember.'

'The patient has been sedated; her recollection of details will be vague,' the nurse said. 'She needs rest. Please say what you need to and then leave her alone.'

Kim touched her mother on the arm; Liz's face was too bruised to touch.

'We've got the best doctor in the hospital looking after you, and one of us will be here at all times,' Kim said, dabbing her eyes with her tissue.

Even Clare felt emotional. Monty Yatton had not fared so well, and if this was an attempted murder made to look like an accident, then the Dundee police had a lot more work to do. First Yatton, now Liz.

Will there be any more? Clare thought.

Clare left Kim and Clive, both sitting quietly on the chairs provided; Liz had gone back to sleep.

Outside, Steve Warner approached her.

'How are you, Clare?' he asked. She had seen him on a few occasions over the last couple of years, but their conversations had been brief, and he had always been with his wife. She felt uncomfortable in his presence.

'Fine. And you? Your family?'

'They're well, another child on the way.'

Clare could be envious of the expected child, not of the life that his wife had chosen for herself. She knew that she was not unique, that others of her age had somehow missed the marriage and the family. She regretted the circumstance, and if she had to choose now between her career and a child, she would choose the latter.

She often thought of Harry, of Steve. One she had loved with intensity; the other love was genuine even if it had come with doubts. It had been more natural on a romantic weekend with Steve to believe that it was love eternal, but back in the police station of a Monday, Tremayne champing at the bit, she found that the love came at a cost, a cost she couldn't afford.

She left the hospital, phoning Tremayne to let him know the situation, and that if it was attempted murder, then Des Wetherell, the great union man, had questions to answer.

Instead of turning right into Salisbury, she turned left.

Harry's grave had been tended; a wilting flower was laid across it. Clare never knew who it was who looked after the grave, and it was three months since she had last visited. She said a few words as she always did and then left.

Before returning to the police station she stopped by her house. The picture of Harry and her that had stood on her dressing table since his death was put into a drawer, face down.

Steve Warner was no longer available, but she did not intend to waste any more time being melancholy, sitting on her own, waiting for love to come. She would find a man on her terms, a man who would accept that she was a serving police officer, and a child would never be neglected, and it would be loved. She had seen Kim and her mother, the love of Clive; that would do for her.

***

Tremayne said nothing when Clare returned to Homicide; he had seen the expression on her face before. He did what he always did; he put her to work.

'You take those files; I'll stay with the others.'

Clare could smell stale tobacco; she would not comment, nor tell Jean. Today was a day for reflection; a day she hoped would pass quickly.

'What are we looking for?'

'Names of interest. Focus on English addresses first. Think of who may have been interested in the burial mound. Was Richard Grantley fixated on ancient English history? If he was, why would someone have gone to the bother of burying him in a mound.'

Clare took her files and worked through them, twice as fast as Tremayne, but he was slower than he had been a year before. She could see him still dozing from the jet lag, feeling the years accumulating.

Clare entered the names and addresses into an Excel file on her laptop; Tremayne wrote them down on a piece of paper.

Subconsciously they were both looking for Des Wetherell, the villain to them. But nothing was proven. Wallace, no longer assigned to Yatton's death, occupied himself with alcohol. Another inspector, this time more agreeable, had been on the phone to Clare as she worked through the files.

'We're checking through Monty Yatton's case file,' Inspector Fiona McAlpine said. Clare imagined her to be young and eager, her enthusiasm apparent on the phone.

'We've had another suspicious accident. This time the victim has survived.'

'Smoke inhalation?'

'A car ran a woman off the road, although there's no proof it was deliberate, not yet. She's in hospital, thankful to be alive.'

'Too many car accidents up here; no doubt you have the same problem.'

'We do,' Clare said, hoping that was what it was. To put a case forward against Des Wetherell would be close to impossible. The man was smart, always distancing himself from the more fractious union disputes with management, coming in at the last minute to forge a compromise. Never to be seen up on the roof of a car rousing the workers to affirmative action, always there to talk to his members about consolidation and harmony.

He was silver-tongued, Clare knew that, and the accident that had put Liz Fairweather in hospital appeared to be just that: a tricky section of road, balding front tyres on Liz's car, one brake light that didn't work.

Jim Hughes phoned. 'I'm here with the accident investigation team, my people as well. What colour did the driver say?'

'Red or blue, but she wasn't sure. Was the car marked?'

'Not from what we can see. We've had a look at the CCTV, and there's no sign of another vehicle.'

Clare was pleased, one less headache to deal with. She phoned Kim who was still at the hospital. 'The doctor said you and he were an item.'

'He wanted something I couldn't give him,' Clare said, disappointed that Steve Warner had brought up the subject with Kim, understanding that the personable young woman was the type of person men like to talk to. 'He's married now.'

'He told me. One child, another on the way. He strikes me as a decent man, the type you should be looking for.'

'I've already found a good man,' Clare said but did not elaborate.

Tremayne drew Clare into his office. 'While you've been chatting, I've found something.'

'Not chatting, doing my job,' Clare's retort. It was part of their usual banter. The day was progressing; it was late afternoon, the jet lag had passed, and Tremayne was wide awake, Clare, who wanted an early night on account of the visit to Harry's grave, was not.

'I've got some names for you to check out. I'll give it to Richard Grantley, he wasn't a man to deal in half-measures. Some of his clients had put millions of dollars through him.'

'Wetherell?'

'Not yet, and what about Justin Ruxton, Wetherell's legal eagle? Anything?'

'We need to talk to him. There are no marks against his name. He's thirty-five years of age, his only job as a lawyer with the Public Services Union. Probably honest enough, but he had made the phone call to Wallace.'

'Any chance of obtaining a record of it?'

'Remote. It's best to ask him straight.'

'Here or in London?'

'London. Organise an interview at the local police station; talk to someone in authority.'

'Tomorrow?'

'Let him stew for a couple of days. Just make sure he's informed and that he's to be ready at short notice. We'll not pin anything on Wetherell, anyway. The man's

gained more political influence, the best legal minds that
money can buy.'

Chapter 22

The case against Des Wetherell strengthened when Clare phoned Justin Ruxton's place of employment, the Public Services Union. The man was no longer there, and as the lady on reception advised her, 'We don't know where he's gone. He mentioned New Zealand, a relative.'

Clare instigated an APW (all-ports warning) for Ruxton. If the man tried to exit the country, or if he had already, which seemed the most likely option, she would be notified soon enough.

Wherever he had gone, one fact was clear: Des Wetherell and Nigel Nicholson were involved in the death of Monty Yatton and the still suspicious accident of Liz Fairweather.

In Dundee, a dissolute and drink-sodden Roddy Wallace found himself at the police station where he had once been a proud officer. This time, though, he was on the other side of the table in the interview room.

Clare had flown up at short notice, and she sat with Inspector Fiona McAlpine. Wallace had chosen not to have legal representation, and besides, he had not been charged with any crime, only suspended subject to an internal investigation. The man's smell was so strong, both of body odour and tobacco, that Fiona McAlpine had sprayed the room with a powerful air freshener. It had helped a little, although it had caused Clare to sneeze, Wallace to turn up his nose at the smell of lavender.

'I don't need to answer to you,' Wallace said. His manner was surly and contemptuous. Both of the women knew that in front of them was a misogynist and a bigot.

Burial Mound

A man who tolerated women only if they were subservient to him, not giving him commands.

Fiona McAlpine was not as Clare had envisaged. She was in her forties with a distinctive style of clothing, tartan and tweed, her hair tied back in a bun. The sort of person who would be hiking up in the Highlands in the middle of winter, not complaining about the cold or the rain or even the snow, but driving forward against the elements, loving every moment, rallying those with her to keep up.

'Roddy,' Fiona McAlpine said, 'your presence here today is to help us with our enquiries. It may well help you in the disciplinary hearing. A good report from us could be advantageous.'

Wallace averted his eyes. 'You reckon,' he said.

Clare could see that the man regarded his Dundee police force counterpart with disdain. She was not his kind of woman: susceptible, young, relaxed with her virtues. He had tried it on with Clare and had received a stern rebuke.

She had not liked him from the first moment they had met; she liked him even less now. He was, to her, all that was wrong with the modern police force.

And now, two women, and Inspector Roddy Wallace was squirming. He had said that his presence in the interview room was voluntary – it was not. If he had not come of his own volition, Clare knew that Fiona McAlpine would have still brought him in. In the back of a police car if necessary, in handcuffs if she could have.

'You've been in communication with Justin Ruxton,' Clare said.

'Who?' the sneering reply.

It was going to be a tough interview. Wallace had many years' experience of grilling people; he knew that

219

non-committal answers, claiming memory loss and ignorance, worked better than being open with those who represent law and order.

'Roddy, what's the point in denying known facts?' Fiona McAlpine said.

'I've never met or spoken to a Ruxton.' the inevitable reply; ignorance clearly the opening gambit.

'We have proof that on three occasions you were contacted by Ruxton,' Clare said. 'He is, or was, in the employ of Des Wetherell, an important and influential man in the trade union movement. You have undoubtedly heard of him.'

'I have, but not Ruxton. What is he anyway?'

'The death of Monty Yatton was suspicious.'

'It was his own damn fault. The man was a drug addict.'

'The man was an acknowledged recreational user of cannabis,' Clare said. 'Why do you say he was a drug addict?'

'He couldn't have stopped, could he?'

'A serving police officer,' Fiona said, 'should know the difference between a drug addict and someone who heavily indulges in drug use.'

'Okay, I'll concede the point. The man was still out of it, no idea what he was doing, burnt the place down or nearly did. Died as a result, open and shut case.'

'Is that what you told Ruxton? Or is it what he paid you to ensure?' Clare asked. Wallace was rattled, in need of a cigarette. His hands were shaking, his face was florid, sweat beads forming on his forehead.

'Being open would make more sense,' Fiona said. 'You did not pass on information to Ruxton and by default his boss, Wetherell, out of a sense of civic duty. You did it for financial gain, and we will prove that. You

220

either lay your cards on the table, make a deal with us, or you'll be charged with a criminal offence.'

'You could be spending time in prison with some of those you've put in there,' Clare said. She had to admit to enjoying the interview. Wallace had thought he was one of Dundee's finest police officers, while Fiona McAlpine, who did not indulge in such arrogance, clearly was.

'You'll not get Wetherell,' Wallace said. He had leant back on his chair, the back of it straining with his weight. One of the buttons on his shirt, close to what should have been his waist, had sprung open. Clare had wanted to laugh but had turned her face away and towards her colleague. She could tell that Fiona also saw the humour in the situation.

But Inspector Fiona McAlpine was also a serious-minded woman who regarded policing as serious business, and Roddy Wallace as a disgrace, the type of person who abuses his position of authority, the type of person who gives the police a bad name.

'Are you acknowledging Wetherell?' Clare asked. She was sitting upright, attempting to stare Wallace down, a tactic that Tremayne would use, but it was not going to work. Wallace was too big a man physically, and he was not going to indulge in posturing.

The hate in Wallace's face was apparent; a desire to strike out, to hit the two women, a possibility. Clare left the interview room. She returned soon after with a uniformed police constable, a larger man than Wallace, but young and fit. The constable took his place close to the door of the interview room.

Wallace made no comment. Intimidation would not work with him, and he was aware that if the situation were reversed, if it were not an interview room, then he would have had no hesitation in ensuring that those opposite him felt the force of his wrath.

'I'm acknowledging no one,' Wallace's eventual reply. 'I've seen Wetherell on the television. He's not the man to respond to threats.'

'Neither are you, Inspector Wallace. We know what you've done, or should I be more accurate, failed to do.'

'We've gone through this ad infinitum, *Sergeant* Yarwood.' A subtle attempt, noticed by the two women, to belittle a lower rank. 'I have at no time had any contact with a Justin Ruxton, a Des Wetherell. Yatton killed himself. Why don't you stop this witch hunt and let me get back to catching criminals, something I'm particularly good at.'

Neither woman had expected Wallace to break under pressure. But without Ruxton and no longer able to be of benefit to Wetherell, the inspector would be aware that he was a threatened species, the dishonest policeman who had been caught out. And prison to Wetherell was anathema, as he had arrested a few whose proof of guilt had been enhanced by his testimony: hard men, violent men, men with nothing to lose, men with long memories and long prison terms to serve, men who would regard retribution against Inspector Roddy Wallace as a pleasant diversion from the monotony of prison.

***

Inspector Ong, a determined individual who prided himself on his thoroughness, phoned Tremayne. It was four in the morning in England.

It was Jean who answered the phone, used to phone calls at odd hours. Tremayne still slept, his snoring only briefly halted when the phone rang.

'Is Inspector Tremayne there?' Ong asked. 'I'm phoning from Singapore. Is that Jean?'

She was surprised that the man knew her name. 'He mentioned me?'

'He said you would have loved it here.'

'Did he?'

'I'm afraid your husband is a stay-at-home Englishman. He'd prefer mushy peas and chips than Asian food.'

'He would; I wouldn't, and yes, I would have loved to have been there.'

'Come when he has wrapped up the current case. Bring him with you, and if he complains, we can always find him an Irish Bar, a glass of Guinness to while away his hours. You and my wife can explore the shops, and we can take you to the best restaurants, the places that locals go to, not the tourist traps where they charge too much.'

'The investigation's not going too well,' Jean said, surprised to receive the call, excited at the prospect of a trip overseas.

'I'm about to make it easier for him. Is he awake?'

'Not yet. Can you phone back in ten minutes?'

Tremayne, initially cranky with Jean waking him up, soon revived.

When Ong phoned the next time, he was sitting downstairs, a cup of tea in his hand, a slice of toast to eat.

'Don't you sleep in Singapore?' Tremayne said when he picked up the phone.

Inspector Ong, used to his English counterpart's dry humour, smiled but did not comment. 'I've continued checking on Richard Grantley. It wasn't mentioned in the files, not at the time. The woman wasn't known to us, not till later, but Grantley had had a girlfriend, the wife of another man.'

'From what we know of Grantley, I can't say I'm surprised.'

'This woman, her name was Veronica Langley, the wife of a highly-influential businessman, vanished seven years ago.'

'The significance?' Tremayne asked as he ate his toast. He was wide awake now.

'She reappeared five months later, or what was left of her was washed up down by the harbour. It was put down to suicide. The woman was known to have had an unhealthy relationship with prescription drugs and a fondness for alcohol.'

'Suicide recorded?'

'There was no reason to doubt it at the time. And no one would have been looking into the Richard Grantley case. It was a sound verdict.'

'The husband?'

'Distraught.'

'So, Veronica Langley had been playing around with Richard Grantley. If that's the case, what about the woman's husband? Did she stay with him? What was his response to her dalliance?'

'She stayed with him. His response wasn't known when Grantley took off. It wasn't known at the time, and her relationship with Grantley was a minor issue; the money he had taken was more important, the crimes he had committed took precedence. It was just when I was running some names through the database that I made the connection.'

'The husband, what about him? Where is he now?'

'He returned to the UK. Anthony Langley runs an investment company, but the man was legit, well known on the social scene in Singapore, a patron of several charities, political influence.'

'That doesn't make him innocent of criminal offences.'

'I know that. Veronica was invariably at his side, before and after Grantley. Always immaculately groomed, the perfect hostess.'

'The prescription drugs, the alcohol?'

'Behind closed doors. The affluent and influential don't air their dirty linen in public.'

'And no one knew about her being Grantley's mistress?'

'If they did, it was never reported, never mentioned. One law for the rich, another for the rest.'

Singapore was no different to England, Tremayne could see; the affluent and well-connected could get away with anything, even murder.

'Where can we find Anthony Langley?'

'The company's name is Langley Investments. I checked his website. He lives in Cornwall; his main office is in London. There's not much more I can tell you. I'll email the case history on the death of Veronica Langley. You can take it from there.'

***

Clive Grantley made his first visit to the council offices since his misguided confession to his brother's murder, the first visit since he had publicly announced that Kim Fairweather, his personal assistant, was his daughter, the first visit since Liz Fairweather had been in a car accident. Liz was now at his home, convalescing, a nurse hired to ensure that she received the best care that money could buy.

Grantley was still a city councillor, if no longer the mayor. If he had been asked, he would have said that he missed the robes of office, the chance to step out of himself, to be someone more open, not the reclusive man that he had always been.

If pressed he would have said being reclusive was an affliction from his childhood; his brother always there teasing him, mocking the stutter that had plagued him until the age of thirteen. The times he had hidden away from his brother – under the stairs, up a tree, in the garden shed – but each time there would be Richard, laughing and teasing, berating him, tears rolling down his cheeks in hilarity, beating Clive with his fists and then a piece of wood or whatever heavy object he could find.

Their mother, sweet and loving, always seeing the best in her two sons, not chastising one for his treatment of the other, not comforting the weaker for fear of showing favouritism. Clive knew that she had been right; Richard would have only treated him worse afterwards when no one was looking. His father knew what was going on, but his solution was to tell Clive to sharpen up, hit back, give his brother a black eye. But he could never do that. It wasn't that Richard was bigger or stronger – on the contrary, he was the smaller of the two – but Clive knew that he was a pacifist, someone who would tend to an injured bird, whereas his brother would have killed it without pity.

He was glad that Richard was dead, had often wondered over the years what had happened to him. That last day in London, Richard had been contrite, acting the perfect brother, Clive wanting to believe it, to hope that he had turned over a new leaf, and that from then on, the two remaining members of the Grantley family could come to a truce.

Neither man was married, and Richard was determined to stay alone, to enjoy what life had to offer, whether it was carnal or financial, preferably both; Clive because he could never trust another woman, not after Grace. He had loved her until his brother had broken the bond between man and wife.

They had parted with a firm handshake: Richard with five thousand pounds, Clive with an overdraft.

When he arrived at the council offices he got a pat on the back, a 'good to see you' from a council employee, the name of the person eluding him. Another person, a rousing cheer, a smile from Clive, a tear from Kim. She enjoyed the new-found fame, the daughter of a respected man, the daughter of a respected mother. Life was good, she knew it, and there was even a new boyfriend, an up and coming dentist, a man she might come to love.

At the house, Kim's mother was slowly improving. Clare was increasingly confident that new information might bring a resolution to the mystery of the death of Kim's wayward uncle, the uncle she had never met.

'You'll soon be mayor again,' a stout man with a walking stick said.

'Let's wait and see,' Clive said. He hoped he would be, but he was too modest to declare that yet. If they wanted him back, he was sure that they would elect him to the position at the earliest opportunity. For the moment, he was content and even pleased that Kim was known as his daughter, yet with Liz in his house, he and she could both see that it was not going to be a happy family of three, the mother and father, the loving daughter.

Kim was an adult, and Liz needed academia, not a man. She never had really; she knew that. In her youth, the exuberance of overactive hormones, the aid of recreational drugs. But Clive knew that her feelings for him had been real, though more emotional than physical, and that the mutual rearing of the child had given them great pleasure.

Another person, then another person, all with the same pleasure at seeing Clive Grantley back again. He had had an excellent record of achievement when he had been the mayor: no trips to exotic locations to check out how their civic responsibilities were dealt with, no ensuring that the roads in the area where he lived, the street lighting, the cleanliness, were given preferential treatment over other areas. He knew that couldn't be said of all the councillors, not that he intended to indulge in denigrating them to regain his position.

A phone call from Clare caused them to leave the council offices.

228

Chapter 23

Tremayne sat back on his chair at Bemerton Road Police
Station, confident that the phone call from Singapore
would lead the investigation into a hitherto unexplored
area. He still harboured a concern that Clive Grantley was
responsible for his brother's death, although the
connection to the burial mound had to be associated with
the picture on Richard Grantley's office wall in Singapore.

Why someone would have seen it as necessary to
bury the man in a mound, and why near Stonehenge, still
made no sense. He was also perturbed by Clare's
closeness to the Grantley family, which had transcended
from professional to personal. To him, it was not a
healthy association, in that one of them could be the
murderer, another an accomplice. His sergeant had been
sorely disappointed by Harry Holchester, the wounds of
that not yet healed; not in him, either. The occasional
nightmare sometimes disturbed his sleep; Cuthbert's
Wood at night; a group of men wearing masks, incanting
chants to pagan gods, full of bloodlust; needing to kill
someone for their beliefs, targeting Clare, Tremayne and
the two uniforms that had been with them.

If Clive Grantley was guilty, then he must have
unusual beliefs as well. Richard Grantley had not, as far as
was known, other than ultimate faith in himself.

The dead man's treatment of his brother, revealed
in small snippets to Clare by Clive, could be enough to
change an otherwise seemingly gentle person into a
savage murderer. Statistically, the possibility of the abused
child becoming the child abuser in adult life was strong;

the neglected child becoming the perpetrator of neglect in adulthood; the child hiding in the cupboard or watching his brother kill a harmless bird was also likely to want to kill the person responsible for his misery.

While the inspector went over the case in his mind, Clare met with the Grantleys at Clive's house. There was a sense of contentment in the air.

Liz was sat upright in a chair in the main room. She was now able to move freely without pain, and the nurse was to leave within a day.

'I'm going back to Cambridge,' Liz said. 'It must have been an accident. Maybe I was neurotic about the woman that I saw.'

Clare said nothing, not sure if Liz was right; no proof had been found to contradict her statement, although no further evidence about the death of Monty Yatton had been found either.

Inspector Roddy Wallace's bank account had been accessed, and his official issue laptop had shown his attempts to prejudice the minds of others that it was a clear case of accidental death.

Wallace would be removed from the police force, and a prison term was a possibility, although the worry of bad press about a corrupt police officer might mean he would be dismissed, but no conviction.

And now Liz was looking forward to going back to Cambridge, back to a place where she would not be protected. The prospect concerned Clare, yet she had no reason to stop her. Liz's memory of the accident was still muddled, having no recollection of veering off the road and into the ditch.

The murder of Richard Grantley was the reason for Clare to be at the Grantley house, although each time she visited she felt as though she belonged.

'I need to ask Clive about Richard's women,' Clare said. The four were sitting around the room. Kim sat close to her mother. Clive had chosen a leather chair, his favourite, and Clare sat on a wooden chair, attempting to affect an air of authority.

'You know about Grace,' Clive replied. Liz pulled a face at the mention of the woman.

'Have you heard of Veronica Langley? He knew her in Singapore.'

'My contact with Richard was intermittent over the years. He occasionally phoned me. Most times he was drunk, wanting to regale me with stories of the good life that he was living, the women, the money, the influential friends.'

'Did you believe him?'

'That was Richard. Either high on life or down and despairing. Yes, I believed him.'

'Veronica Langley?'

'I don't remember the name, but he wasn't the sort of man to be satisfied with one. He enjoyed the chase, the capture, the seduction. Whoever she was, she wouldn't have lasted long.'

'Inspector Tremayne's contact in Singapore came up with the name.'

'Married?' Liz asked.

'Yes,' Clare's response.

'That'd be Richard,' Clive said. 'The more elusive, the more exotic, the more desirable, then he'd be there. What about the woman's husband?'

'Anthony Langley. Do you know him?'

'Not that I can remember.'

Clare sensed that Clive had not been candid with her. She didn't know why and it troubled her.

'Why is this important?' Kim asked. Fifteen minutes earlier, as she had left the council offices, she had been happy; now she was not. It was as if a blanket had come down over her.

'Veronica Langley was fished out of the water in Singapore, the verdict given as suicide,' Clare said. The focus was the woman's husband: his reaction to his wife's affair with Richard, the death of his wife and how he had taken it, whether he could be implicated.

'Richard?'

'It wasn't Richard. It was years after he had left Singapore. The woman had a history of alcohol and drug abuse. The verdict of suicide would have been correct, given that there were no other extenuating circumstances. But now, with Richard and Veronica Langley, the net gets tighter. If the woman's death was not suicide, then who killed her and why? And there was a picture in Richard's office, a burial mound, Stonehenge in the background.'

'Where is this leading?' Kim asked.

'To the truth, I hope,' Clare said. She was feeling uncomfortable, concerned that she should not have revealed a new avenue of enquiry, especially if Clive and Liz were involved. And now, Kim was interceding, asking questions that could not be answered.

'The woman died, but when?'

'It was years after she had finished with Richard, and she had stayed with her husband, the loving wife in public, the wild woman at home. If Anthony Langley had arranged for his wife's death or had hired others to deal with her, he could also have had Richard killed. It would answer the uncertainties that we have, but your father is still the most likely suspect.'

'Father would never do such a thing.'

'A daughter's belief in her father will not help in court. Proof of who is responsible is what we need.'

'Very well,' Clive said. 'Richard did mention the woman on one of his drunken phone calls.'

'Why didn't you mention it? Why lie?'

'He was serious about her, or so he said to me. Not that you could ever place faith in what he said. He had made a career out of deception.'

'You've not answered why you lied.'

'Because it would further prove my guilt.'

'Why?'

Liz and Kim sat mutely watching Clive shift uneasily in his seat. He stood up and moved closer to the large window; its curtains were drawn back to let in the sun.

'She was another woman that Richard took from me.'

'In Singapore?'

'What do you know about Veronica Langley?'

'English, born in Bristol, grew up there. Her surname back then was Cuthbertson.'

'We were boarded there, Richard and I. An exclusive college in our early teens.'

'You knew Veronica?'

'We both did, but we were younger then. She was my friend more than Richard's. Our friendship was prepubescent, harmless and sweet. Nothing overtly sexual.'

'Love?'

'Childish make-believe, the sort that does not harm. Pledging each to the other until eternity.'

'What happened?'

'We left there after eighteen months and returned to Salisbury, went to Bishop Wordsworth's grammar school.'

'And what of Veronica?'

'We kept in contact by letter for a few months, and then she stopped writing. I never thought any more about her, not until Richard phoned up, bragging as he always did, putting me down, giving me graphic details of him and Veronica.'

'What did you do? What did you say?'

'He had come across her at a function. She was married, a plus in her favour, she was someone who had preferred me to him, although we weren't much more than children then, and her husband was a powerful man. The challenge would have been irresistible.'

'You never answered my question. What did you do?'

'Nothing. I let him have his say.'

'Are you telling me that you felt nothing that he was charming a woman who had loved you, admittedly a childish love, still important though. He was sleeping with her, using her for his own gratification, not caring for her, a woman you had cared for.'

'I was angry. I'm sorry to hear of her death.'

Clare left the house confused and concerned. The visit had not helped to clear Clive Grantley; instead, it had further condemned him.

***

A sweeping driveway, a grand mansion at the end of it, reflected the success that Anthony Langley had achieved for himself.

Tremayne was impressed with the man, dressed as a country squire, who welcomed them. Langley was in his early sixties, yet his head of hair was still full and not totally grey, only streaking at the edges. Clare thought it was a contrived look, designed to impress those that knew the man and those that didn't.

'Inspector Tremayne, Sergeant Yarwood, please come in. It's always a pleasure to meet members of our excellent police force'.

The silver tongue, the elegant manners, the fashionably decorated mansion, the trophy wife, all contrived to convey the aura of success.

Clare looked at Langley's wife, Lady Sally Langley, her husband having been tapped on the shoulder for services rendered to charity.

'Sir Anthony, you're aware of why we're here?' Tremayne said, a cup of coffee in one hand. A butler stood nearby awaiting further instructions.

'Sadly, it's to do with Veronica.' The right air of sorrow shown by Langley.

Clare recognised that he was attractive, but distrusted him. The man's wealth, the aristocratic accent, the 'butter wouldn't melt in his mouth' demeanour may have convinced many; it did not convince her.

Prior to the trip down to St Austell – Clare had driven as usual – she and Tremayne had read up on Sir Anthony Langley: his humble working-class background, the son of a train driver and a shop assistant, his scholarship into one of the best schools in the country, his academic success, the two degrees in economics and finance, both honours. And then at the age of twenty-four, he had struck out on his own. First in real estate development, making a fortune, going broke when the market collapsed. And then at thirty-four moving to

Singapore, finally returning to England after Veronica, his wife for nineteen years, committed suicide.

Lady Langley sat quietly, smiling as she was expected to. She was younger than Clare and was dressed in designer labels. Her history was well known: a successful model, she had walked the catwalks of the major fashion houses of Europe, minor parts in three movies.

The butler, resplendent in tails, continued to hover.

'We need to talk about your time in Singapore,' Tremayne said, lifting his head in the direction of the butler.

Langley dismissed the man. 'I'm an open book. Ask me what you want.'

'Your wife?' Clare asked.

'My wife can stay. There is nothing hidden in my past, and most of it is in the public record. No doubt you can tell me more about myself than I can,' Langley said convincingly.

'Very well,' Tremayne said. 'Veronica, your first wife died. A tragic accident, or…'

'Suicide, Inspector. Don't try to make it out to be anything else.'

'Did you know Richard Grantley?'

'I knew a Raymond Alston, although your sergeant told me that was the name he was using there.'

That was something Tremayne and she hadn't considered, Clare realised. If Veronica had known the man as Richard Grantley as a child, then why had she accepted him as Raymond Alston in Singapore.

'They are one and the same.'

'Then I knew him. I liked him at first, but then I realised he was an opportunist, always pushing, aiming to get an edge on other people.'

'Including you?'

'Including me, but he never succeeded. I played hard but fair, more profitable in the end.'

'Tell us about him.'

'A good-looking man, confident, an air of authority about him. A man you instantly like, but in time, some see through the veneer.'

'Your wife never did.'

'My wife had issues. A loving woman and we were happy, but she was weak of spirit. Life had dealt her a bad hand.'

'What does that mean?'

'Let me tell you the events leading up to her disappearance,' Langley said, an attempt to deflect the conversation.

'I'd prefer to focus on the time that Richard Grantley was in Singapore. Both you and your wife knew him.'

'We did, as a business colleague on occasions; as a friend on others.'

'Do you want me to spell this out, or do you wish to explain the relationship between Grantley and Veronica?'

'My wife was weak.'

'You've already said that.'

Langley took no notice of Tremayne's impatience, only taking a casual sip of his coffee, looking at his second wife, glancing back to the police inspector. 'Veronica always needed crutches in her life. Not that I ever knew why as her parents were perfectly sensible people. In her childhood, she had her school and her circle of friends. In her later years, a boyfriend, a casual lover, always something to keep her steady.'

'Did you know Richard's brother?'

'I never met him, and remember, we didn't know him as Richard Grantley, only as Raymond Alston.'

'There's more, isn't there?' Clare said, as anxious as Tremayne for Langley to get on with it.

'I was a few years older than Veronica when we met. I had only just arrived in Singapore. She was upset due to a lost boyfriend. We hit it off, moved in together after three weeks, married in six months.'

'You're in Singapore. What then?'

'I went into business. I didn't have much money, but I had contacts. Within a year I had an office, a staff of eight. Veronica had been the receptionist, accountant, even the tea lady for the first couple of months. I made a few good calls on the market, made several people richer than they had been before. After two years we had enough to splurge out on a penthouse flat. Life was good, we were good, but then Veronica, who had had a full life, had time on her hands. She took to the shops and then to the golf course or whatever diversion she could find.'

'Drink?'

'She always drank more than I did, but with her life of leisure, the drinking became heavier, and then it was cocaine. Soon her life was spiralling down, and there wasn't much I could do. After all, I couldn't use her in the office again.'

'Richard Grantley?' Tremayne asked.

'An alcohol and drug-dependent person always needs the next fix. I ensured that Veronica didn't progress to heroin; my efforts, however, did not stop her from becoming involved with the man.'

'What did you do?'

'What could I do? I had no option but to continue with the business. I became a workaholic, only coming home when the desk was clear, no loose ends. I couldn't stand to see what Veronica had become; powerless to stop it.'

'Did you try?' Clare asked.

'I did the best I could. Not the best excuse, I know, but what else was there for me to do. She hung onto Grantley, discreetly, although everyone knew, and if we needed to attend somewhere as the loving married couple, she'd stop the alcohol and the drugs for a few days before.'

'She wasn't addicted?'

'An event to attend, and she had the distraction. I don't think she saw Grantley at those times, and then he was gone. She was inconsolable, not because she loved him, but he had become one of her three crutches.'

'Your marriage continued?'

'For a long time. The same routine as before.'

'Another lover?'

'There was one. By then, I had come to realise the reality. There was no point in trying to stop her.'

'And then she committed suicide?'

'She disappeared. No one knew where she had gone, and for months, I did what I could. I thought she had gone overseas, but nothing. Life eventually moved on, and I continued with my business.'

'The day your wife was found?'

'There wasn't much to identify. She always wore a necklace that I had given her, so that gave them the first clue. DNA checking confirmed it was Veronica. That's all I can tell you about Veronica and Grantley.'

'A sad story,' Clare said.

'Sad, as you say, but life goes on; it must.'

Clare could agree with Langley's outlook on life, although he had not convinced either her or Tremayne as to his innocence in the deaths of two people.

Chapter 24

Not only had Justin Ruxton phoned Roddy Wallace's mobile number, Ruxton's number visible in the received calls list, but after checking into a hotel in France under a false name – no one was checking passports – he had started using his English credit cards.

It was Clare who received the first call about him, from a town in the south of France. Ruxton was spending time enjoying the hospitality of the French police, his confinement at the police station a result of the APW that Clare had organised in England. It applied equally well in France, and while Ruxton had not been charged with any crime, he was still a person of interest in the cases of Monty Yatton and Liz Fairweather.

Inspector Fiona McAlpine in Dundee had secured an open verdict on Yatton, the final police report stating that there was no evidence to confirm that the man had died as a result of criminal activity.

The man's death was suspicious, however, and it was believed that Montgomery Yatton, a timid man, would in time have revealed all that he knew.

Ruxton, from what Clare had deduced, was of the same ilk: a smart man, but not strong-willed and indeed of a nervous disposition. And now he was in France, and no charge could be levelled against him. Phoning a police officer was not a crime, only what he may have said or done.

Ruxton's detention caused elation in one place, fear in another.

Nigel Nicholson was concerned. It had been him that had instructed the young lawyer to deal with the police inspector in Dundee.

It was clear to Tremayne that Ruxton needed to be interviewed and soon. Liz Fairweather was heading back to Cambridge, Anthony Langley was using his wealth to secure a team of lawyers in case the police needed to speak to him again, and Clive Grantley was more visible in Salisbury. Amongst the people identified, one, probably two, were murderers.

Moulton had given his approval, the tickets had been purchased, the flight was later that day. Tremayne knew that he'd have to break it gently to Jean that the trip to the south of France was not a holiday and she wasn't going. He knew she'd understand, but she'd been the one wanting to travel, him resisting. So far, he had been to Singapore, and now France, and all she had had was a trip to the supermarket of a Saturday.

Clare was ambivalent about the trip. She had travelled around Europe with her parents, and then on school trips. Cultural tours to visit art galleries, a chance to immerse the pupils in the local languages. The pupils had seen it differently, and whereas most of them had been interested in the culture and the languages of the places they'd been to, the highlight for most had been getting drunk on the local wine, flirting with the local youths, one or two experiencing a cold marble floor underneath them, a more intimate exchange of cultural values.

Clare could admit to the first two, not the third, although her friend had had a rude awakening of cultural values when, nine months later, she had given birth.

***

Anthony Langley, calm when meeting Tremayne and
Clare, did not stay that way for long; not after receiving
word from Singapore that the reopened case into the
death of Veronica, his first wife, was likely to head into
hitherto unexplored areas.

The veneer that he had developed to protect
himself would crack under the modern surveillance
techniques used to look into financial dealings. He had
known Raymond Alston for the villain that he had been,
having sussed out the man early in his time in the former
British colony. Not all of Langley's contacts were above
suspicion. One of them, a casino owner in Macau, had a
gruesome record of dealing with those who opposed
him, a reputation of benevolence towards those who
helped him.

Langley pondered the situation at his mansion in
Cornwall; his wife nearby dutifully honouring her part of
the deal. Pretty though she was, he had to respect her too;
she was as mercenary as him.

If his dealings with the casino owner and one or
two others became known in England, his credibility
would be threatened. That was why he had passed them
over to the man the police now referred to as Richard
Grantley; forty per cent of a great deal was better than
nothing.

Grantley had played his part; played it well, up
until he had seduced his wife, Veronica, with his charm
and wit. Langley had known that it had hurt him, not
emotionally, not as much as it should have, but because
he was the man they laughed at behind his back. The man
whose wife would be there with him at the various
functions, at Government House, at home when they
were socialising. The perfect hostess, the attentive wife,

the trollop who lay on her back for Grantley, the two of them not aware that he noticed their exchanged looks, the gentle touching when they thought no one was looking. But he, Anthony Langley, always was.

He had decided to rid himself of her, but then Grantley made the ultimate error; he had become arrogant, and with arrogance comes sloppiness, failure to grease the correct palms, inattention to detail and failure to keep the records of who and what he was dealing with as secret as they should have been.

And then, no Grantley, only a distraught wife who had seen love. A reconciliation, professional help to deal with her loss and then her drinking and drugs. The marriage had lingered on; the intimacy no longer possible.

For him, the solution had been a succession of lovers, trips out of the country, the rendezvous where they would not be seen; Veronica oblivious to what he had been doing.

A private investigator had revealed that she had found someone else to take Grantley's place.

Her disappearance one night had caused a panic. A phone call to a chief inspector of Langley's acquaintance had ensured a thorough police investigation into the woman's movements, eventually leading to the water's edge, her handbag in a rubbish bin, the coat she had worn discarded at the scene, the open verdict recorded as suicide, though no note had ever been found.

Langley, suitably bereft and full of sorrow, had stayed another eight months in Singapore before relocating to England. A move that on reflection had been worthwhile, but now came the re-examination of Veronica's death, the questions, the suspicion, and Grantley dead in Salisbury, supposedly in a location where he should have never been discovered.

'Don't worry, Anthony,' Lady Langley said as she came over and sat by him, kissing him on the cheek.

'It's one more complication I don't need,' Langley's reply. He saw his second wife as decorative, and her comment, encouraging or otherwise, was not needed. She had a purpose in the relationship. As long as she kept to that, then she could stay. If she did not, then to hell with her.

Anthony Langley, for all his piety, was not a good man. He knew that Grantley had suspected it, Veronica had not cared, and his current wife neither had the intellect nor the wisdom to see the truth.

Langley picked up the phone and made a call.

***

Justin Ruxton never met Tremayne and Clare. He had been released on his own surety with explicit instructions to remain at his hotel. He had agreed, a French lawyer arguing his case.

The suicide letter found in his room stated that he was sorry, but he could not go on. He felt worthless, isolated and lonely. His struggles with bipolar and mood swings were documented: the depths of depression, the periods of normality, and as his letter stated, 'It all seems so pointless'.

Tremayne, as he sat in the hotel restaurant, saw it as further justification for the view that Des Wetherell was a murderer.

If Wetherell and Nigel Nicholson were guilty of murder in Dundee and a faked suicide in Nice, France, then that was a matter for the authorities in those two locations.

Ruxton's body was discovered later that day at the bottom of a cliff no more than five hundred yards from where Tremayne sat. Clare phoned Kim to find out about her mother.

'She's on the way to Cambridge. I'm with her,' Kim replied.

'Turn around, go back to Salisbury now,' Clare said forcefully.

'Mother won't be deterred.'

'Another person has died. The man worked for Wetherell.'

'Murder?'

'It's murder, we're sure of it, but there's a suicide letter. We must assume duress was applied. Stay with your mother if she won't listen to common sense.'

'I will, not that I can do much. Are you sure about this? Is it this dangerous?'

'It's dangerous in Salisbury, but I can ensure some protection at your father's house. I also suggest that you hire a security company. Not a cheap one out of the phone book, only the best.'

'Do you have a suggestion?'

'I'll text you one,' Clare said. 'Now, get your mother to turn around. This is serious. I don't want her dead, not now.'

With Liz returning to Salisbury, Clare rejoined Tremayne. With him was Inspecteur Michel Villedo, a smartly-dressed man who shook Clare's hand. His English was perfect, with a soothing French accent. He was an impressive man next to Tremayne, who after the flight and the disappointment sat in the early afternoon heat in his crumpled suit, his tie askew, although Clare wouldn't have changed him. The man was what he was, take him or leave him, and he was still the best investigative police officer she had met and the most dogged at following through to the conclusion of the murder enquiry.

'The body has been recovered,' Villedo said. 'The circumstances are suspicious.'

'Proof of murder?' Tremayne asked.

'There are signs of a scuffle at the top of the cliff, and the dead man had been drinking.'

'Is the drink relevant?'

'I phoned the local police where he lived in England. They checked, and Justin Ruxton, it has been confirmed, never drank alcohol, not even when he was at his most depressed.'

Both Tremayne and Clare were impressed by Villedo's proactive style of policing.

'Is the man's identity confirmed?'

'We phoned when he became of interest to us. His body had not been found then. His passport was in his room, and the face is still recognisable. It is him, even before we conduct the formal identification. I am afraid, Inspector Tremayne, that you and your sergeant have had a wasted trip.'

'It's not been wasted. The man was killed to stop him talking to us. It confirms our suspicion that Montgomery Yatton was killed on orders.'

'Do you know by who?'

'By who, no. For who, we do. The murder investigation will be with you and the Dundee police, an Inspector Fiona McAlpine,' Clare said.

After Inspecteur Villedo had departed, once again shaking Clare's hand, even kissing it gently, she phoned Fiona McAlpine to pass on the details and Villedo's contact number. She would feel flattered by the French inspector; Clare was sure of that.

Chapter 25

It had been five days since Tremayne and Clare had returned from France, and the Grantley murder case was stagnating. Outside Bemerton Road Police Station, the weather was poor, and a mist hung over the city.

Liz Fairweather was back at Clive Grantley's house and not enjoying it there. Clive was more visible in the city, having attended another council meeting, Kim by his side.

On the streets of Salisbury, the almost universal belief was that Clive could not have been responsible for his brother's death: 'such a nice man', 'a lovely daughter, so well brought up', 'the best mayor we've ever had' were the comments most often heard.

Fiona McAlpine had been down to the south of France to meet with Inspecteur Villedo, Clare teasing her after the woman had had her hand kissed as well.

'Yatton's not so easy to prove,' Fiona said.

'You're meeting with Des Wetherell?'

'The French police will be; I'll be with them. We can't prove a case against anyone for the death of Montgomery Yatton. Sorry, but that's the truth, and no one's likely to confess. Even the French police are not sure where to go with Ruxton's death. They'll try, of course, but what can they do at the end of the day?'

'Any clues as to who pushed him off the cliff?'

'According to Inspecteur Villedo, finding someone to commit murder is not the issue; not if you've got money.'

'Which Wetherell has. It appears that the man will remain free.'

'It's not the first time, is it?'

'More crimes are committed by those who make the laws than those who break them. The way of the world, unfortunately, but you and I will not change that. We still have the question of who killed Richard Grantley.'

'Another unsolvable crime?' Fiona said.

'Inspector Tremayne will never give up,' Clare said.

Tremayne, even though he had not been privy to the phone conversation between Clare and Fiona McAlpine, was considering the options. Wetherell and Nigel Nicholson were unlikely to make any mistakes that could link them to Grantley's death, and Clive Grantley had adopted an air of innocence which seemed unshakable; his earlier confession to Richard's murder was filed in the 'too stupid to be true' cabinet.

And as for Liz Fairweather, she was anxious to get back to Cambridge and her academic work, not to be confined to a house in Salisbury, a security company ensuring the premises were secured, the woman inside safe. She had spent her time compiling course notes, preparing lectures, discussing with her students over the internet.

Clare had met with Kim socially on one occasion, but not for long. It was still not time for Clare to tell Kim what had happened to Harry; that was for another time.

***

It was Inspector Ong who provided a breakthrough. His brief conversation with Tremayne was succinct. 'Get out here as soon as possible,' he said.

Tremayne had been sitting in the office, his knee troubling him on account of the damp weather. He remembered how much better he had felt with the heat on his body the last time in Singapore.

'What is it?' Tremayne asked.

'The investigation into Veronica Langley's death was badly handled. We've re-examined the case files, found inconsistencies. We're exhuming the woman in two days. It would be best if you're here while Pathology and Forensics check it out.'

'Is there much they can do after so many years?'

'You saw the photos after she was fished out of the harbour. But we've got modern technology on our side. It's worth a shot.'

Superintendent Moulton reluctantly agreed to another trip for Tremayne.

Tremayne left the police station at three in the afternoon and drove down Wilton Road towards his house and Jean. He found her in the kitchen.

'Pack your bags. We're going on a trip.'

'Where? For how long?'

Tremayne sat her down and explained that it wasn't customary to take the family along on a police investigation, but he had suggested it to Moulton, who had agreed. Ong had made it clear that Jean would be looked after by his wife while they were involved on official business.

Jean was excited, gave her husband a hug before rushing upstairs to pack. The flight to Singapore was at four in the afternoon the next day, the cost of Jean's ticket paid by Tremayne. He was pleased that she was going, but worried that her presence could encumber the investigation, although Inspector Ong was adamant that it would not.

Clare learnt of the trip after Jean had been told; she was delighted.

Not only was Tremayne taking Jean, but there was a possible breakthrough. Clare phoned Kim, more confident than ever that Clive was innocent. They arranged to meet at the weekend. Clare intended to drink more than she should.

***

Anthony Langley reacted with alarm at the news of the exhumation of his first wife. He had been informed officially as the next of kin.

His second wife tried to console him. It had not worked. Langley knew that for all her faults, Veronica had been a woman of substance who in her lucid moments he could turn to for advice. But the second wife, as pretty as she was, could offer no intelligent comment. Langley knew that he had married her out of loneliness, the need to have a woman in his life.

Sally Langley realised that she was only the icing on the cake, the adornment of a wealthy man, the country squire's wife.

She was trapped in a marriage where the love of one for the other was now a pretence; her husband had revealed the truth. Unable to rationalise the situation, she walked out of the front door of the house, got into her car and drove away. There was only one solution, she knew of: shopping. It would make her happy; it always had in the past.

Langley, free of the house, walked around the grounds of the mansion. He checked that the expansive garden was well maintained; he checked on the deer that roamed freely, the sheds where the gardening implements were stored, the outside of the mansion, but mostly he thought. He thought about Veronica and when they had first met. He remembered setting up the business in Singapore, how hard she had worked, and then the success, the wealth. But mostly he thought back to the later years, when he had been too busy to give her the attention she wanted, and then the drink and the drugs. And finally, Richard Grantley.

Langley looked around at all that he had. He wondered whether it had all been worth it. Life was a journey; a journey he had started on his own, a journey that he would end in a similar manner. He grabbed a small bag, his passport, and got into his Mercedes. It was a long drive to London, but it was quicker than taking the train.

***

Des Wetherell acknowledged the applause at the TUC general meeting. It was his first meeting as Deputy Secretary General; his last if the incumbent Secretary General stood down within the next year.

Wetherell had made an impassioned speech in defence of unionism and how it remained the buffer between the injustices of the past and the future: the children down the mines and in the sweatshops, always at the mercy of the money-grabbing and uncaring, ruthless aristocrats and landowners, the mine owners, the mill owners, the savage landlords who bled them dry, left them to rot. He spoke about the Tolpuddle Martyrs, humble agricultural labourers who in the nineteenth century had protested against the gradual lowering of agricultural wages, only to be sent as convicts to Australia for making an oath of allegiance to each other and their cause.

He spoke of Thatcherism and the ongoing battle to reduce the influence of the unions, to make them irrelevant when they were needed more than ever, as the living standards of many were threatened by a weakening economy, cheap imports, the restrictive trade practices of other countries.

Wetherell spoke for almost an hour, the audience riveted as the man told stories of the past, of the injustices committed against many, the sacrifices of some of them, the gains made by a few. Each and every time he hammered home a point, he paused to allow those listening to show their appreciation of him.

An astute observer of people and the lost identity of the United Kingdom, Wetherell had structured his speech accordingly. To him, it was not only a speech for the faithful; it was a party political broadcast, he the only candidate. It was to show the union movement that he was the man to succeed the Secretary General; it was to show that the choice of a safe seat for him to enter Parliament was critical. He had set himself one year, two years at the maximum with the TUC, another year as a member of her Majesty's loyal opposition, and then a cabinet post or the prime ministership.

As he sat down and took a sip from the glass of water in front of him, he realised that loose ends still needed to be dealt with. He messaged Nicholson from where he sat high above the membership, isolated from those whose support he needed. He despised many that he could see down there waving their banners, talking amongst themselves, working themselves into a fervour.

Wetherell knew that he was a political animal and that an animal uses whatever he can. Unionism would serve him well. It would give him what he wanted; it would give him what he had fought all his life for.

***

As fate would have it, while Tremayne and Jean were back in economy on the flight to Singapore, eating their meal off a plastic plate, at the front of the plane in first class, Anthony Langley ate the gourmet meal placed in front of him, a glass of champagne beside him in a champagne flute of the finest crystal.

It should have been Langley who was enjoying the flight the most, but it wasn't. It was Jean who was excited about the places she intended to visit, the shops she planned to explore. Tremayne was pleased for her, but full of trepidation that caution might be thrown to the wind and his meagre finances would be left with a hefty bill to pay afterwards.

He had become absorbed by her enthusiasm, although she was to see the beauty of Singapore, he was not. He was to see the long-dead remains of a woman, not a pleasant sight at any time.

Tremayne had seen Langley at London Airport as the first-class passengers were boarded first. He had looked his way, seen Tremayne standing there, a brief nod of the head from both men.

There was no reason for Langley not to be making the trip, Tremayne understood. It was, after all, his wife that was being removed from her resting place. Tremayne had no idea of what importance to attach to

Langley. Whether he was innocent or whether he had been responsible for Veronica's death. The truth would be revealed soon.

On arrival, Langley left in a chauffeur-driven limousine; Tremayne and Jean were met by Ong. That night they dined at Ong's house, Tremayne once again attempting to eat with chopsticks, Jean accomplishing it successfully.

The two men spoke of their respective investigations; the women spoke of what they were going to do the next day.

Tremayne had already had a brief encounter with the heat in the country and he handled that first day with Jean better than she did, although by the next morning, she was ready to get started, pleased that she was in the country.

Tremayne left with Ong for a brief visit to police headquarters to coordinate activities from the time of exhumation to completion.

At the headquarters, the news that Langley had obtained a court order delaying the exhumation of his wife's body. It was not unexpected.

There was only one action, Tremayne knew; he and Ong had to meet the man, attempt to instil in him that delaying tactics were just that. There was no way that he would ultimately succeed in holding up the exhumation by more than a few days.

That wasn't the exact truth, both Tremayne and Ong knew. If the man claimed a religious prerogative, a wish to maintain the dignity of his wife intact, a smart lawyer could string out the delay of the exhumation for months.

Before meeting Langley, Tremayne and Ong decided to visit some of Veronica Langley's friends. The only ones they could find, due to the expat nature of a lot of the English in Singapore, were a retired businessman and his wife.

They met them in their modest flat not far from the hotel where Tremayne and Jean were staying.

'We decided to stay on. The climate's good for my rheumatism,' Lilith Hempel said. She was a woman in her seventies, well-tanned, her skin taut on her face. Tremayne thought she had had a facelift.

'Veronica Langley, what can you tell us?' Tremayne asked.

'It was a long time ago.' The clipped speech of the woman was distracting, as though she affected her speech to impress.

Lilith Hempel's husband sat by her side. He was in poor health. Compared to his wife he looked fifteen to twenty years older, but the difference was only four. His complexion was pallid, and a walking frame was close by.

To Tremayne, the man had the look of impending death. George Hempel did not take part in the conversation.

'Whatever you can,' Ong said.

'Very well. We used to meet, a group of us, every Wednesday for tennis. She was an attractive woman, but then she changed.'

'Only on Wednesdays?'

'Most weekends at the club as well, but I can't say I knew her, not really.'

'Why's that?'

'She had hidden depths to her. She was a smart woman, though. If you wanted to know about geography or history, even archaeology, she would be able to tell you what you wanted to know. If we ever had a game of Trivial Pursuit at the club, I'd want her on my side.'

'Tell us about the archaeology. It was never mentioned at the time of her disappearance; not at the inquest after her body was found.'

'A dreadful business,' Lilith Hempel said. 'Dying like that.' She leaned over and wiped the dribble from her husband's chin. 'He'll never see England again,' she said.

'I'm sorry for your troubles,' Tremayne said.

'You spend life striving, trying to improve yourself, guiding your children, hoping they'll make good decisions with their lives, and then, what you see with George. Regressing back to his childhood.'

'You must be upset,' Ong said.

'My husband will not be here for much longer, and then I'll go and live with my sister in England. Sadness doesn't enter into it.'

Tremayne reflected that but for Jean and Clare, his life would be close to its end, but in Singapore, the sun beating on his back, he felt better than he had for a long time.

'Were you interviewed when she disappeared?'

'Not that I can remember. One day she was there; the next she wasn't. We always thought it was to do with the marriage.'

'What about the marriage?' Tremayne asked.

'Veronica had issues.'

'Substance abuse?'

'She was a drinker, even on our Wednesday get-togethers. I asked her once why she drank so much. Her reply, "because it makes me feel good".'

'Was that a sufficient answer?'

'It was the only one I was going to get. The expatriate community was insidious; plenty of unusual characters with hidden backgrounds, stories that would never be told. If Veronica didn't want to say more, that was fine by me.'

'Anthony Langley?'

'He was always polite, charming and generous. He'd buy the drinks at the weekend. We didn't see as much of him after Veronica disappeared. We heard he had a girlfriend somewhere, but we never saw her.'

'Coming back to Veronica. What else did you know about her?'

'Why the interest? You never said.'

'We have reason to dispute the circumstances surrounding her death.'

'George could have told you more about Anthony, but I'm afraid he's beyond telling you anything now.'

'What do you believe your husband would have told us?'

'He would have told you that Anthony was tolerant in accepting his wife's behaviour. George didn't like Veronica.'

'Did you?'

'It wasn't for me to judge. As I said, expatriate communities are insidious. Everyone has a tale to tell, skeletons they'd rather keep hidden.'

'Why the tolerance? You've said she was a drinker; we know she was more than that.'

'She was involved with Raymond Alston.'

'Involved?'

'An affair, screwing the man, whatever you want to call it. Everyone knew, but no one ever said anything.'

'You said she was smart. Tell us about archaeology.'

'She was always reading books on the subject, watching documentaries on the television. God knows why, but that was Veronica, a frustrated academic, I suppose.'

'You're aware that Raymond Alston, although his real name was Richard Grantley, is dead?'

'It's not been mentioned before. How?'

'He was murdered. Anthony Langley is in Singapore.'

'We've not heard from him. Why's he here?'

'We intend to exhume his wife's body.'

'But why? She committed suicide. She sometimes spoke about the futility of her life, especially after a few drinks. Do you think Anthony killed Raymond Alston?'

'Not yet,' Ong said. 'What else about archaeology and history?'

'She used to put pictures on her wall at home of ancient sites in England.'

'Stonehenge?' Tremayne asked, more intensely focussed than before.

'She had this hideous one of a burial mound. I don't know why; none of us liked it.'

Tremayne took out his phone and scrolled through the photos. He showed the picture of the burial mound to Lilith Hempel. 'That's it. Positively hideous, so depressing.'

'She gave it to Richard Grantley, sorry, Raymond Alston.'

'It's not much of a present.'

'It was on the back wall in his office. He didn't like it either.'

Chapter 26

Tremayne and Ong visited the Choa Chu Kang Cemetery Complex in the west of the island of Singapore, close to the Tengah Air Base, and now the only place that allowed burials in the island state.

Veronica Langley's grave was located in the Christian section, a small marble plaque with her name and dates inscribed on it. There were no other inscriptions, no mention of 'beloved wife' or 'sadly missed, never forgotten'.

It was, to Tremayne a sad grave. Fresh flowers rested on top of it.

'Langley's been here,' Ong said.

'Was it him?'

'I've got a person keeping an eye on him. Very discreetly, but from what we heard from Lilith Hempel and from what you've told me, the man must be frightened.'

'He would have been better staying in England. We can't prove that he killed Richard Grantley, and if it's found that Veronica Langley's death is a result of foul play, then extradition from England to Singapore would be difficult and could take years.'

'Even if we find proof of foul play, it doesn't mean that he was responsible. Quite frankly, I reckon we've got our job ahead of us.'

'Where is Langley now?'

'The Fullerton Bay Hotel on Collyer Quay. Way out of our salaries. He's taken a suite. He may be on a mission, but he's not going to do it on a shoestring.'

'His legal team?'

'The best. They'll hold up the exhumation for as long as they can. And then if we have proof of murder, they'll drag it out in the courts.'

'Which means he'll have to stay in Singapore.'

'Not necessarily, and besides, what are we going to confront him with? His wife disappears, she's subsequently found dead. She's an alcoholic, into recreational drugs, and she had a history of illicit love affairs.'

'Did she?'

'A smart lawyer will raise the possibility. From what I've found out, there was Grantley, and then after he left, another man.'

'A name?'

'One of her old friends may know.'

'What do you suggest?' Tremayne asked. It was good to have someone to bounce ideas off. In Salisbury, it would have been Clare, but she was back in England.

'We'll go and visit him,' Ong said. 'Lay the facts on the table, see what his reaction is.'

They found Langley on a recliner at the side of the hotel's infinity pool. He did not appreciate the intrusion, but he remained cordial.

Tremayne introduced Ong to the man, a shaking of hands.

'My lawyer is dealing with the matter,' Langley said. Which to Tremayne meant that he didn't intend to say too much.

'Do you need him here?' Ong asked.

'Not at this moment. I regard the desecration of Veronica's grave with alarm. I will object to it strenuously.'

'That is your legal right,' Tremayne said. 'However, we have uncovered more in the last couple of days that should be of concern to you.'

'Such as?' Langley said. Tremayne had met the man before; he knew of his arrogance, his self-belief. The man shouldn't be speaking to him and Ong, but it appeared that he was going to. A waiter walked by, Langley ordered a drink for himself, ignored the two police officers. It was to Tremayne a sign of implied strength, similar to sticking out the chest to make a person to look stronger than they actually were. It was a wasted exercise. Neither he nor Ong wanted to spend time drinking pina coladas with a man who was more than likely a murderer.

'Veronica was interested in history and archaeology.'

'In her more lucid moments. That's true. Is it relevant?'

'On the wall of your house, you had several pictures. One of them was of Stonehenge, a burial mound in the foreground.'

'I don't remember it, but it may have been there.'

'Richard Grantley was buried in a burial mound. There's a significance in that, wouldn't you agree?' Tremayne asked. He paused to allow Langley to digest what had just been said.

Langley took a sip from his drink, stood up from the recliner and dived into the pool. Tremayne and Ong did not move from where they were sitting, although they wished they could. The sun was beating down on their heads, and it was uncomfortably hot.

If Jean had been there, she would have made Tremayne move under a shade nearby. 'You'll get sunstroke, and then what will we have,' she would have said. Tremayne was glad she was not there, not when Langley attempted to act nonchalant; he and Ong intending to press the advantage.

Langley returned after five minutes and lay back on his recliner. 'Sorry about that. I needed to cool off.'

'And how long do you intend to stay in Singapore?' Ong asked.

'As long as necessary. My business will continue without my constant input. Now if you don't mind, I would appreciate being alone.'

'Lady Langley, is she well?' Tremayne asked.

'She is in England. This does not concern her.'

'It will if you are arrested for murder, won't it?' Tremayne had crossed the line between questioning and intimidation. He expected Langley's reaction to be immediate and for the man to retreat from the pool and to the security of his room.

There was no visible reaction as Langley calmly said, 'Are you accusing me of killing Grantley?'

'I'm more interested in Veronica,' Ong said. 'After Grantley left, why did you and she stay together for so long. Her affair with the man was well known, and you must have been a laughing stock.'

'You will find out, or maybe you know already, that I am not a man who cares what other people think of me. Veronica had her faults, we all do, but I had loved her, still do.'

'Lady Langley?'

'The current Lady Langley knows her place. I hope that you two do.'

'Veronica gave a picture to Richard Grantley, or as Inspector Ong knows him, Raymond Alston. I put it to you,' Tremayne said, 'that you are a vengeful man, and that murder is not only the act, but it is also a statement.

You're also a man who cares what other people think, regardless of your insistence to the contrary.'

'This is nonsense. Please leave,' Langley said as he picked up his phone.

'I would suggest you hear me out. This act of indignation does you no credit. You want to know where we stand with the investigation into the two crimes. You want to make decisions based on facts. Facts that we have.'

Ong did not like the direction that Tremayne was taking. He respected the English police inspector, but a confession made under duress would not hold up in Singapore, and a poolside interview would be discredited, any information obtained deemed inadmissible.

Ong's concerns did not worry Tremayne. He was on a roll; he was not going to stop.

'Richard Grantley had dented your invulnerability. You had watched Veronica transfer her affections from you to him. You did nothing, waiting for the ideal time to act, not sure what to do. And then the man left Singapore, his departure at short notice. It may be that you were somehow involved with that.'

'He was gone; Veronica was back with me. We staggered on for a long time, but she was a weak person. She would drink and take drugs, but that's already known and on the public record. And yes, I was angry with the man, wished him harm. But that's a long way from murder.'

'Not that far. Grantley's gone, but not forgotten. Somehow, you must have discovered his true name. You find him in England; you exact your revenge. That awful picture that no one liked, but which Veronica had, and which she had given to Grantley, the poetic justice that you craved.'

'It makes no sense.'

'As you say, it makes no sense, not unless the murderer is a control freak. Are you that sort of person? Would the current Lady Langley agree with my definition of you? Would Veronica have? Is that what drove her to destroy herself, to have an affair with Grantley? We know the man could be charming, but he was not a decent person. He was callous and unfeeling, and to him, Veronica was just a plaything, the affair something to rub your nose in. He would have enjoyed seeing your friends, business colleagues, laughing at you behind your back. Anthony Langley, tell us straight, did they laugh?'

'Of course they did. There is one factor that you've not taken into account. I loved Veronica. We were together during the early days when we had no money, only a lot of ideas.'

'The connection between you and Grantley has been made; the picture of the mound the final link. It is only your confession that is needed.'

'You have no proof, and let me reiterate, I did not kill the man. I hated him, but that's not murder, and you know it.'

Tremayne did. All the evidence pointing towards Anthony Langley as the murderer of Richard Grantley was circumstantial. It would have been enough to bring the man into Bemerton Road Police Station for questioning. However, without concrete proof, the progression to a murder trial would never occur.

***

Clare met with Kim one day earlier than planned. A phone call from Singapore had convinced both her and

Tremayne that Clive Grantley and Liz Fairweather were innocent of the murder of Kim's long-dead uncle.

It was premature, Clare realised, and further evidence could well come forward to point the murder investigation in another direction, but the need for her to unburden herself of the past was paramount.

With the turning down of Harry's photo on her dressing table at home, with the guilt she had felt over his death finally lifted, with the need to move on with her life, the time was right for her to tell someone. She was pleased that it was Kim.

The two women met in the Pheasant Inn, where they had met before. Clare had left her car at the police station; she would be too inebriated to consider driving. She felt emotional yet nervous. A sense of trepidation, a sense of fear about what she was about to reveal. The dark clouds, the lightning, the rustling of the leaves in the wind, the deaths that had occurred, still fresh in her mind.

Kim had also chosen not to drive, although the walk from her father's house in the Cathedral Close was a lot closer than Clare's home in Stratford sub Castle.

For some time, the women just spoke in general terms. Kim about how her mother was dealing with the confinement in Salisbury, away from where she wanted to be in Cambridge with her books and her students, in her untidy house.

Clare told Kim about her life growing up in Norfolk; a father that she was fond of, a mother who she cared for, but not with the love that she thought she should have for her. How her mother was always matchmaking, telling her to stop wasting her time with an old man, to stop being a police officer and to accept that the normality of a home and a family were more important than chasing after criminals.

Kim listened attentively, aware that today was not for her to talk about herself and her blossoming romance in Salisbury; the fact that she thought it was love, and if it was, then it would be the white wedding.

It was on the second glass of wine that Clare started to talk. A pub lunch was on its way, and Clare was beginning to feel the effects of the alcohol. She realised that the drink had been a crutch; she didn't need it now. She put her wine to one side.

'It was my first case with Inspector Tremayne,' Clare said. 'A body in a house up on Castle Road. You may have read about the case.'

'There are plenty of references to it on the internet; even to you. It's your story I want to hear, though.'

'The body wasn't there, just the legs. The man had been a heavy drinker and a smoker, obese as well. The verdict was that he had set himself on fire and because he was old and infirm, and clearly overweight, he had just burnt out. You would not believe the temperatures involved.'

'But nothing else was burnt.'

'Nothing. The man had burnt from within. It wasn't my first dead body, but it was the one that affected me the most. It was during the investigation that I met Harry. He was the landlord of the Deer's Head. At first, I thought he was just working behind the bar that night, but it turned out that he had inherited it from his parents. It was Inspector Tremayne's favourite pub at the time.'

'Now?'

'Neither of us enters it. After the first death, there were murmurings of strange rituals, pagan beliefs.'

'Did you believe them?'

'A total sceptic, at first; but then there were blasts of cold air when they weren't expected, the lightning striking the house of an old lady that I had become fond of. She was murdered, face down in a water trough at the back of her house, a few days later.'

'Avon Hill?'

'How much have you read?'

'When Clive's body was found, and you and Inspector Tremayne started questioning us, mother took it on herself to research you and the inspector.'

'As the investigation progressed, Harry and I fell in love. I was spending increasing amounts of time with him, sometimes at my place, sometimes upstairs at the pub. We were, barring our respective responsibilities, inseparable.'

'Something changed?'

'There were more deaths which led us to Avon Hill. A vicar at the church in Stratford sub Castle, not far from where I live, told us of strange events. We were there with him in the church when the door slammed, and an eerie feeling came over the building. Tremayne always scoffed at such nonsense, and so did I, at first.'

'What made you change your mind?'

'The old lady I mentioned. I was in the house when it was struck by lightning. It may have just been a freak occurrence, but it scared me, and then the vicar hanged himself in the church. It's not been used since.'

'Avon Hill?'

'The clues kept pointing back to the village. The village at the end of the track like you see in horror movies. That was Avon Hill. It was an incestuous place, a core group of families from centuries past, people who had not travelled out of there apart from schooling and the occasional shopping trip. Each time we went there, we felt the enmity of the villagers. They would huddle in the pub, small groups talking in low voices when we were there. If we spoke of strange happenings and mysterious disappearances, they would talk to us in a roundabout manner. "Old wives' tales", "You don't want to believe in that sort of thing". But we did. Not in the supernatural or pagan gods, but in the mysterious. The old woman in the water trough, her husband had disappeared, never found. It was the vicar who told us some things; the woman some more, but she was mortally afraid.'

'Do you believe?'

'Did you ever watch a late-night horror movie? One so scary that for a few hours you were putting the light on in a room before you entered it, looking under the bed, just in case?'

'I would have.'

'That's what it was like. You knew there was nothing that couldn't be explained, but you were still frightened, unable to rationalise it. The mind can play powerful tricks on us.'

'Harry?'

Clare took a sip of her wine, finished her meal.

'We were discussing our future together, getting married. I didn't know for a long time that Harry's family traced its ancestry back through Avon Hill.

'There was enough evidence to investigate the area behind the church in Avon Hill. A wooded area and we believed there were bodies there. We brought in a full team of crime scene investigators and secured the area. It was at night when the trouble occurred. It started to snow heavily, the roads out of the village were impassable. Our phones weren't working, and we had sent one of the uniforms in a car to try and get further assistance for us.'

269

'You could have stayed in the pub or the church,' Kim said.

'We could, but the investigators had started finding bodies. The evidence against the village was damning. The rituals, gods or no gods, were malevolent, people had been killed, and more than one person was responsible. The pub was up the road, its lights on. And then a group of men started coming down the road. They had masks on; they were chanting. The investigators took off across the fields, one didn't make it. It was Tremayne and me and two uniforms. As the men got closer, we could see the evil in their eyes.'

'But why? This is the twenty-first century.'

'The question to us wasn't why. It was who. We had long suspected one of the villagers as being the leader, and old beliefs die hard. Most are harmless, but some are not.'

'Devil worshippers?'

'Not devils, ancient gods of England. Okay, you can make light of it, so can I now.'

'Where does Harry come into this?'

'The situation was grim. We knew that people had been killed before; we knew that deaths had occurred that night. We got into one of the police cars, the four of us, and drove through the mob. Unable to take the main road, we took a side road. We drove as far as we could and then on foot hurried up to Cuthbert's Wood at the crest of the hill.

'We were ahead of those following by a long way, and in the distance, we could see the car lights on a busy road down below. We set out through the wood, becoming hopelessly lost. By that time, those following had caught up with us. We were restrained, and the leader was driving them into a frenzy. We can only put it down to centuries of isolation, the impact of the twentieth and twenty-first centuries not able to overcome the beliefs of the past. Apart from that, they were all mad.'

'What happened then?' Kim asked.

Clare realised that she was being unemotional as she told the story. As if it had happened to someone else; as though it was only fiction.

'The mob chose me to die. They had knives. Tremayne was furiously trying to free himself, as were the uniforms. My time was up, I knew it.

'And then one of the group told them to stop, to disobey the leader. It was Harry. He had been there all along. He was one of those who had indulged in murdering others. It was he who was going to save me. A fight broke out between those who wanted me to die and those who wanted me to live. The secret of the village had been revealed; there was no way that they could keep the outside world away from them forever. Avon Hill was hardly Brigadoon.'

Kim smiled at the comparison of the violent Avon Hill with the fantasy sugary-sweet Scottish village.

'Harry saved me, saved us. Outside of Cuthbert's Wood, we were soon joined by other police and an ambulance. Harry had not come out. He was a murderer, that was known, and he would not be free again. Tremayne told me not to go back into the wood, but I had to. I had to understand. I found him in there sitting quietly. He got up to meet me, but a branch from a tree fell on him. He died there, the branch piercing his chest.'

Kim's earlier smile had been replaced by a tear.

'That's the story,' Clare said. 'I will never speak of it again.' She ordered a brandy each for her and Kim; they both needed it.

Chapter 27

Anthony Langley's disappearance from his hotel in Singapore was not altogether unexpected. Tremayne had thought that after laying out the investigation to Langley beside the hotel's swimming pool, the man would react.

The first that anyone was aware that he had gone was at a hearing into the exhumation of Veronica Langley; the opportunity for the police to put forward their case, the time for Langley's lawyers to raise their objections.

Langley's non-attendance caused his lawyers to ask for an adjournment, which was granted. Tremayne could see them attempting to contact the man. His presence wasn't vital, but it would have lent strength to their argument.

Tremayne and Ong, noticing Langley's no-show, had phoned the hotel, found out that he had checked out. Further investigation had shown that he had taken a flight to Thailand. From Bangkok, the man had headed north and disappeared. There was no case against him, but because he had been so determined to prevent his wife's exhumation and had then left the country in haste, the police efforts to exhume the body intensified.

Langley's lawyers withdrew their services four days after the court appearance. With the money deposited in their trust fund by Langley exhausted, they had no intention of continuing.

On the seventh day after Langley had left the country, the body of Veronica Langley was raised from her grave. Two days later, Pathology submitted their report. The effects of the extended period in Singapore Harbour and the body's time in the ground meant that standard testing for DNA and poisons was not possible. Ong knew that already.

Tremayne realised the remains that he viewed, barely human in appearance, would challenge the most competent pathologist, but the facilities and expertise in Singapore were first class.

'What can you tell us that wasn't known before?' Tremayne asked the pathologist.

'There's no question that these are the remains of Veronica Langley. The cause of death was originally stated as suicide. That was based on no other extenuating circumstances.'

'It was not known that her husband may be implicated in a murder in England,' Tremayne said.

'Precisely,' the pathologist said. 'Our initial examination of the body was thorough. However, advances in technology allow us to examine a body in more detail than would have been possible when the woman died.'

'Are you saying that you've found proof of murder?'

'That is not what I said, Inspector.'

'My apologies. What have you found?'

'Disregarding the new evidence, it must be remembered that the initial examination of the woman's body was to ascertain the cause of death. There was no concern raised at that time that she may have died as a result of violence. The DNA testing was not as well advanced, either.'

'This investigation is not a reflection on either you or your profession,' Ong said. 'It is only the facts that we need. Whether we have enough to change the woman's cause of death from suicide to murder.'

'The answer is not that positive. We have found skeletal trauma on the skull consistent with a heavy object. However, that could have been caused in the water with the current slamming the body up against rocks. Also, there are signs of skeletal trauma on the body, the eighth rib. I should caution you from drawing conclusions from these. The body had been in the water for a long time. It's possible that the damage is the result of natural action.'

'But it could be murder?'

'It's possible.'

Two days later, Tremayne and Jean left the heat of Singapore for the inclement weather of Salisbury. Jean had enjoyed herself and was more determined than ever that she and Tremayne would wander the globe as latter-day Marco Polos. For Tremayne, he was disappointed that the cause of Veronica Langley's death remained unknown, although, with what he knew of Langley, what experience told him, the man was capable of murder. He had either killed two people or one. The number wasn't important; apprehending the man was.

***

In Salisbury, the murder investigation ground slowly to a halt. Tremayne and Clare continued to go over the evidence, the possible suspects, but each time the clues led back to Anthony Langley. Clare had been down to Cornwall to meet the man's wife. She was a happier woman without the presence of her husband.

'I can't believe him capable of murder,' the young woman said.

'You're married to him. Have you ever seen signs of anger or violence?' Clare asked. Without her husband present, Lady Langley preferred to be addressed as Sally. Clare thought the name suited her, and she could see why she had been successful as a model, and why a man such as Langley would have chosen her.

'Sometimes he would be dismissive of me as if I wasn't smart enough for him.'

'You're a smart woman, Sally.'

'I was smart enough to marry a wealthy man. We both knew what our marriage was. He wanted me on his arm; I wanted a man who could provide for me. Love is for those who can afford it. I grew up on a council housing estate. It was a tough upbringing: a drunken father, a weak mother.'

'It's not an uncommon story.'

'It probably isn't. My sister, prettier than me, is stuck there, three children, an abusive husband. Regardless of what we say, we repeat the mistakes of our elders. My sister fell into the trap; I was determined not to. Modelling was my way out; Anthony, my salvation.'

'No love?'

'A different kind of love.'

Clare could only reflect that with Harry it had been an intense romantic love, but she was getting older. She was ready to compromise the love that came from respect and closeness.

If Anthony Langley came back, then Sally would have to deal with it. But she would, the same as Clare knew that she would deal with whatever life threw at her.

***

Tremayne had finally been forced to admit to the pain in his knee. In Singapore, it had improved, but the underlying ache had remained. As expected, Jean had taken him to the doctor; Tremayne continuing to say it was a waste of time.

The doctor had not agreed and tests had revealed that he was suffering from mild osteoarthritis, and that exercise coupled with rest would assist. Also, he took to wearing a compressive bandage on the knee. He had to admit that it all helped, apart from the nightly walk around the area. After a hard day at work, all he really wanted was good English home cooking, Jean by his side, a pint of beer down the pub.

It was in the fourth week since Langley's disappearance that Clare received a phone call from Sally, Lady Langley.

'Can you come down? Bring your Inspector,' Sally said.

'What is it?'

'Anthony phoned. I don't know where from.'

'We can check.'

'It was a Skype call.'

'Probably not, then. Where are you?'

'At the mansion. If he comes here, I don't know what to do.'

'Do you have somewhere else that you can go?'

'I have a friend, but I don't think I should be with him, not if Anthony's returning.'

Clare realised that Sally Langley needed a man in her life, whether it was Anthony or not, rich or poor.

'Go now. Is he watching you?'

'I wouldn't know. I'm frightened to leave the house.'

'We can't be there for three hours.' Clare phoned the police station nearest to the Langley mansion, asked them to station a patrol car at the premises.

Tremayne had a doctor's appointment which was cancelled at short notice, and Clare already had an overnight bag in her car, just in case. They called in at Tremayne's house, Jean at the gate with a bag for her husband.

The trip down to Cornwall took longer than expected; close to four hours, an accident on the M5 motorway near to Burnham-on-Sea in Somerset.

As they drove, Tremayne checked with immigration. Anthony Langley had landed at London's Heathrow Airport at 8.45 that morning. It was 6.20 p.m. when the two arrived at the front door of the impressive mansion. The patrol car was parked outside the building, one officer in the vehicle, the other in the mansion with Sally Langley.

'Am I glad to see you,' Sally said. 'Sergeant York and Constable Jones have made sure that I'm safe.'

'You've taken another lover?' Clare asked.

'He's a good man,' Sally said.

'He's a target, so are you,' Tremayne said. 'Your husband is in the country. He arrived this morning. Time enough to have made it to Cornwall.'

'Will he come here?'

'It seems logical. A migrating bird always returns to the same place. This is his home; this is where he'll want to be.'

'He'll not want to be arrested.'

'That's a hurdle we'll cross when we come to it.'

Outside Sergeant York got out of the patrol car. He walked around the grounds, checking. It was going to be a cold night, the probability there'd be a frost on the ground in the morning. All those in the house knew that Langley would reappear at some stage.

Tremayne phoned Ong in Singapore to tell him about the developments. Ong updated him that the investigation into the death of Veronica Langley was to be put on the backburner. With no sign of her husband, no further evidence, then the case was cold.

Tremayne understood the actions being taken in Singapore; he had seen murderers go free over the years due to no evidence; some had even gone on to murder others. It was the legal system that he believed in; the system that sometimes got it wrong. The system that could still see Anthony Langley walk free.

As Sally prepared a meal for all those at the mansion, the local police officers as well, it was Sergeant York who came bursting into the kitchen. 'Where is Inspector Tremayne?' he asked.

'In the other room.'

Tremayne and Clare, on hearing the voice of the sergeant, came into the kitchen.

'In the shed, around the back.'

Sally ceased what she was doing and dashed out; Clare in hot pursuit. Tremayne, not as nimble, kept up as best he could.

'Sally, stop. You don't know what you're walking into,' Clare shouted.

'She'll not come to any harm, Sergeant,' Sergeant York said. He was standing by the door of the shed. He grabbed hold of Sally as she tried to enter. 'It's better if you don't.'

Clare, appreciative of the sergeant's strong arms, entered the shed. A lawnmower was to one side. On the shelves were jars of nuts and bolts, a wheelbarrow was upended against a far wall. On a wooden chair sat

Anthony Langley. His head was resting on a wooden bench, his legs were askew.

Tremayne entered, quickly accessed the situation, and left.

'I'm afraid your husband is dead,' he said to Sally.

The woman burst into tears, desperate to see her husband. It was Clare who grabbed her the second time, the woman not resisting as she had before. Clare led her back to the main house.

'You've called an ambulance?' Tremayne asked.

'And our crime scene team,' Sergeant York said.

'Good job. Messy business, though.'

'Suicide?'

'The cuts on his wrists, I'd say so.'

It was another ninety minutes before Tremayne re-entered the shed. This time he was kitted out in coveralls, overshoes and nitrile gloves. The senior crime scene investigator handed over a letter written in Langley's hand. It was enclosed in a clear plastic bag; it was readable with difficulty without removing it.

Tremayne took the letter to the mansion. Clare and Sally Langley sat close to one another; Clare giving support to Sally who was very emotional. 'I did love him, you know.'

Clare knew that she had in her own way. And as the letter was read, it was clear that Anthony Langley had reciprocated her love.

Tremayne cleared his throat, trying, as always, to hide his emotions.

I write this in the hope that there can be forgiveness for what I have done. I loved Veronica intensely, Sally with an enduring passion. It was Grantley, or Alston as we knew him, who destroyed what we had in Singapore. Veronica was a person who thrived on attention, and I had let her down.

Grantley filled the vacuum in her life. I accepted it for a long time, and I had hoped that she would have tired of the man, but then he left. Life moved on as it always does, but Veronica still suffered from the frailties that blighted her. The second time she strayed, I had to do something. We were out on the harbour in our boat. It was night time. We started arguing, Veronica out of control, drunk as usual. She lunged at me, and she fell over, falling on a fishing knife, and then getting up and banging her head on a capstan. I tried to save her, but she died in my arms. I then put her over the side of the boat, knowing full well that blame for what had happened would fall on me.

Grantley was not an accident. I had followed him to England. I could not accept the humiliation he had caused me; the emotional conflict he had inflicted on Veronica.

And yes, Inspector Tremayne, if you are reading this. It was that depressing picture. I killed Grantley in London and transported the body to Wiltshire. It was not that hard to find a suitable place to bury him. That picture became the focus of my anger. Each time in his office, there it was on the wall, not even in reception but hiding around the back.

I needed to make a statement, not to anyone else, but to myself. It was a perfect crime, so I thought, but I did not count on the body being disturbed.

For the last few weeks, I have been in a remote location in Thailand, pondering the future. But there is no future without hope, no life without love. Sally, I thank you for the time we spent together, but I could never come back, not the way it could have been.

I returned to the place that I loved most in the world with the intent of ending what had been started. If this letter is being read now, then I have been successful.

'It's signed at the bottom,' Tremayne said.

It was not how Tremayne and Clare had expected the murder of Richard Grantley to be solved, but solved it had been. There would be no arrests made; the confession in Langley's letter made it clear that he had indeed killed the man.

Both Tremayne and Clare spent the night in the mansion, Sally staying close to Clare.

The next day, Sally left the house and returned to her mother's council house. She had not seen her for five years.

Langley was buried in the local churchyard, a quiet ceremony with only Sally, Tremayne, Clare and Jean in attendance. Jean had insisted, as she felt that after her time in Singapore, she was an integral member of the team.

Richard Grantley, his burial long delayed while the murder investigation progressed, was given the honour of a funeral service in Salisbury Cathedral, not that he necessarily deserved it. There were over a hundred people there; not for Richard, but out of respect for Clive.

A reception was held at Clive's house later that day after Richard had been finally buried in the family plot. The black sheep of the family would only be remembered in death as a Grantley, not as what he had been in life. Of those who had been at the cathedral service, sixty of them were at the house, drinking and laughing and reminiscing, but only Clive and the man who had sold Richard the jacket could remember him. It was a sad indictment of the murdered man's life.

Eventually, the guests left, some the worse for the alcohol, all impressed with Clive and his daughter; also, with her mother.

Only the Grantley family, Clare, Tremayne and Jean remained.

Tremayne knew the truth. After all, that was what he had been trained to do: to observe, to pick up the body language, the secret signs that people make to each other. He had not told Jean what he knew as Clive rose to speak.

'This is addressed to Tremayne and Jean, as the others know what I am to say. Liz is to return to Cambridge tomorrow. We believe that she has nothing to fear. As for Kim, she will stay here in Salisbury with her boyfriend. As for me, my story is well known. Kim is now an adult, and I have honoured the agreement I made willingly with Liz to look after our daughter to the best of my abilities; to not confuse it with another relationship, not to get married, not to become involved in any romance.

'Today, I am pleased to say that the pledge I made all those years ago no longer applies. I have asked Clare to marry me; she has agreed.'

Jean burst into tears; Tremayne leaned over to Clare and whispered in her ear, 'Your mother?'

'She'll hate it. Clive's nineteen years older than me. He'll never let me down, and Kim and Liz are family to me now.'

Clare went and joined Clive, her arm in his.

'How long have you known?' Jean asked Tremayne.

'The signs have been visible for some time. I wasn't expecting marriage, but there you are. It's not often we get a happy ending.'

The End.

ALSO BY THE AUTHOR

Death in the Village – A DI Tremayne Thriller

Nobody liked Gloria Wiggins, a woman who regarded anyone who did not acquiesce to her jaundiced view of the world with disdain. James Baxter, the previous vicar, had been one of those, and her scurrilous outburst in the church one Sunday had hastened his death.

And now, years later, the woman was dead, hanging from a beam in her garage. Detective Inspector Tremayne and Sergeant Clare Yarwood had seen the body, interviewed the woman's acquaintances, and even those who had hated her.

None professed to having murdered her, but when the body count starts to rise, secrets start to be revealed.

Death by a Dead Man's Hand – A DI Tremayne Thriller

A flawed heist of forty gold bars from a security van late at night. One of the perpetrators is killed by his brother as they argue over what they have stolen.

Eighteen years later, the murderer, released after serving his sentence for his brother's murder, waits in a church for a man purporting to be the brother he killed. And then he too is killed.

The threads stretch back a long way, and now more people are dying in the search for the missing gold bars.

Detective Inspector Tremayne, his health causing him concern, and Sergeant Clare Yarwood, still seeking romance, are pushed to the limit solving the murder, attempting to prevent any more.

Death at Coombe Farm – A DI Tremayne Thriller

A warring family. A disputed inheritance. A recipe for death.

If it hadn't been for the circumstances, Detective Inspector Keith Tremayne would have said the view was outstanding. Up high, overlooking the farmhouse in the valley below, the panoramic vista of Salisbury Plain stretching out beyond. The only problem was that near where he stood with his sergeant, Clare Yarwood, there was a body, and it wasn't a pleasant sight.

Death and the Lucky Man – A DI Tremayne Thriller

Sixty-eight million pounds and dead. Hardly the outcome expected for the luckiest man in England the day his lottery ticket was drawn out of the barrel. But then, Alan Winters' rags-to-riches story had never been conventional, and there were those who had benefited, but others who hadn't.

Death and the Assassin's Blade – A DI Tremayne Thriller

It was meant to be high drama, not murder, but someone's switched the daggers. The man's death took place in plain view of two serving police officers.

He was not meant to die; the daggers were only theatrical props, plastic and harmless. A summer's night, a production of Julius Caesar amongst the ruins of an Anglo-Saxon fort. Detective Inspector Tremayne is there with his sergeant, Clare Yarwood. In the assassination scene, Caesar collapses to the ground. Brutus defends his actions; Mark Antony rebukes him.

They're a disparate group, the amateur actors. One's an estate agent, another an accountant. And then there is the teenage school student, the gay man, the funeral director. And what about the women? They could be involved.

They've each got a secret, but which of those on the stage wanted Gordon Mason, the actor who had portrayed Caesar, dead?

Death Unholy – A DI Tremayne Thriller

All that remained were the man's two legs and a chair full of greasy and fetid ash. Little did DI Keith Tremayne know that it was the beginning of a journey into the murky world of paganism and its ancient rituals. And it was going to get very dangerous.

'Do you believe in spontaneous human combustion?' Detective Inspector Keith Tremayne asked.

'Not me. I've read about it. Who hasn't?' Sergeant Clare Yarwood answered.

'I haven't,' Tremayne replied, which did not surprise his young sergeant. In the months they had been working together, she had come to realise that he was a man who had little interest in the world. When he had a cigarette in his mouth, a beer in his hand, and a murder to solve he was about the happiest she ever saw him, but even then he could hardly be regarded as one of life's most sociable people. And as for reading? The most he managed was an occasional police report, an early morning newspaper, turning first to the back pages for the racing results.

Murder in Hyde Park – A DCI Cook Thriller

An early morning jogger is murdered in Hyde Park. It's the centre of London, but no one saw him enter the park, no one saw him die.

He carries no identification, only a water-logged phone. As the pieces unravel, it's clear that the dead man had a history of deception.

Is the murderer one of those that loved him? Or was it someone with a vengeance?

It's proving difficult for DCI Isaac Cook and his team at Challis Street Homicide to find the guilty person – not that they'll cease to search for the truth, not even after one suspect confesses.

Murder has no Guilt – A DCI Cook Thriller

No one knows who was the target or why, but there are eight dead. The men seem the most likely, or could have it been one of the two women, the attractive Gillian Dickenson, or even the celebrity-obsessed Sal Maynard?

There's a gang war brewing, and if there are deaths, it doesn't matter to them as long as it's not them. But to Detective Chief Inspector Isaac Cook, it's his area of London, and it does.

It's dirty and unpredictable, and initially, it had been the West Indian gangs. But then a more vicious Romanian gangster had usurped them. And now he's being marginalised by the Russians. And the leader of the most vicious Russian mafia organisation is in London, and he's got money and influence, the ear of those in power.

Murder of a Silent Man – A DCI Cook Thriller

No one gave much credence to the man when he was alive. In fact, most people never knew who he was, although those who had lived in the area for many years recognised the tired-looking and shabbily-dressed man as he shuffled along, regular as clockwork on a Thursday afternoon at seven in the evening to the local off-licence. It was always the same: a bottle of whisky, premium brand, and a packet of cigarettes. He paid his money over the counter, took hold of his plastic bag containing his purchases, and then walked back down the road with the same rhythmic shuffle. He said not one word to anyone on the street or in the shop.

Murder in Room 346 – A DCI Cook Thriller

'Coitus interruptus, that's what it is,' Detective Chief Inspector Isaac Cook said. On the bed, in a downmarket hotel in Bayswater, lay the naked bodies of a man and a woman.

'Bullet in the head's not the way to go,' Larry Hill, Isaac Cook's detective inspector, said. He had not expected such a flippant comment from his senior, not when they were standing near to two people who had, apparently in the final throes of passion, succumbed to what appeared to be a professional assassination.

'You know this will be all over the media within the hour,' Isaac said.

'James Holden, moral crusader, a proponent of the sanctity of the marital bed, man and wife. It's bound to be.'

Murder in Notting Hill – A DCI Cook Thriller

One murderer, two bodies, two locations, and the murders have been committed within an hour of each other.

They're separated by a couple of miles, and neither woman has anything in common with the other. One is young and wealthy, the daughter of a famous man; the other is poor, hardworking and unknown.

Isaac Cook and his team at Challis Street Police Station are baffled about why they've been killed. There must be a connection, but what is it?

Murder is the Only Option – A DCI Cook Thriller

A man, thought to be long dead, returns to exact revenge against those who had blighted his life. His only concern is to protect his wife and daughter. He will stop at nothing to achieve his aim.

'Big Greg, I never expected to see you around here at this time of night.'

'I've told you enough times.'

'I've no idea what you're talking about,' Robertson replied. He looked up at the man, only to see a metal pole coming down at him. Robertson fell down, cracking his head against a concrete kerb.

Two vagrants, no more than twenty feet away, did not stir and did not even look in the direction of the noise. If they had, they would have seen a dead body, another man walking away.

Murder in Little Venice – A DCI Cook Thriller

A dismembered corpse floats in the canal in Little Venice, an upmarket tourist haven in London. Its identity is unknown, but what is its significance?

DCI Isaac Cook is baffled about why it's there. Is it gang-related, or is it something more?

Whatever the reason, it's clearly a warning, and Isaac and his team are sure it's not the last body that they'll have to deal with.

Murder is Only a Number – A DCI Cook Thriller

Before she left she carved a number in blood on his chest. But why the number 2, if this was her first murder?

The woman prowls the streets of London. Her targets are men who have wronged her. Or have they? And why is she keeping count?

DCI Cook and his team finally know who she is, but not before she's murdered four men. The whole team are looking for her, but the woman keeps disappearing in plain sight. The pressure's on to stop her, but she's always one step ahead.

And this time, DCS Goddard can't protect his protégé, Isaac Cook, from the wrath of the new commissioner at the Met.

Murder House – A DCI Cook Thriller

A corpse in the fireplace of an old house. It's been there for thirty years, but who is it?

It's murder, but who is the victim and what connection does the body have to the previous owners of the house. What is the motive? And why is the body in a fireplace? It was bound to be discovered eventually but was that what the murderer wanted? The main suspects are all old and dying, or already dead.

Isaac Cook and his team have their work cut out trying to put the pieces together. Those who know are not talking because of an old-fashioned belief that a family's dirty laundry should not be aired in public, and never to a policeman – even if that means the murderer is never brought to justice!

Murder is a Tricky Business – A DCI Cook Thriller

A television actress is missing, and DCI Isaac Cook, the Senior Investigation Officer of the Murder Investigation Team at Challis Street Police Station in London, is searching for her.

Why has he been taken away from more important crimes to search for the woman? It's not the first time she's gone missing, so why does everyone assume she's been murdered?

There's a secret, that much is certain, but who knows it? The missing woman? The executive producer? His eavesdropping assistant? Or the actor who portrayed her fictional brother in the TV soap opera?

Murder Without Reason – A DCI Cook Thriller

DCI Cook faces his greatest challenge. The Islamic State is waging war in England, and they are winning.

Not only does Isaac Cook have to contend with finding the perpetrators, but he is also being forced to commit actions contrary to his mandate as a police officer.

And then there is Anne Argento, the prime minister's deputy. The prime minister has shown himself to be a pacifist and is not up to the task. She needs to take his job if the country is to fight back against the Islamists.

Vane and Martin have provided the solution. Will DCI Cook and Anne Argento be willing to follow it through? Are they able to act for the good of England, knowing that a criminal and murderous action is about to take place? Do they have an option?

The Haberman Virus

A remote and isolated village in the Hindu Kush mountain range in North Eastern Afghanistan is wiped out by a virus unlike any seen before.

A mysterious visitor clad in a space suit checks his handiwork, a female American doctor succumbs to the disease, and the woman sent to trap the person responsible falls in love with him – the man who would cause the deaths of millions.

Hostage of Islam

Three are to die at the Mission in Nigeria: the pastor and his wife in a blazing chapel; another gunned down while trying to defend them from the Islamist fighters.

Kate McDonald, an American, grieving over her boyfriend's death and Helen Campbell, whose life had been troubled by drugs and prostitution, are taken by the attackers.

Kate is sold to a slave trader who intends to sell her virginity to an Arab Prince. Helen, to ensure their survival, gives herself to the murderer of her friends.

Malika's Revenge

Malika, a drug-addicted prostitute, waits in a smugglers' village for the next Afghan tribesman or Tajik gangster to pay her price, a few scraps of heroin.

Yusup Baroyev, a drug lord, enjoys a lifestyle many would envy. An Afghan warlord sees the resurgence of the Taliban. A Russian white-collar criminal portrays himself as a good and honest citizen in Moscow.

All of them are linked to an audacious plan to increase the quantity of heroin shipped out of Afghanistan and into Russia and ultimately the West.

Some will succeed, some will die, some will be rescued from their plight and others will rue the day they became involved.

ABOUT THE AUTHOR

Phillip Strang was born in England in the late forties. He was an avid reader of science fiction in his teenage years: Isaac Asimov, Frank Herbert, the masters of the genre. Still an avid reader, the author now mainly reads thrillers.

In his early twenties, the author, with a degree in electronics engineering and a desire to see the world, left England for Sydney, Australia. Now, forty years later, he still resides in Australia, although many intervening years were spent in a myriad of countries, some calm and safe, others no more than war zones.

Made in the USA
Coppell, TX
18 April 2020

20541404R00173